Secrets We Keep

by

Valeriya Goffe

This is a work of fiction. Names, characters, places, and incidents are either the product of the author's imagination or are used fictitiously, and any resemblance to actual persons living or dead, business establishments, events, or locales, is entirely coincidental.

Secrets We Keep

COPYRIGHT © 2023 by Valeriya Goffe

Cover Art by *The Wild Rose Press, Inc.*

The Wild Rose Press, Inc.
PO Box 708
Adams Basin, NY 14410-0708
Visit us at www.thewildrosepress.com

Publishing History
First Edition, 2024
Trade Paperback ISBN 978-1-5092-5246-6
Digital ISBN 978-1-5092-5247-3

Published in the United States of America

The Indian Ocean was gorgeous, with its bright and clear turquoise waters, and they were passing a lot of different, interesting vessels. Some of them were ordinary boats and yachts which Anna was used to seeing in the States, but others had triangular lateen sails and sharp bows. These boats were both big and small, and some were tiny with just one fisherman sitting in them.

"These are called dhow boats," Jean said, pointing at a few of the traditional vessels sailing by. "It is a typical East African boat. In the past, merchants were traveling in such boats all the way to and from India carrying all kinds of heavy items—fruit, water, different merchandise—"

"I love these," she interrupted with excitement. "They are so beautiful and romantic. They look like the vessels from fairy tales."

By now, Anna was no longer scared; she even got up and walked around the boat, enjoying the scenery around her. The boat was moving at a good speed and would be reaching the destination in no time.

Anna tried not to look at Jean but eventually she could not help taking a peek at him sitting on the bench, totally in his element, relaxed with his blond hair flowing in the wind. He took his T-shirt off, and Anna was able to see he had a deep tan and was muscular—maybe a couple of inches shorter than David and also thinner.

How would David carry himself in Tanzania?

Dedication

To my family

Prologue

Kyiv, Ukrainian Soviet Socialist Republic, January 3, 1973

Solomon picked up a framed photo from his desk and looked at it with a long, wistful gaze. His eyes moistened around the edges. Gloria appeared so vivid, so incredibly beautiful with long hair cascading down her shoulders like frothy waves. Her smile was electric and her laughter contagious. Whether they ran along the beach under the robin's egg blue sky or swam in the turquoise ocean waters, Solomon could never keep up with her.

My little sister must have grown a lot during these six years… Just a few more weeks, and we'll be together again.

He smiled for a brief second, imagining his wife in Africa for the first time. This was going to be quite a sight! Maria would freak out once she saw their grand family mansion overlooking the Indian Ocean… But she would love it, no doubt about it. Together, with Maria, he would explore his native land all over again—listen to the trumpeting of mighty elephants, admire the flame-colored acacias, and breath in the aroma of cloves and other spices in the vast plantations.

Solomon reached into his pocket and rubbed a small bag with sand. A gritty piece of the beach from his native country. Soon enough, he'd be walking down his favorite beach again—this time with his wife.

Thinking about Maria, it was definitely time to go home now. He looked at the clock. It was already eight pm. Maria never complained that he stayed late at work—he was saving lives here after all—but tonight he felt a sudden urge to embrace her and also press the little Olena against his heart. Solomon quickly packed his things up and started shutting down the office at the Happy Meows Veterinary Clinic.

"Doctor, I beg you, do not leave!" a woman who must have been eighty years old forced her way into the clinic. She grabbed on to the sleeve of Solomon's dove-gray jacket. "Please, can anything be done?"

She held out a basket with a small white cat who was meowing weakly under a soft pink blanket. "Murka is all I have, please rescue her."

Solomon lifted the miserable cat out of the basket and started carefully examining her. "How did this happen?"

"Oh, it is all my fault. I was cooking some fish for us on the stove, but I forgot to switch it off. The fish got burnt. So, I opened a window to get a little fresh air in the kitchen. I did not see that Murka was right there. I assumed she was asleep… She accidentally slipped on the icy windowsill and fell down. We live on the fifth floor, doctor. I heard about the miracles you perform from my neighbors many times. So, I put Murka in the basket and rushed here as fast as I could. I thought this was the only place where my kitty could be rescued."

Solomon finished his examination and carefully put the cat back in the basket. "Yes, there is a chance to save Murka."

The old lady's face lit up with a glimpse of hope.

"Murka did not manage to land on her feet, but being a cat, she suffered much less damage than a person would. I will have to perform surgery, however. Every second counts. I must warn you that this will be an expensive procedure, and Murka will need a lot of medicines right after to ensure recovery. I will write a prescription for you, so you can go to the 24/7 pharmacy around the corner. The medicines would cost at least one-hundred rubles. Is this fine?"

The light of hope disappeared from the old lady's face, and she started crying bitterly. "Doctor, I understand, the surgery is the only way to go. And this is fine with me. But… I would not be able to pay for all these expensive treatments. This is all I have—" And she took out all the contents of her antique wallet, mostly coins and a few crumpled small bills.

"Please take it all. I wish I had more. Maybe I can try to sell some things from my home in the market tomorrow. I do not have anything valuable, but it could yield some money. We live far away, though. It took us over two hours to get here, and it is already evening. We first took a bus and then walked for at least thirty minutes from the bus stop. Luckily, many people had been to Happy Meows and showed us the way. I have no friends or relatives to borrow from nearby. Today, I have nothing else."

Solomon shook his head. Without the urgent intervention, the cat could not be saved. She suffered too much damage. "I am sorry. Tomorrow will be too late. You would put Murka through a lot of pain, without any chance to rescue her. It would be unkind. Please think about that. We cannot be selfish when a loved one is suffering. We have to act now."

The old lady's body trembled and she stood there motionless for a minute or two. Her face was struck with immense pain and she seemed to age another decade in those brief moments. Eventually, she gave the cat a long farewell kiss.

"It is all my fault…" she repeated with the same sadness in her voice. "I will never forgive myself. I do not know how I will live now. Please, put Murka to sleep, doctor. I do not want her to be in any more pain. She does not deserve it. One day, we will meet again, my dear friend. I will cherish every moment we shared."

Solomon wrapped his arm around the fragile old lady to give her the support she so desperately needed, as she was plunging deeper and deeper into the world of grief. He then quietly picked Murka up and carried her to the operation room. The cat owner did not object. She just stood there without movement, tears flowing down her cheeks.

Solomon made up his mind quickly. In a few minutes, he performed the most difficult operation of his career, without a single ruble paid by the pet's owner.

"She will be sleeping for a few hours, this is totally fine," Solomon announced to the astonished old lady, as he was handing Murka back to her, as well as a small bag with all the necessary medications. "The operation was successful. Murka is expected to make a full recovery. Please make sure to give her these medicines."

"Thank you, thank you, doctor," the cat owner mumbled, as her eyes were filling up with tears of joy and her lips spread in a smile. She was stroking the cat's fur frantically, while her whole body was shaking. "You brought my little girl back… from the grave. And me together with her."

"I was just doing my job," Solomon said calmly.

"You are young enough to be my grandson, yet I can now see for myself where your tremendous fame came from… Not only do you have the golden hands, but also the golden heart. I will never forget your kindness. May God bless you for all your good deeds."

Solomon ushered the old woman and her pet out and finally closed up the clinic. As he was walking towards his car, he felt a strong urge to turn around. He looked at the Happy Meows building and stood in silence for a brief moment. The simple two-storied construction was illuminated by the silver moonlight, making it look not like a clinic but a divine castle. A place where love prevailed over death. The good prevailed over evil. The light prevailed over the darkness.

Soft tenderness filled up Solomon's heart and streamed down his veins. The memories of animals he had rescued during his career slowly flowed in front of his eyes.

Finally, he started walking towards his car, the sparkling firm snow crunching under his boots.

I will miss this when we go back to Africa.

Peace and quiet reigned over the city at this late hour. The strong wind died down, now tenderly caressing the branches of the leafless trees. The full moon gracefully rose up high, illuminating the dark velvet of the sky. A few light snowflakes circled in the air like skilled ballerinas and fell effortlessly on the cold ground, their short dance over in a flash.

The roads were wide open, with just a handful of cars here and there, probably driving home to their loved ones, minding their own business. Sidewalks, bustling with pedestrians in the daytime, were completely empty. Many Kyiv residents were inside still celebrating the New Year or out of town visiting their friends and relatives.

As Solomon was serenely cruising along the wide streets in his snow-white Volga, his gaze accidentally fell on a car which was right behind him. It seemed to keep some distance, but whenever Solomon changed lanes, the car also moved; whenever he turned, it also turned. The dark gray Moskvich moved steadily and calmly along the road, like a giant spider, getting closer and closer to its victim.

Solomon's mouth suddenly became dry and his throat tightened. The Moskvich was now only a car length behind, with its lights glowing menacingly, like rings of fire.

What do these people want from me?

He pressed on the gas pedal as hard as he could. His faithful Volga was flying through the city like a white swan being chased by a relentless hunter. Solomon finally made it to the Taras Shevchenko Boulevard. He was now just a few minutes away from his home on the historical Ivanka Franka street. His family was but a stone's throw away.

Solomon glanced in the rear-view mirror, as he was trying to fight off the sense of disquiet. He sighed with relief; the road behind him was now empty. Maybe it was just a mistake and he had imagined everything.

Right at that moment, an incredible force shook Solomon's body and tossed him up in the air, as a huge blow struck his car. A million broken glass pieces flew by his eyes and dug into his skin. Cloying darkness enveloped him until the moon briefly cast a ghostly glow on his pale face.

After overcoming the initial shock, Solomon desperately tried to get out of the car. But it was all in vain. His legs felt completely numb, and no matter how hard he tried to pull himself up with his arms, he could not move an inch.

Several images raced through Solomon's mind. One was of little Olena in her bright-red suit extending her chubby arms to him and another one. Another one of Maria standing by the window, cooking borscht and smiling gently, illuminated by the silver moonlight.

"If only I had time to tell them," whispered Solomon as he squeezed the small bag of sand in his pocket.

Solomon made a grave mistake. He knew this now. He'd waited too long. His beloved Ukrainian family would now never know who he was and where he came from. Maria and Olena would remain just ordinary people living in the colorless, cold USSR for the rest of their lives, and never witness the glory of Africa.

He watched, immobile, as the gray car quickly turned around and fled in a matter of seconds, its tires squealing on the icy road. For a time, there was nothing but silence. Then, sound. The air filled up with the piercing howl of sirens. The long-awaited ambulance arrived, illuminating the coal-black night sky with frightful bloody-red lights.

Solomon's heart thumped in his chest. Maybe, just maybe, he still had a chance to reveal the truth to his family.

PART I

Under the lying stone the water doesn't flow
Ukrainian proverb

Chapter 1. The High Stakes

Indian Wells, California, present time

"Here you go. Thanks a lot for coming!" Anna smiled warmly and handed the signed tennis ball to the kid in the navy-blue shirt, standing up straight like a little soldier.

She loved the thrill of a tennis match, but she also savored these more relaxed moments. An opportunity to interact with tennis fans and get to know people who supported her during tennis tournaments—those who yelled "Go Anna!" from the stands, or applauded loudly after her winners, or quietly sat in their seats and simply bathed her in their positive energy.

Kids were especially precious—waiting so seriously and patiently for their turn, extending their short arms with tennis balls and other gear, smiling pleadingly: "Can you sign mine, please?" Anna always looked at their faces and wondered: who in this group was the future Grand Slam winner? Was it this curly boy in glasses and bright blue sneakers, holding out his marker with so much determination? Or maybe that pale little girl in the back, clinging to her mother, wearing a pink tennis dress and blond hair in cute pigtails?

Of course, not every kid asking for an autograph

would be famous one day, but beyond doubt, a few of them would be. A decade or so later, they would be on a big stage, holding a shiny trophy. Signing autographs the same way Anna was doing today. Tennis was such a non-stopping machine, churning new champions out year after year. One player's star went down, another player's star rose up. Some champs stood on the pedestal only once, others would do so many times, bathing the spectators in the rays of their awe-inspiring glory.

Anna fixed a stubborn lock of her chestnut hair sticking out from underneath her tennis hat and glanced around. The square was empty. By now, all the fans had left. Everyone had gotten what they needed—autographs, selfies, or any tennis advice they were looking for.

Phew, she was all done for the day. Except for one thing. The most significant one actually.

Tonight was the all-important dinner with Donna McGreevy, the renowned agent from the Sierra international agency. They represented some of the best tennis players of the world. Donna was not just an agent. She was a fairy godmother. She held a magic wand which had the power of changing Anna's life forever.

Could Donna possibly represent Anna?

Without a doubt.

Last year, when Anna won the Wimbledon junior title, Donna was incredibly impressed by Anna's performance and had reached out to her. They immediately began discussing the possibility of representation. However, the process dragged. No offer was put on the table, and Anna had started losing hope.

But a couple of days ago, Donna called again and asked for a meeting at a restaurant. Yay! She'd probably made up her mind. *Why else would she want to meet up, right?*

Anna texted her mom as she was getting into a cab:
—*Leaving for the restaurant*—

The reply buzzed almost instantaneously:
—*Donna's already here, fifteen minutes early! Hurry up*—

—*Chatting about the weather for now. She is in good spirits*—

Wow. Donna had come *early*! The blood rushed to Anna's face and her pulse started racing. The fairy-tale was about to begin. She would be the first Ukrainian tennis player ever to get signed by the Sierra agency. No more pinching pennies. Anna would finally have the money to support her own training, travel to tournaments, eat dinner at nice restaurants, receive medical care, you name it.

Tennis was so incredibly expensive, especially when you came from a country like Ukraine… People always had this mind-boggling misconception—that a promising young tennis player like herself was leading an easy, luxurious life. But it couldn't be further from the truth. She needed the Sierra agency to give her wings and take her further.

Anna felt her hands getting sweaty and her heart jumping out of her chest as she was entering the high-end restaurant. It must have been picked by Donna. Anna's mother and coach, Olena, was sitting down at the table near the window, smiling at Anna as she walked in.

OMG, Mom is wearing a dress… And are those high heels under the table?!

Quite a contrast to her usual "uniform"—a dark-blue sports suit, at least ten years old and sewn up in a couple of spots, and worn-out sneakers she would normally wear to all places. Did Mom even have this type of outfit in her suitcase? Very unlikely. Maybe she just went to the mall this afternoon and bought it? Of course, she was taking this dinner very, very seriously.

I'll have to tell Mom after dinner how beautiful she looks. She totally needs to start wearing such outfits more often. Once we become rich, she'll be finally able to afford some!

Donna, a chic woman with short choppy black hair and alabaster skin, was sitting next to Olena. She immediately rose up from her chair and gave Anna a big hug.

"Sweetheart, I saw you play against Millie Thomas in the second round! To be completely honest, I didn't expect you to win. I thought that maybe you'd resist well and there would be three sets… But you played such a flawless match and won so quickly! This is incredible. Millie is such a fierce competitor and won several big titles!"

Anna's mouth curled into a wide smile.

"This was a real clinic," Olena cut in. "The stats speak for themselves: sixty-three minutes, six zero in the second set. Anna only had five unforced errors and twenty-six winners."

"It's hard to imagine such perfection is even possible!" Donna said incredulously. "This brings me to the main point of our conversation. The contract."

Right. The elephant in the room.

Anna closed her eyes for a second. Her stomach tightened into a knot. *Here it comes! Please, please, please, say something really good!*

"I've discussed with our executives," every single

word Donna said echoed in Anna's head, " and everyone is supportive of signing a contract with you. But a little concerned that you don't have enough track record. You're still so young, only seventeen… In the end, we've decided the following. We'll sign a contract with you, *if you win your match tomorrow*. The win would put you right inside the top one-hundred of the best tennis players in the world. A sufficient guarantee to us that you would do well."

Anna pursed her lips, both thrilled and shocked at the same time. The contract was very, very close. She could literally touch the paper it would be printed on. Quite possibly, she would be signing it tomorrow.

For a brief second, however, she wished that she didn't have to wait another day and climb another mountain.

Anna and Olena exchanged looks. In the grand scheme of things, it seemed doable. Anna had been on fire these past couple of weeks, with a ten-match winning streak. And by a stroke of luck, her opponent tomorrow was nobody famous. Anna was a definite favorite. But still…

"I'm not sure why age is an issue here," Olena finally spoke up with a quivering voice, swallowing her words.

Anna felt a pinch in her heart as she watched her mom struggle at this important moment. Of course, she was not used to negotiations at this level. What experience did she have? None.

"Plenty of teenagers did well on tour… Martina Hingis, the Williams sisters, Jennifer Capriati went on to win Grand Slam titles."

"True, but these are more exceptions rather than the

rule." Donna narrowed her eyes. "You have mentioned really big names here. Let's hope Anna is one of them, but we don't know that yet. These days, tennis players peak at twenty-four or twenty-five. I've seen many great juniors in the last several years, but will any of them make it on tour? It's a question. I haven't signed any of them."

"Oh, come on! Anna's is so different from all these other juniors!" Olena yelled, but caught herself and quickly lowered her voice. "She could beat them with her eyes closed. Even the tennis commentator Helena Johnson prophesied that Anna would become the first Ukrainian to win the Grand Slam one day! Did you know that?"

"No, I didn't. Helena sure can smell the talent a mile away." Donna smiled cunningly. "But Helena is a tennis commentator, not an agent. She can make these bold statements; she doesn't have to invest in Anna's career."

"All right." Olena sank into her chair, all her energy drained as if she had just finished a three-set match. She was not here to argue, but to make a deal. "I think it's fair. Anna will play one more match tomorrow. If Anna wins, then what happens next?"

"Well, we'll discuss it in much more detail tomorrow. Together, we'll come up with a budget which will fully support Anna each year. This money will need to be paid back if she makes it as a pro. We'll help to facilitate endorsement deals with various companies. I can tell you that your daughter can expect a whole new life. Today, it's just the two of you, right? You as the coach, Anna as the player. And I know your family has… very limited means. Tomorrow, Anna will have a whole world class team supporting her! It will be a whole new level."

"But what if Anna... loses tomorrow?" Olena's voice was cracking with emotion. Her chicken burger still stood in front of her, untouched.

Donna gave Olena a non-committal look. The one she probably used with parents of all the other tennis wannabes. "Nothing. We'll just have to wait till another tournament. Or another. She gets in the top one-hundred; she gets the contract. As simple as that."

As Anna was drifting off to sleep that night, she heard the rain drops chime against the windows. Rains at Indian Wells were extremely rare. It was the first time Anna could remember it raining at the tournament.

Maybe it was the golden rain? It would wash off her old life. And tomorrow her new life would start. Full of shiny trophies, new friends and rivals, glamorous boyfriends, fancy dinners, and new dresses for Mom. Lots and lots of dresses.

Anna's eyes closed and she plunged into a deep, restful sleep.

****

The early morning sun hovered over the peaks of Santa Rosa Mountains, bathing the slender palm-trees and the lush gardens of Indian Wells in a golden gaze. As the soft sunlight started streaming through the narrow windows of the little budget hotel, crawling over the faded carpets and the unpretentious furniture, Anna's eyes opened instantly.

This is my big day! Nothing is going to get in my way.

Anna climbed out of bed in a flash and tried to stretch and move her arms around. But the pain in her right shoulder was not going away.

This was not the first time Anna had felt pain in this area. She'd experienced occasional discomfort in her shoulder over the last several weeks during serves and high backhand volleys. With her long winning streak, she had so much adrenaline in her blood during the matches that she easily ignored it. Fans, interviews, dreams of fame, the meeting with Donna McGreevy— Anna was too busy to listen to her body. But now it was clear that something might have happened to her shoulder.

"Mom, I don't want to scare you, but something is wrong," Anna said quietly. Olena was just coming out of the bathroom with a towel on her head.

"Hah? What happened?" Olena gave Anna a frightened gaze, the towel flying off her head and landing on top of one of the suitcases standing by the bed. The hotel room barely had room to walk around the beds.

"I might have pulled a muscle. In my shoulder. I don't know what to do now."

"I don't know either." Olena looked at Anna tentatively and patted her shoulder softly. "Maybe… it will get better? How about we try to tape it up? You just have to get through today. You know, this is the most important match of your career."

"I don't know, Mom," Anna said as her heart beat faster and faster. "Could we… go to some doctor here? Get it checked out?"

Olena jumped up as if she were just bitten by a bee. "Anna, are you out of your mind? Where would we get the money to pay the doctor in the US? For one X-ray they'll charge your dad's annual salary."

"Yes, I know… But what if the shoulder gets even worse during the match?"

"Let's stay positive," Olena protested. "You're a teenager. Not a middle-aged woman like me. Your body is young and flexible. I can't imagine you having any major injury. Let's do some treatment first and see. If you feel better, then we'll go to the practice court and hit some balls. We still have a few hours before the match. If the shoulder still bothers you, we'll just call it quits. How does that sound?"

Anna nodded in agreement. That kind of made sense.

Before Anna knew it, Olena got down to business. First, she gave Anna some ibuprofen and also fish oil—this was her favorite remedy for everything! After, she massaged Anna's shoulder, put on some ice, then some gel, and finally taped it solid. The shoulder now smelled disgusting and looked bulky and ugly, with the black chunks of tape sticking out from underneath Anna's tennis dress. But looks and smells aside, Anna seemed to feel a million times better.

"Thanks, Mom. The treatment helped a lot." Anna sighed with relief.

Practice went fine. She felt a bit of dull pain nagging somewhere deep inside the muscles, but it was minor.

"Okay, I'm ready for the match," Anna declared confidently as she hit the last practice ball perfectly down the line.

"Great!" Olena gave her a thumbs up. "Don't worry about things outside of your control. Just play your game. I have no doubt that you will win. And from there, we will have a new life."

Anna's match was being held at one of the side courts, not the central court which was reserved for a top ten player's match that afternoon. Maybe it was for the better. She'd already had her sixty-three minutes of fame at the central court earlier when she beat Millie Thomas. With the Sierra contract in sight, Anna just wanted to concentrate on her game today. All the bells and whistles could be saved for some other occasion.

She marched on to the Stadium five court with the usual fire and determination in her eyes, her head up high, earphones in her ears, confident in her every step. She needed to appear relaxed and poised. The opponent could not possibly see that she was injured.

As Anna was thoroughly arranging her things on the bench—water bottles, rackets, towels, all needing to be in a specific order—she subtly glanced at the stands packed with spectators and bit back a smile. The fans didn't disappoint. The gorgeous blue and yellow colors of the Ukrainian flag popped up here and there. She also spotted quite a few posters supporting her. All these people had come to see her win.

Hopefully, I'll put together a good show for everyone!

Anna happily jogged to the net where the umpire was ready to toss the coin to determine who would be serving first. She couldn't wait to start.

She won the first set easily. Her game was far superior to her opponent's, an average twenty-something year old. Anna hit winner after winner. The crowd applauded energetically.

In an effort to protect her shoulder, she made sure to somewhat reduce the speed of her serve. Why put unnecessary pressure on her arm? Things were going her way. There was no need to serve aces.

However… the second set was a lot more challenging. Her opponent did not want to lose. She was one of those grinders who just refused to go away.

Ugh, this girl is just circling around non-stop and trying to retrieve every single ball! Anna hated these types of players, who only thrived on the unforced errors of their opponents and didn't hit any winners themselves. *Go ahead, take a risk, earn your win!* No, this girl was not doing that. She would scramble all match long and wait till Anna made a mistake. Typical cowardly behavior.

Eventually, the second set went into the tiebreak. After a few long, heated rallies, Anna found herself on serve, a couple of points away from winning the match.

She started bouncing her ball ten times, like she always did before each serve. It calmed her, let her focus.

Finally! A couple of strong first serves, and I'll be done.

Anna's favorite tune switched on in her head loud and clear. She tossed the ball up high, arched her back and hit it with all of her power. The ball went flying like a rocket and hit the corner, right where she was aiming. Her opponent helplessly extended her arms; there was no way in hell she could return that ball.

But at that same moment, a burning pain enveloped Anna's shoulder. It was throbbing like it just went up in flames.

The rest was a blur. The music stopped. Everything went quiet. Anna discerned some "Ohhhh" and "Ahhh"'s from the crowd, maybe even the voice of her mom, but they were so echoey, so distant and indistinct, as if she'd suddenly went underwater. The world around Anna faded to the singular sensation of the sharp, intolerable pain… A strong force was pulling her into a deep black hole, and she did not have enough strength to climb out.

"Medical timeout."

She was stretched out helplessly on the court, looking into the blue sky, while all the moments from her tennis life were rushing in front of her eyes.

Will I be able to finish this match? Will I play any more matches? Is this my last tournament… ever?

It can't be over so soon.

Finally, the match was over, and all that was left was returning to the dark, cold hotel room. And a night filled with tears of despair, tears of pain, tears of broken dreams.

****

The year dragged on like a snail. It felt like a lifetime. Every day looked the same and smelled the same. Green spring, bright summer, colorful fall—they all melted into one continuous cold and gray existence.

The bright and thrilling life on the tennis tour carried on—its heated matches, electrifying victories, and excruciating defeats. The enthusiastic fans streamed to tournaments, and new champions were crowned every week. Anna just wasn't part of this delightful world. Not anymore. She now lived in a parallel universe.

After another sleepless night, she poked her head out from underneath her checkered blanket and slowly reached for her phone. She'd finally made up her mind. She couldn't continue like this forever. No matter how much she loved and desired it, a professional tennis career was now out of reach. Anna needed to let it go—throw her dream up high and let it fly, like a beautiful white dove cruising in the blue skies. It was time to pursue a new profession, something else which could make her adrenaline run. But first, she needed to do one important thing.

Valeriya Goffe

Reluctantly, Anna sent out a text and immediately dialed a familiar number.

"Anton, I finally have an update for you," she said, her voice breaking and a sudden chill shooting down her spine. "Just sent you a text. I'm really sorry. I know you've been reaching out to me for a while, I just wasn't ready. You should post the update as soon as possible. And I also attached a photo I wanted to share with the… fans." Anna swallowed hard as she pronounced the last word.

She sat motionless for a few minutes, glancing at the photo she had just shared with Anton—a selfie she had taken in the middle of her room, holding a book titled "Finance" in front of her chest. Did she look happy enough? Hopefully. Anna wanted everyone to remember her just like that—with the bright, radiant smile, exactly like the one which crowned her face in the early rounds of the Indian Wells.

Anton didn't disappoint. The update went live in the space of thirty minutes. Anna's tennis era was officially over.

Ukraine Tennis Blog // Latest tennis news

Many of our readers have been wondering how our beloved *Anna Levenko* is doing.

Relax guys. I finally have an update for you. Although, I'm afraid, this might not be quite what you wanted to hear. I'm still shocked myself. I wish I had better news… Don't kill the messenger!

Back in June, Anna underwent a surgery to treat a torn tendon in her right shoulder. She was hoping to return to the practice court in several months.

Unfortunately, it wasn't in the cards—it's now apparent that the operation turned out unsuccessful.

Anna won't be returning to competitive tennis after all. She is now planning to start a new career.

Let's wish her the best of luck at the business school in Washington D.C. !

Comments (1,378):

Mikhailo P: I can't believe the news… I was positive Anna would win a Grand Slam one day. We'll miss her bright smile at the tennis court!

Linda H.: What a bummer! Anna was a real star. I saw her play in London. Good luck with the business school. Xoxo

Teresa J.: Dear Anna, it's such a pity. My daughter Erica keeps the ball autographed by you at Indian Wells as her greatest treasure. P.S. Erica is doing great at her tennis lessons. Thanks for the inspiration.

Tai C.: Anna, you were my favorite tennis player of all time. If you'd like to go on a date, message me at tc98@hotmail.com

Click to view more comments…

Chapter 2. Uncle Stepan's Store

Kyiv, Ukraine, six years later

Late Sunday morning the business channel was broadcasting their segment on cryptocurrencies in Latin America. Anna was in the kitchen, a bright red apron tied around her waist and a subtle smile on her lips, busily preparing borscht for the family.

Cooking a delicious dish while listening to an interesting reportage—what could be better? Cryptocurrencies were a hot topic these days. She could not wait to dig her teeth into such a difficult subject and learn more.

"This is amazing—El Salvador now accepts bitcoin as a real money. I wonder if this will last?" Anna kept peeking at the TV over and over again while carefully peeling golden onions, carrots, beets, and other vegetables.

The next program was equally interesting—"Green Energy in Africa." Thanks to her constant encouragement, her parents recently installed solar panels on the rooftop of their country house. Recycling was also a must in their household. The next item on the family's agenda was reducing plastic consumption to zero as soon as possible, if she had any say in it.

"Wow! This is exactly the type of project I'd love to do," Anna whispered in awe as the program started showing the new Mekdela Solar Park in Ethiopia—ten thousand acres of land with rows upon rows of solar panels. The TV commentator took the viewers on a brief tour of the solar park, currently one of the largest in Africa, and announced that it was financed by a top development agency—Polaris International Corporation. It cost four billion dollars, according to the Vice President, Eduardo Martinez, who gave a brief statement during the program about Polaris and their portfolio of investments.

"Is the continent of Africa a priority for Polaris, Mr. Martinez?" asked the commentator.

"Absolutely. We have recently doubled our investment in Africa and are planning to continue increasing our presence on the continent and financing more and more projects." Eduardo Martinez nodded proudly. "Polaris currently has offices in twenty-eight African countries, and we are preparing to open several new offices in the next six months."

"What are some of the key areas of focus for your company?"

"We work in many different areas—developing the technology and tourism sector, deepening financial inclusion, supporting small business, improving healthcare and education... A large share of our portfolio is in clean energy investments, similar to the park we financed in Ethiopia. At Polaris, we take climate change very seriously. We have supported many governments in meeting their green energy targets."

Anna's head started spinning with excitement. What a wonderful company Polaris was! Of course, this was not the first time she'd heard about them. Their fame preceded them. Polaris was the *crème de la crème* in international development, a highly selective organization headquartered in Washington. It was consistently ranked as the top company to work at for people under thirty. All the graduates from top schools all around the world applied there, hoping to get a coveted position. But Polaris's doors were closed for most mortals—only the best and the brightest got an opportunity to work there. No exceptions. It didn't make sense to even fantasize about getting a job there.

Olena slowly strolled into the kitchen and sat down right next to Anna, distracting her from the program.

"Please make sure you put more meat in the borscht. Last time Dad was complaining it came out a little bit too light. He was still hungry," Olena commented, closely watching Anna's manipulations. "Do you want me to help you?"

"Mom, believe it or not, I'm perfectly capable." Anna dropped the first batch of cut vegetables in the boiling water. Her family was very picky when it came to borscht. It needed to be absolutely perfect, or somebody complained.

But somehow Anna had a feeling that her mom did not come here to talk about borscht. Usually, she did not venture into the kitchen when some boring—from her point of view—TV program was on. Olena normally watched sports competitions, game shows, occasional adventure movies, and daily news. Obviously, none of those programs were on at the moment.

Anna didn't have to wait long for Olena to cut to the chase.

"I assume Dad told you that Uncle Stepan agreed to hire you as his sales associate?" Olena grabbed a green apple from the counter and bit through its crispy flesh with a loud cracking sound, juice drops spilling in different directions. "Finally, you will be getting a paid job. And working for your own super successful uncle. You'll be making good money. I think it's fantastic."

Anna continued chopping her vegetables, not lifting her eyes. Her knife was glittering bright and pounding the wooden board.

She had been trying to avoid this conversation. And now she had no place to hide. Her mom had her cornered.

"Of course Dad told me. But I don't see anything fantastic in this. I want to keep working as the research assistant at the Energy Institute, that's what I told Dad."

Olena crossed her arms. "Anna, we talked about it twenty times before. I know how much you enjoy working at the institute, and it has been a great experience for you, but this is an *unpaid* job. When you just started there, I thought it was okay to do it 'pro bono'—let them see how brilliant and hard-working you are, so they can decide if they want to keep you or not. But it's been a while, and nothing has changed! You don't have the luxury of working for free anymore! Neither your dad nor I are earning enough money now to keep us going." Olena pointed at the old cookware and ancient refrigerator in the kitchen.

Anna swallowed. They were in a desperate need of some new pots and pans, that's for sure. The refrigerator was also falling apart. Its door wouldn't even close properly; one needed to hit it really hard. And don't forget the stove—among the four burners, only two smaller ones were working. The whole sight of the Levenko kitchen was rather depressing.

But in the large scheme of things, did any of that matter when her dreams and life goals were on the line?

And even more so, when the whole world was in tremendous jeopardy because of climate change? *Heck no!*

"Yes, Mom, I realize all of that," Anna said calmly. "But why do I need to work for Uncle Stepan? He just owns several shops, that's all. What kind of career can I build there? It's a good position for a high school graduate, but I went to a prestigious business school in the US. I'd like to get a job that has an impact. I want to help improve the lives of people and save the planet— like I'm doing at the Energy Institute. We're working on projects to scale up the use of renewable energy in Ukraine. Do you know how important this agenda is for combatting climate change? Our whole world is in danger! People are suffering from terrible disasters— extreme weather, the fires, the floods—I want to do my part, or I'll never forgive myself!"

Olena took a deep sigh. "I know all that, sweetie. And with all of my heart, do I wish that things were different. But you sent out your resume to many companies, both local and international, and there was no result. Not even a single interview! It has nothing to do with your intelligence, there are just too many business graduates and not enough jobs. Uncle Stepan seems to be the only one who actually wants to hire you. He is a respectable businessman. The Ukrainian Business magazine even published an article about him a few months ago."

"Yes, I read the article... I read all the business magazines from cover to cover, you know. Well, let me tell you, I am *this* close to getting a full-time job at the Energy Institute. They said a couple more months, and they would have an opening for me. My name is already on several important research papers. All the management knows me. It's just a matter of time—"

Olena dismissively waved her hand. "Anna, you are naïve like a baby. Don't believe in these fairy-tales. They said that many times before, but we know very well that their budget had been cut. How could they finance a new position? I'm positive they'd never pay you for your work, no matter how many late nights you spend there. Just go to Uncle Stepan tomorrow. Please? Have a look. See what he is offering."

"Fine," Anna said, gritting her teeth. She didn't see the point in arguing with her mom any longer. She'd go to Uncle Stepan's shop and just tell him directly—*sorry, this job is not for me. Period.* Problem solved.

Olena picked up a newspaper from the table and glanced through it. The cultural section held a myriad of photos catching her eye.

The Bright Colors of Ruslan Petrenko
By Hanna Moroz
Last night, Ukraine's biggest stars gathered for the opening of Ruslan Petrenko's latest art exhibition at the Ukraine House, and this was no surprise. The young "Ukrainian Picasso" has already conquered the hearts of many with his brilliant portrayal of Ukrainian landscapes and animals (both real and fantastic) using his unique colorful and expressive style. Ruslan Petrenko was raised by his grandparents in a small village, and his meteoric ascent to the top of the Ukrainian contemporary art scene has been so much talked about in the recent days.

The attendance at the event didn't disappoint. *Marina Zaiko*, a famous singer and a music award winner, looked incredibly fit after spending just three months on the ketogenic diet, the latest diet craze. Be sure to try it for yourself! Several powerful politicians were also in attendance, including *Artem Slusar*, *Pavlo Trudnev* and, most importantly *Igor Banduchenko*, People's Deputy of Ukraine representing the Svyatoshyn district. His girlfriend, *Sveta Levenko*, drew gasps of delight after appearing in a cobalt-blue mini-dress and ultra-high gold stiletto boots, her ears adorned with the show-stopping ruby earrings. It's common knowledge that Mr. Banduchenko has left a long trail of broken hearts in Ukraine and beyond, but this immaculately chic young lady has nothing to worry about, with her confidence and incredible charm.

"Just look at this!" Olena pointed at Sveta's picture and shook her head subtly as she glanced at Anna's casual T-shirt and shorts. "Your cousin is not even half as pretty as you, but she plays her cards right. Aunt Motria has been telling me that Sveta is getting closer and closer to the engagement with Mr. Banduchenko. And you don't even have a boyfriend. What a mistake it was to let David Thompson go, I can't tell you…"

Anna sat down next to her mother. The cooking was all done. The kitchen gradually filled up with the delicious smell, making Anna's stomach rumble.

"Mom, you know that ship sailed—we separated such a long time ago. He moved to the NYC for work; I kept studying in Washington. A long-distance relationship was not for me. David was a nice guy, but I didn't think he was the one."

"I still wish you gave him a chance." Olena sighed. "Sometimes, you can grow into loving a person. Love doesn't always strike like a thunderbolt. That was my perfect son-in-law… I don't know what you are looking for in a man!"

****

Anna was supposed to meet Uncle Stepan at ten am. She was walking through the Svyatoshyn market in search of Uncle Stepan's store. Along the way, she'd prepared a few opening sentences to jump-start the conversation. Like that she greatly valued his support, but working at a small store was really not something she wanted to do at this time. Maybe later. If the Energy Institute job didn't work out, she'd call him.

The market was located right next to the railway station and a lot of passengers had just gotten off the latest train. Many of them were *babusias* (old ladies) who wore colorful headscarves. These women lived in the neighboring villages and commuted to Kyiv to sell different goods. They all had a sturdy build, strong legs, and carried humongous baskets of fresh milk, meat, fruit, and vegetables which they were planning to sell in the market.

It's supposed to be right… here. But wait. Is this really his store?

Uncle's Stepan new shop looked surprisingly bright. And modern. It stood out among all the other stores in the market. A large sign "*Chervona Ruta*" with a gorgeous bright red flower ornamented the structure. Anna instinctively looked up and shrieked in excitement—the roof was covered with a row of silver solar panels! How delightful. The last thing she expected to see. Uncle Stepan clearly passed the litmus test with flying colors.

The door of the store was open. She carefully

glanced inside. The space appeared warm and hospitable. It was designed in the unique Ukrainian style and reminded her of an authentic Ukrainian *hata*. Walls were decorated with pictures of charming ladies wearing traditional Ukrainian *vyshyvankas* and bright poppy wreaths, young men moving to an electrifying *hopak* dance, and children playing in the golden fields of sunflowers. In addition, lovely indoor plants adorned various parts of the store, making it look thriving.

"Anechka, welcome!" Uncle Stepan came running to the door. Anna flushed with happiness at the familiar nickname. He immediately opened his arms wide and tightly embraced his niece. "So, what do you think?"

"Looks really nice!" Anna confessed as she could not hide her surprise. "I was expecting something a bit more like... the other stores I've seen in markets. More old-fashioned, if you will. This one looks like a museum of Ukrainian culture, not a store."

"Well, glad you like it. I have put my heart and soul into this store. I want it to be my flagship. Not only is it carbon neutral, but five-percent of all our proceeds will be going to charity—a small orphanage in the suburbs of Kyiv. Come, look at everything, walk around. From tomorrow on, you will be in charge. I know that this might not be the job of your dreams and you will be looking for another one. It's fine with me. In the meantime, I'd be delighted to have you working here."

Uncle Stepan was saying all the right things. Hitting all the right buttons. Anna took a quick look at the neatly packed shelves. The store held a lot of stuff—food, electric appliances, toys, diapers, stationery... Everything a family would need. The merchandise in colorful packaging seemed of high quality. The selection pleasantly surprised her. Even from the first glance, Anna was able to discern a lot of healthy low-calorie snacks and items made from recycled materials. Most of it looked made in Ukraine, supporting the local producers. Somehow she and Uncle Stepan turned out to be on the same wave length.

Of course, this was still not the type of job Anna would want to have in the long run. There was no question about it. But for today, it was not the worst option… And most importantly, her family would be happy.

"Have you ever worked at a store?" Uncle Stepan asked.

"As a matter of fact, I did. During my freshman year I worked at a book store at the business school."

"Excellent. Then it won't be too hard for you to master this craft." Uncle Stepan smiled. "A few important things, which probably did not come up in business school. First, watch out for any counterfeit money. A few times we had a problem at my other stores. Second, keep an eye on any rats or rodents. There is a chance they will run in from the market. Third, no animals. Dogs, cats, you know. One time my sales associate in the clothing store in Petrivka market brought her dog to the store for only thirty minutes. She needed to take her to the vet later. Well, the dog managed to chew on the most expensive sheep coat and designer leather boots we had in the store! We posted a big loss that month."

"Oh, don't worry, Uncle Stepan. I don't have any pets right now. So your merchandise is totally safe!"

"Fourth, don't pay any attention to people working at other stores around here—they are nosy and will try to sabotage our success. I think one of these individuals is coming through the door right now."

"E-e-excuse me?" an old lady walked into the store and stopped near the door, carefully examining everything. She was probably in her mid-sixties, strong and stocky. "So the shop is finally ready to open? And let me guess—you are probably plotting how to steal all the customers away from me?"

Uncle Stepan sighed. "This is Baba Kateryna from the *Chudo* general merchandise store next door. A competitor," he explained to Anna in a lowered voice.

"No, Baba Kateryna, we're not plotting anything," he said. "It is fair competition, you know. Let the best one win."

"Right... And how am I expected to compete with you? Your store is double the size and looks so trendy, while mine is falling apart. I also hear that you will be selling merchandise online, is that true?"

Stepan shrugged. "Obviously, we have an online store as well. Customers can shop online and have items delivered to their home or pick up here at the store. It's the twenty-first century, you know. We are trying to deliver the best experience for our customers. Ukraine will be part of the European Union one day, and Ukrainians demand quality."

Baba Kateryna shook her head. "Value for customers? Who cares about them. All we need is to make a living. Life was so much better during the Soviet Union times. I could buy a whole bun for three *kopijkas*. You're just creating more work for all of us, that's all..." she mumbled as she left the store.

Uncle Stepan just rolled his eyes.

"Anna, make sure to watch out for Baba Kateryna

and her like. These are 'old school' people who are trying to take us back. Instead, we are trying to build a new Ukraine," he noted. "You know, I'm so glad to have you working here. I think we'll make a good team."

"You can definitely count on me, Uncle Stepan," Anna said cheerfully. "I'm ready to start tomorrow."

"Excellent." Uncle Stepan gave her a hug. "Are you going home now? If you'd like, I can give you a lift. I had promised to pick up Aunt Motria from the beauty salon, and I still have some time to kill before her appointment is over."

"Sure, if it's not a big imposition." Anna nodded. Normally, she'd take a yellow minibus to go back home from the Svyatoshyn market, but naturally, riding in the car with Uncle Stepan would be much fancier. At least she'd be getting some perks from this job.

Anna installed herself comfortably in Uncle Stepan's brand-new glacier-white SUV and diligently put on her seat belt. What a lovely car it was! She held her breath as it started moving so quietly and smoothly along the road.

Uncle Stepan has sure done well for himself, Anna thought. He was definitely one of those Ukrainians who didn't give up till they succeeded. Some years ago, he ditched the dreaded factory job, took a risk, and started a small store with his life savings. Bingo! Turned out, commerce was his true calling. Uncle Stepan quickly opened several more retail stores and started building an empire. He proudly called himself a "new" Ukrainian— somebody who reinvented himself and achieved great success.

"How's my cousin Sveta doing these days?" Anna asked for the sake of politeness.

Stepan could not respond right away—all of a sudden, a gold colored convertible cut in front of him rather impudently. With the burgeoning Ukrainian economy, there were so many new expensive cars on the roads of Kyiv these days. Many of them did not observe the rules and only knew one thing: *"I've bought a luxury car, I need to go over there, so it's permitted."*

"Sorry, Anna, I got distracted because of that stupid *kozel*…" Stepan grumbled, using the Ukrainian word for goat. "Svetochka is off to a big reception at the Emerald Hotels and Resorts tonight with Mr. Banduchenko. You know, it's one of the largest hotel chains and they just opened their first hotel in Kyiv. Everyone who is anyone will be there. I bought a big emerald necklace for Sveta so she looks irresistible at the reception… As of late, I hardly even see my daughter anymore! She leaves for the university in the morning, and then attends an important event almost every night."

"It's quite an exciting life Sveta is leading." Anna sighed, thinking of her own miserable fate. Tomorrow she'd be starting her first paid job, in the Svyatoshyn market of all places. Not exactly what she expected to ever happen to her.

"Sveta's life sure is exciting. But you know what, I often wish Sveta were more like you," Uncle Stepan said kindly. "Hard-working, goal-oriented, good student… Sveta attends the Taras Shevchenko University, but how much studying does she actually do? Not much. I haven't seen her with a book for a long time! I understand, she has too many other temptations, like social media, beauty salons, coffee shops, fashion boutiques. But still… I had suggested many times for Sveta to do a semester abroad in the UK. I'd pay for all her expenses."

"And what came out of this idea?" Anna asked.

"Not much, to be honest." Uncle Stepan shook his head. "In Sveta's words, it was too complicated... She didn't speak good enough English to understand the lectures... Eventually, she just went on a trip to London with a couple of friends and did a lot of shopping. That was the end of it. All right, we're on the Hnata Yury street. Where do you want me to drop you off?"

"Right here, near the kiosk, please. I need to buy the Ukrainian Business magazine—a new issue is supposed to be out today. Thanks so much for the lift Uncle Stepan! My best wishes to Aunt Motria and Sveta. I'll see you tomorrow."

Chapter 3. The Rainy Day at the Svyatoshyn Market

Kyiv, Ukraine

Anna spotted the two furry newcomers near her store as soon as they passed by her window. The first dog, orange and gray, was medium-sized and bore some distant resemblance to a rough Collie. She had an abundant and soft coat, muscular legs, and almond-shaped dark-brown eyes. The origins of the second dog were completely unclear. She was small and scrawny, with scruffy fur and bushy eyebrows hiding her eyes. One ear was lying flat and another one was standing up.

Anna's lips quirked slightly at the corners while she watched the newcomers hesitantly walk around the market, looking around and sniffing everything while investigating their new territory.

These dogs are in a dire need of some good names. How about Zirka and Lapa? I think these names perfectly match them!

Zirka was the indisputable leader of the two, marching proudly in the front, and barking loudly from time to time to announce her presence to the bystanders. Lapa was running behind Zirka on her short legs and barking in a shrill voice.

Zirka and Lapa eventually stopped at the shawarma stand where a couple of customers were waiting in line. The dogs wiggled their tails and gave people a pleading look: *"Can you spare some shawarma for the two hungry dogs?"* When none of the customers responded to their plea, the animals plopped down and put their muzzles on the ground.

Anna approached the stand and motioned to the dogs to come closer. They jumped up in a flash and took a place next to her, their mouths wide open.

"Two shawarmas, please!" Anna announced loudly, as she waved her smartphone with the magic digital wallet.

"This is a total waste of money," lamented Baba Kateryna, as Zirka and Lapa were digging their muzzles deep into their shawarma meals.

"These stray dogs in the market come and go. Most likely, they will get run over by a car tomorrow. I would definitely not recommend forming any kind of attachment to them."

"Thanks, Baba Kateryna, but I will still feed them," Anna objected. "Hopefully, they will be around for a while and nothing will happen to them."

"Well, do as you wish. Don't tell me I didn't prevent you. And one thing for sure—I won't let them come anywhere near *my* store."

****

It was raining so hard in the afternoon that the market flooded and all the customers quickly scrambled away. Anna watched hundreds of bright umbrellas pop up outside in a flash and listened to the soothing sound of the rain drumming on the roof. What a quiet and relaxing afternoon it was going to be in her dry and warm shop.

Suddenly Anna discerned something outside which made her heart sink. The two lonely figures were huddling under one of the market tables, soaked to the bone and absolutely miserable. The rain kept pouring down on their heads and bodies, forcing them to shake their fur off from time to time, but there was no better place to hide.

One second, and Anna was already outside. The wind was piercing through her chest and heavy rain drops were banging all over her body like heavy rocks.

"Girls, get in!" Anna yelled as she ushered Zirka and Lapa into her store. "You are staying here with me." She poured the water out of her shoes and then grabbed a big towel and wiped the droopy-eared friends. Immediately their fluffy tails were wagging non-stop and black eyes were shining brightly again.

"Sit here in the corner and please—don't even think of shaking off your fur! Uncle Stepan will kill me if we ruin the merchandise or the decorations inside the store. I am not allowed to keep animals here—I could lose my job if somebody finds out."

Zirka and Lapa curled up in the corner. But just as Anna started cleaning the wet paw prints on the floor with the towel to hide all the evidence, the door of the store opened wide. A gust of wind blew in and the dogs jumped up in fear.

Crap!

She sighed when she looked over. It was just Dima Kudermet, her old friend from high school. He entered the store nonchalantly, dragging his drenched shoes all over the floor and splashing everything with the water as he closed his giant umbrella. In his hand, Dima was holding a large cup of double decaf macchiato, his all-time favorite.

"Dimochka, what are you doing here in such terrible

weather?" Anna closed the door and carefully wiped off the wet merchandise.

"Well, I had something important to tell you, so I had to come without delay. I don't care about the rain, my SUV drives perfectly in any kind of weather... But wait a minute, who are those two wet brats huddling in the corner?" Dima pointed at the two dogs, who immediately perked up their ears.

"Not only do you have to work at a store, now you also are pet-sitting?" Dima shook his head and took a large sip of his coffee while loudly smacking his lips and moving around his tongue.

Lapa and Zirka subtly growled and instantly lifted up their upper lips, displaying a row of white, sharp teeth.

Anna frowned at them before turning to Dima. "These are just two dogs from the market, no big deal. I am giving them shelter from the rain," Anna explained.

She waved her finger at Lapa and Zirka. "Girls, calm down. Sit. This is a friend. *Supposedly*. He is not a big fan of animals, as you can see, but otherwise he is not that bad. One can get used to him, so to say. We used to date back in high school... Okay, what were you going to tell me about, Dima?"

Dima handed a couple of glossy and colorful brochures to her with a big grin.

"I have some great news to share. Tonight, I will be featuring exciting new food recipes on my social media channel. The recipes are inside the brochure, but make sure you don't miss the demonstration! Also, I added a new post to my travel blog about my recent trip to Peru. It has a lot of photos of me sporting the latest resort fashions. You should check it out just in case you will be going to Peru soon."

Dima slid off his rain jacket and twirled around, showing off his nut-brown tan.

"Thanks… I'll have a look. Of course, I urgently need to know everything about Peru. Where else would I be going, right?" Anna sighed. She could not even dream of going to Peru. The best vacation she could afford would be to the city of Odessa on the Black Sea. Dima, on the other hand, always managed to travel to faraway places. Thanks to his successful travel blog, hotels let him stay for free in exchange for publicity.

Dima leaned against the counter, took the last sip of his drink, and tossed the empty cup in the corner.

"I have one more thing to tell you. The most important one actually, but the most delicate." Dima lowered his voice a notch. "I saw that today is the last day of applications for the Global Associates Program at Polaris International Corporation. You HAVE to apply. This year, they are looking exactly for young people like you—those who are interested in working on projects to protect our planet. Just look here!"

Dima held out his tablet and scrolled through the colorful ad on social media featuring smiling young people of different nationalities.

"Anna, this would be a perfect job for you!"

She glanced through the ad. "Dima, of course I would love to work at Polaris. Who wouldn't? But believe me, I don't have the right credentials to get in. Do you think anybody would invite me to an interview with my background? A sales associate at the Chervona Ruta store? I don't think Uncle Stepan's stellar reputation has reached Polaris yet."

"No, Anna, I'm totally serious. I have an idea. You

are not going to put Chervona Ruta as your current position."

"Then what should I put? The Energy Institute?" Anna looked at her friend expectantly. "I suppose I could do this. But I doubt this would impress them either."

"Of course not. I looked up profiles of successful candidates on the Polaris website. Clearly, all of them held very important leadership positions in other organizations prior to being selected. So, you also have to state in your CV something outstanding which Polaris could never resist: that you are an adviser to the Minister of Finance of Ukraine!"

Anna burst out laughing.

"Dima, this is the craziest thing I have ever heard. I don't even want to discuss it." She turned away and walked to the opposite side of the store, trying to occupy herself with something useful like organizing some new merchandise on the shelf.

"I don't think it's crazy at all!" Dima's eyes were burning with excitement. "I know the Minister and people from his office. I can help with the reference if Polaris asks for one."

"Dima, this still makes no sense. To lie on the application? I could never do that." She shook her head. Only a delusional person could come up with a plan like this, really. Nobody else's could even fathom something close to it.

"Okay, fine." Dima snorted, angrily kicking a box of diapers which was laying on the floor. "Just bury yourself in this shop. Bury your talent, your brilliance, your dreams. Do you think the most successful people have always taken the high road? Not at all. That's the whole point—you need to know when to cheat, maybe just a little, for the greater good. Otherwise, you'll end up a total loser. You used to be a tennis star—now look where you are, thanks to your fame-obsessed mother who made you play through that shoulder injury, destroying your chances for greatness."

"Dima, it's not my mom's fault that I turned out a failure," Anna exclaimed as the emotional pain cut her deep. "It's nobody's fault. That's just the way the stars aligned. It wasn't meant to be."

"Well, maybe you were not meant to be the tennis champion. Fine. But you shouldn't be working at the Svyatoshyn market either! This gig might be good for a few months, but then what? You want to become another Baba Kateryna, working here till the end of your days? You know the Ukrainian proverb—under the lying stone the water doesn't flow. No pain, no gain. Success doesn't just come to you by itself—you have to act!"

"But I already sent out resumes to so many companies—and none of them even invited me to an interview!" Her heart ached as she spoke.

"So what? It's their loss. Don't give up... You were destined for great things. You were the best in your class at the business school with a perfect 4.0 GPA. All the professors thought you were brilliant, right? You belong at the top company like Polaris, *I know that*, Anna! You'd ace their interview, no doubt. And you refuse to act. What a waste of my time."

Dima stormed out of the store and slammed the door shut, without saying so much as a goodbye.

"And now it's just us." Anna wiped away her tears as Zirka and Lapa approached her and licked her hands.

"Maybe Dima has a point," Anna said weakly as she was tossing his empty cup into the trash. "Polaris is such a great company. Girls, they are the best of the best! I would fit in perfectly. I… I suppose I could try to follow Dima's advice… I could submit the application. He is right—sometimes a small lie can really help you get ahead. I just need to take a chance, buy a lottery ticket, so to say."

The dogs wagged their tails. In their view, nothing Anna was going to do could possibly be wrong. She was likely the best person they had ever met. Period.

The rainstorm had almost passed; tender rays of sun looked into Anna's window. Lapa and Zirka stood in the middle of the store hesitantly, unsure whether they should stay a bit longer or get going. Anna caught their gaze and thought for a minute.

"You know what," she finally said, "I'll just take you home with me today. How about that? I'm sure my parents won't be thrilled in the beginning, as we'll have two more mouths to feed, but they'll understand. Afterall, I'll be finally making a decent salary here at the store. Let's get you washed and coiffed, buy you some lovely soft beds, a bunch of balls and toys. From now on, you'll be enjoying the life of complete leisure."

****

This is simply unbelievable. Dima's diabolic plan… worked.

Frost spidered across her window, snow blowing outside while Anna sat inside, her computer in front of her. In her email mailbox, glared the coveted email from the Polaris Human Resources.

Somebody named Michelle Miller was inviting her to Washington D.C. for an interview. Next week. All travel expenses would be borne by Polaris.

For a few minutes, Anna sat motionless and just

stared at the screen. Up till this moment, she had never lied in her life. And yet, she had not accomplished any of her goals. Everything seemed to go wrong for her. But the one and only time she tried to cheat, she seemed to get what she wanted. How could life be so incredibly unfair?

Well, in any event, she couldn't possibly go ahead with this lie. She was a good, *honest* person. People like that did not lie on job applications. Never.

Anna immediately clicked the "Reply" button.

I'll send a polite response to the Polaris folks. Say that I had a change in plans and no longer want to apply for their program. That's the right thing to do.

But her fingers typed a completely different message.

In a few short days, the evening of her departure for the Polaris interviews arrived. By nine in the evening, Anna was standing in the middle of her room, putting a few final things in her suitcase, looking around the room and wondering what else she might need. This was a short but potentially life-changing trip, so she needed to make sure she had everything.

Lapa and Zirka were lying stretched out on her bed after a big meal and observing Anna's movements with one eye. Lapa was slowly chewing on her favorite elephant stuffy. Olena was relaxing in a rocking chair, drinking her beloved tea with rosehips she had collected at the end of the summer, and giving Anna interview advice.

Anna's father, Ivan, was also in the room, making occasional comments, although he was paying much more attention to the heated hockey match on TV than to Anna's preparations for the trip.

"Sorry, girls," he said earlier that evening, "this is a big match today. Ukraine vs. Russia. It's a life-or-death situation. I must watch it, or I am not a patriot."

"Don't worry, Dad," Anna said softly. "Mom and I both know what this match means. Please, concentrate on hockey, we'll take care of all the preparations."

That evening reminded Anna of the good old times. Some years ago, their family used to sit just like this, strategizing about Anna's upcoming tennis matches and assessing strengths and weaknesses of various opponents. Lapa and Zirka didn't exist back in those days, but Anna had a different partner in crime: Porky the bulldog. He usually sat right next to her on the sofa, listening carefully to what was being said. Anna wiped away a tear as she remembered Porky. When he passed away, the whole family was devastated for months. They still visited him at the pet cemetery.

"What are you planning to wear on the interview day?" Olena asked, stretching her neck out and trying to see what Anna had put in her suitcase. "Appearance matters. Don't forget about that."

"My dark-red suit. The one with the knee-high skirt. That's the only appropriate suit I have," Anna said. Her wardrobe did not have suits from the major brands, but she hoped this outfit would make her look presentable enough.

"Okay, that should work. The dark-red color projects seriousness, sophistication, and responsibility. Interviewers will notice you."

"I hope so. I also hope to answer all the questions right."

"That's the most important part, of course. Think of the interviews like the final of the US Open. You have to beat a lot of strong competitors in order to win."

"Absolutely," Anna agreed.

"I am positive that some candidates at your interviews will be the cream of the crop," Olena said as she took the last sip of her tea. "They have impeccable credentials and are expected to get the slot in the program no matter what. But there will probably be a few random people like you—dark horses who nobody expects to do well."

"That's for sure. I am probably the darkest horse they have ever invited to the interviews," Anna said gloomily and turned away from Olena, fiddling with her clothes in the suitcase. She immediately thought about her lie on the application. She did not want her mom to notice her hesitation and become suspicious.

Over the years, they had often criticized famous athletes who had taken performance-enhancing drugs. Both Anna and Olena found it mind-boggling that somebody could put their career at risk and cheat like that. It was not worth it! When Anna was playing competitive tennis, she'd never considered cheating a possibility. Not even for a second. It was a taboo in their family. Their philosophy was that winning could only be accomplished by working. Hard. And now, after a moment of weakness, Anna had ended up going against everything she stood for.

"You okay, Anna?" Olena asked. "I can imagine this time must be very stressful for you."

"Yeah, I'm fine," Anna said in a trembling voice, making sure she did not meet her mom's gaze. She was a terrible liar, and Olena could easily spot something was fishy had she looked over then. "Just a little worried, that's all."

Anna's phone suddenly beeped and flashed. She was happy to change the subject.

"Uncle Opanas will pick me up at two in the morning in his minibus to go to the airport. He just texted me to confirm," Anna said after looking at her phone. Uncle Opanas was a mini-bus driver Anna knew from her job in the market. "This will be fifty dollars, much cheaper than a taxi, plus much safer. I know the driver well, he's never had an accident."

"Great. Is this enough time though?" Olena closed her eyes, trying to estimate how long it might take to get there. "The airport is far away. Your flight is at six, and what if there is some problem with immigration?"

"This should still be plenty of time, even if something happens. Normally, it takes just two hours. I wouldn't worry."

"I hate these morning flights," Olena grumbled. "You don't get any sleep, and then you end up on the plane in coach and you still can't sleep either. You will be exhausted. You should go straight to bed when you get to Washington."

"I was actually planning on seeing a couple of friends from college. I'll be fine, don't worry."

"I'm not sure if that is such a good idea. You need time to rest and get over the jet leg before the interviews…" Olena shook her head. "Well, it's your choice. By the way, do you want to take some borscht with you to eat on the plane? I could put it in a neat jar for you."

"No, Mom, you must remember that they don't allow any liquids on the plane. They would confiscate the borscht!"

Right at two am, Anna climbed into Uncle Opanas's

yellow minibus with her suitcase and got comfortable by the window. It was snowing a little, but not a blizzard or anything serious. Olena waved a tired goodbye from the window and switched off all the lights. Everyone else was asleep in the house.

As the minibus was moving slowly and smoothly along the snowy streets of Kyiv, with hardly any other cars in the streets, Anna was excited and proud of herself for embarking on such an adventure. She was going to an interview with one of the best companies in the world! She hoped she would do really well at the interviews and get the coveted Global Associate spot. She definitely deserved it, with all her hard work she had put in at the Energy Institute.

Anna started dozing off a little, but about thirty minutes into the drive, she woke up and decided to check her documents, just in case. Both the e-ticket and the passport were in her handbag, so everything was fine. Anna then opened the passport to look at her visa, and suddenly froze. There was no visa. *This is the wrong passport!*

Last month, Anna had needed to get a new passport as her old one expired. They allowed her to keep the old one, even after the new one was issued. She must have grabbed the wrong one from the drawer.

"Uncle Opanas, we have a problem here," Anna said quietly, as her heart sank and she felt sick to her stomach. "We need to turn around and go back. I forgot something."

"Are you sure?" Uncle Opanas turned to Anna, puzzled. "We have already driven pretty far away from your house, we might not make it to the airport on time. I suggest to keep going. We are making good time now."

"Doesn't look like we have a choice. I have the wrong passport here."

"Well, we can try, of course. But no guarantees. The roads are covered with a lot of snow and ice. We cannot go too fast, or the bus will slide off the road…"

Anna suddenly got a feeling that maybe the universe was trying to tell her that she was not welcome at the Polaris interviews. She shouldn't have lied on the application. Now she would miss her flight. She would never even get a chance to show her knowledge.

To Anna's despair, the snow was starting to fall heavier and heavier, like a thick white wall. The wind became stronger, and it was hard to see anything through the window. How Uncle Opanas was driving in such weather was a complete mystery to her. On any other day Anna would have admired the snow, but now she so wished it would stop! She felt powerless, unable to change anything about the forces of nature.

As the minibus clung to the road as it continued forward, she kept peeking at her watch every five minutes. Eventually, she gave up and surrendered to her fate. There was simply no way they would ever make it on time.

And yet—an hour later than she had planned, right passport in her hand, the yellow minibus still arrived at the Boryspil airport forty minutes before Anna's flight. She still had a chance. But she needed to move. Fast.

"Good luck!" yelled Uncle Opanas. "I will stay in the parking lot for now just in case. Hope you make your flight!"

She ran into the airport at full speed, dragging her suitcase behind her. The check-in for her flight was still open. *Phew!*

After dropping her bag off, she rushed over to passport control. The long line swirled around like a snake. It would take at least an hour to get through. If Anna chose to stand in the line, the best thing she could do would be to wave her plane goodbye from the window.

She begged the people in line in front of her to let her go first. She explained that she was about to miss her flight, and she was heading to an important job interview in the US.

"*Dobre*. Please go ahead!" Fellow passengers seemed quite generous that morning. "Good luck with the interview!"

When Anna finally took her seat on the plane, she sighed with relief. *Ugh, this was close!* But she would make the interviews after all. Despite the scare, she was destined for the US. For now, there was nothing more she could do. She slept through the whole flight.

Chapter 4. The Good Old Friends

Washington, D.C.

It's 6:59 pm. I'm perfectly on time! Like always. Emily Roberts pulled up to the restaurant in her silver Mercedes-Maybach, grabbed her studded, leather handbag from the front seat, and walked in confidently. One glance around the dining area, and she immediately spotted her former college classmates—Katie Gardiner and Anna Levenko.

"Anna, what a surprise! Last time we saw each other was at our graduation, right? Didn't expect to see you in Washington!" Emily said loudly, giving her old friend a double-cheek kiss and subtly peeking at her *vyshyvanka* embroidered with the patterns of red flowers, branches, and leaves.

They were such a work of art! A few years ago, Emily had been in Paris and witnessed for herself the success of couture collections featuring vyshyvanka patterns. Given all the buzz, she'd acquired a couple of peasant blouses, but her collection looked bleak compared to the masterpiece Anna wore now.

"I'm so happy you could make it, Emily!" Anna said in a perfectly smooth and melodic voice. Her Ukrainian accent always made everything she said sound like sweet music. "Wasn't planning on coming back to the States at all, but suddenly everything changed. So good to see familiar faces—both you and Katie."

Emily gave Katie a tired look. It had been a couple of years since they graduated, and somehow she had very limited interest in seeing Katie again. With her nose piercing, a giant butterfly tattoo on her arm, overall geeky look, and a lowbrow public accounting job, she was not quite the crowd Emily wanted to associate with.

Well, if Katie had to be here tonight, fine. It was just one dinner and Katie would have a lot to dish about their former classmates. She'd likely kept in touch with everyone over the years.

Katie announced that the majority of people in their class were doing quite well. Several classmates ended up in public accounting, similar to Katie, as these were some of the easiest jobs to get right out of college. A few guys, including the ingenious and handsome Forrest Lamm—Katie's unreciprocated love at one point—scored big and landed great jobs in investment banking. Jason Schubert, a failed marketing manager, somehow made it to the semifinals of the talent show with his ventriloquist act and was now a big celebrity.

"Any big news on the relationship front?" Emily checked. "Nobody's married yet, right?"

"Well... I assumed you knew about Laura?" Katie gave her a puzzled look.

"She got married!" Anna squealed.

Apparently, Laura Newbury, one of the most popular girls in the class, had married picture-perfect Italian diplomat Giuseppe Ferraro, ten years her senior, and moved to the splendid and romantic city of Rome. Emily felt a pinch of envy squeezing her heart as she listened to Katie's story. *WTH?* Laura was getting married, everybody knew about it, and not a single soul bothered to alert her?

"I went to their wedding last June," Katie declared proudly. "The wedding took place on the marvelous island of Capri, where Giuseppe's family is from. They own this gorgeous villa overlooking the Tyrrhenian Sea. When the invitation came, I was like, okay, I'm going to Italy for the first time. Let me arrive a week early and explore the island. There turned out to be so much to see! My favorite thing was sitting at La Piazzetta, Capri's famous square, where one can see movie actors, billionaires, princes, and princesses who are visiting Capri. You'd fit right in, Emily."

"Guess so. Come to think of it, I have not been to Capri yet," Emily admitted through gritted teeth. The mere fact that Katie Gardiner, who rarely travelled past the Maryland border, went to the island of Capri first annoyed her beyond belief. "Maybe I should go there this summer."

"Oh, you'll totally love Capri. The weather there is unbelievable all summer—sunny, in the eighties, with a slight breeze."

"In the eighties? Then Capri must be one of the few places in the world that have not yet been hit by climate change! I used to spend a lot of weekends sailing, but we hardly even went out this past summer. It was either unbearably hot, or raining heavily," complained Emily.

The bad weather in D.C. was really getting on her nerves. She detested both hot and cold, but especially the heat. She hated when the steamy air enveloped her soft skin, infiltrated her nose and eyes, and melted her carefully applied makeup.

However, the one who suffered the most from the recent heat waves was Fofo—Emily's Pomeranian. His abundant double-coat, which made him look super cute and fluffy, was a huge liability during the D.C. summers. Luckily, Fofo was perfectly equipped for winter and was now absolutely happy, enjoying his walks in the chilly D.C. weather and especially an occasional snowfall. Till next summer.

"The climate here will only get worse," Katie nodded. "We already get terrible floods. And I read in a magazine that by the year 2100, the river level in the Washington area could rise so much that Reagan National Airport and the National Mall could be under water! Seriously, guys, this climate change is no joke."

"Unbelievable." Anna shook her head. "In Ukraine, we now get horrendous heat waves too. My Grandma hates air-conditioners, nonetheless we had no other choice but to install one last year—Grandma now sits under it in a hat and scarf... So, returning to the Capri trip, did you meet any celebrities while you were there, Katie?"

"Gosh, let me think... Well, 'meeting' is a bit of a stretch, but I did see Bradley Cooper and Tom Cruise, right there at La Piazzetta. In fact, I have a picture with Tom Cruise now! Let me show you... The local photographers were taking photos of him and I was like—let me try to sneak in..."

Emily and her friend Anna looked at the pictures in Katie's phone with interest. Yes, indeed, Tom Cruise was standing in the front and right behind him was Katie, smiling widely and waving her hand. Pretty lucky. There were some other nice pictures as well—Katie on the beach, Katie at the wedding, Katie at the botanical gardens, and even Katie with some tan and handsome guy.

"Now who is that?" Anna asked cheerfully. "Did you also find a boyfriend while in Capri? How romantic would it be to go to a beautiful island and meet your true love there—like a movie star or a prince!"

"Oh, this is definitely not a prince. It is Alessandro, a tour guide in Capri," Katie said sadly, the spark in her eyes fading. "I went on a group tour of Capri together with other people from my hotel, and he was our guide. We had a few very romantic dates in Capri, and I thought he might be my person. But then he got interested in another girl from our group. Why can't I be as lucky as Laura?"

"Oh, don't worry. You'll meet somebody much better very soon!" Anna said, tightly hugging Katie. "I must confess that I have not had much success with guys lately either. I dated a few guys in the past year, and nothing came out of that."

"For your information, I heard that David Thompson left his job in New York and is now back in Washington," Emily stated meaningfully, looking straight at Anna. Finally, she managed to think of some important news to share as well. David and Anna had a hot romance back in college.

"I see," Anna said calmly, although she blushed slightly. "I have not seen him ever since I broke up with him. Hope he is doing well."

"More than well. I hear he opened his own consulting firm and enrolled in the PhD. program. Still think it was a huge mistake for you to let him go."

"Well… At that time, I felt I was doing the right thing by letting him go," Anna said with a long sigh. "David was a bit boring. He worked and studied, that was pretty much it. I thought I would soon find the guy of my dreams—romantic, fearless, adventurous…"

Emily shook her head. Hands down, David was Anna's best shot. Describing him as "fearless" or "adventurous" would be a stretch, but he had many other good qualities. Beggars like Anna couldn't be choosers.

"How about you, Emily, seeing anyone special?" Anna asked.

"Not at the moment. I'd met a really gorgeous man some time ago, but guess what? He started dating my sister and now they're engaged."

"That's a bummer," Katie said sympathetically.

"Well, let's hope we all meet some great guys very soon. *Bud'mo!*" Anna said as they clinked their drinks. "By the way, do you want me to tell you why I am here in the States?"

"Of course!" Katie yelled. "I'm dying to know what is going on."

Anna paused dramatically. "Okay, let me explain," she started in a whisper, looking at her former classmates triumphantly. "I got invited by Polaris International Corporation to interview for a spot in their prestigious Global Associates program! Can you imagine? Emily, you and I might be working there together soon!"

Katie froze with her mouth open and her face expressing unbelievable delight and euphoria. At the same time, Emily bit her lip. Hard. Her throat suddenly felt tight and scratchy from disappointment. How on Earth did *a Ukrainian* get an interview for a slot in the Polaris flagship recruitment program? That was completely unacceptable. What was HR thinking?

"Look, Anna, I had no idea you were pursuing this," Emily finally said in the kind of soft voice used to talk to little kids. "You must know that Polaris is one of the most elite companies in the world, right? And that your chances to get in are—let me check my notes—nil?"

"Not true!" interjected Katie. "Come on, Emily. Anna was the top student in our class. She'll get in."

"Oh sure she will," Emily replied, pretending to fix her hair but in reality giving both Anna and Katie a good view of her latest purchase—a new ring with an immense black opal she just bought last week. The opal glowed like a big star on her finger, so dark and mysterious.

"They have tens of thousands of candidates from different countries applying every year. Seriously, ladies, it's nearly impossible to get a spot in the Global Associates Program. Even for people who are highly qualified."

"I know it's very hard to get accepted." Anna nodded, her look serious and focused. "I participated in the monthly chats Polaris holds for candidates where they discuss the application process and what to expect at the interviews. It's really very challenging. But I hope I have a tiny chance to get in? I've been preparing very diligently, studying every day."

"Sure, you have a good chance. Emily, it can't be that hard to get in!" Katie protested so violently that she even accidentally spilled her drink all over her top. Anna quickly picked up a napkin and started helping Katie clean up the mess.

"Of course it can be, sweetie." Emily wrinkled her nose, observing Katie's and Anna's frantic attempts to clean up Katie's old baggy sweater.

"You know, ladies, I've been working at Polaris since graduating from the business school. Even with my superb intelligence and great credentials, I didn't get into the Global Associates program. It's completely impossible, believe me! Instead, between us, my dad managed to pull some strings and I got a staff position."

Emily took a sip of her champagne and continued in her traditional fake-friendly tone mixed with disdain. "On the Global Associates Program, I can tell you for a fact who normally passes the grueling interview and gets the slot. People who went to Harvard, Yale... those who worked on Wall Street at the top investment firms. Also, the company is starting to get very focused on Sub-Saharan Africa. Our management is looking for people who have connections to the region. Why on Earth would they hire Anna, who has never even been to the African continent?"

"That's a good point, I heard about it on TV," Anna said softly. "But—surprise, surprise—I do have a connection to Africa. My grandfather happens to be African."

Emily rolled her eyes. "Gosh, Anna! No, this is obviously not the kind of connection we're looking for. I am talking about *work experience* in Africa. Got it?"

This girl is so clueless! Clearly, Anna would never pass the interview at Polaris. The rejection email would be in her mailbox in no time.

As soon as the bill was paid (split three ways, out of principle, to compensate for the tremendous waste of her time), Emily quickly drove off in her fancy car. She noticed that Katie and Anna stood in front of the restaurant, watching her beloved Mercedes-Maybach speed away. Most likely, she'd never see either one again—unless they'd have a school reunion or something. Good bye ladies, thanks for a lovely evening!

****

"Best of luck at the interviews, Anna," Katie said,

as Emily's car disappeared. "You'll get the position, I know it. Can't wait to have you in Washington again."

"Thanks, Katie. If the stars align, the job will be mine."

"When you come to Washington next, I'll show you my new pet. A red-eyed tree frog. I named him Freddie. He is super cute."

"Definitely! When did you get Freddie?"

"A couple of weeks ago. I decided to get a pet finally and I thought a frog was a perfect idea. He is super easy to take care of compared to a cat or a dog, very low maintenance."

"Oh, I don't know about that," Anna objected. "They are actually quite sensitive creatures and can easily get sick, from what I have seen. My friend Dima has some unique variety of a tree frog. He always needs to be different and impress everyone, so a regular pet did not work for him. I have to take care of the frog during Dima's constant trips, and there is always something wrong. One time the frog ate too big of a cricket and had a stomachache; another time he swallowed a pebble."

"Luckily, Freddie has very good health," Katie said proudly. "Ever since I got him, he's been in perfect shape, happy and jumpy!"

"This is good to hear. All right, give Freddie a hug from me. Until next time!"

"Catch you later! Blow them away, girl."

Chapter 5. The Big Day

Washington, D.C.

The morning of the interviews dawned cold, gray, and rainy. It was December after all. Anna quickly jumped out of bed, brimming over with anticipation, and immediately got into her interview clothes which she had diligently spread out on the bed last night.

Now, where is my lucky charm?

Anna took out from the safe her necklace with a pendant—a most gorgeous, deepest-blue sapphire in the shape of a star, surrounded by iridescent pearls, rubies, and diamonds. The jewel also had an uncommon engraving in the back of the pendant, but Anna could not read it.

Many years ago, Grandpa Solomon gave this necklace to Grandma Maria on their wedding day. Anna found it in the back of one of the drawers, and was astonished by the shiny stones whose glitter had not faded even under a thick layer of dust. Nobody in the family thought that the necklace was valuable, but Anna still took it into a jewelry store in downtown Kyiv to check. Turned out, these were all precious gemstones of the highest quality. Where Grandpa could have possibly gotten them, was a complete mystery.

It was still dark outside when Anna climbed into the taxi. Pretty soon, she was rushing through the Polaris lobby, shaking off her wet umbrella. She presented her ID to the guard with a proud smile and announced loudly: "Good morning to you! I'm Anna Levenko. I am here for the Global Associate interviews, Mister…?"

"Mr. Washington." The guard yawned loudly and looked at his watch. "You are too early, Anna Levenko. You know what time it even is? Six thirty. The interviews are not till eight."

"I couldn't sleep, Mr. Washington—too excited to come to Polaris!" Anna confessed. "And it's so rainy out there…" She anxiously looked outside. If the guard kicked her out, her only good suit would get wet.

"Fine, sweetheart, I'll let you in," Mr. Washington agreed reluctantly, looking Anna over from head to bottom. "I guess we shouldn't penalize you for having a lot of enthusiasm."

He ushered Anna to a waiting area where all the candidates were supposed to gather. The room was nice and cozy.

She browsed through the latest finance news on her smart phone to kill some time. Also, she read a bunch of cheerful texts which came in from Dima:

—You can do it, I believe in you!—

—Don't forget to look at my new blog tonight! Xoxo—

—Some new items in my store - check them out!—

Eventually other candidates started to trickle in. A British curly red-haired guy came first, then came two girls from Spain, a girl from the Philippines, a guy from India, a Frenchman, an Australian, several Americans, and a few extra people whose nationality Anna did not get a chance to find out.

In order to avoid appearing anxious or nosy, Anna

indiscernibly observed everyone, while carefully listening to what they had to say. Hopefully, at least some of the candidates came from a modest background.

The girl from Philippines, Rosie, was simply a knock-out, shooting bright smiles in every direction and chatting non-stop. Apparently, she had been working at a large development bank in Asia for several years after graduating with a PhD in energy policy from Yale.

A Spanish woman, Mariella, sat quietly in the corner, with her eyes down. Anna's face lit up. *Maybe this one is not an overachiever?* But it turned out, Mariella had a perfect pedigree: her whole family was in finance back in Madrid, she held a Stanford MBA, and had been working on multi-billion-dollar deals in investment banking in NYC for several years.

Other candidates also appeared highly accomplished. The name of the Frenchman was Jean. He'd graduated with an MBA from INSEAD, one of the world's top business schools, and worked on various projects funded by the French government. The Australian guy, Thomas, held a PhD in economics from Harvard and was a department head at Australia's securities and investments commission. The British guy, Alistair, was a Professor of Finance at Oxford and an author of four books and ten articles published in top academic journals.

Anna sank deeper and deeper into her armchair every time she heard some new important credential announced by one of the candidates. Why on Earth had she ever agreed to Dima's crazy plan, let alone come here? She was a total imposter at these interviews! If only she could shrink into the size of a tiny mouse and find her way out of Polaris, before she made an embarrassment of herself. She'd fail the interviews, for sure, and everyone would be laughing at her.

The organizers soon arrived and announced the rules. Two hundred contenders had made it to this stage. Interviews of small groups of candidates, like today, would continue approximately till the end of February. After that Polaris management would deliberate on the lucky fifteen candidates who would make the final cut. The new batch of Global Associates would join the company in mid-September.

"How many candidates who are interviewing today are expected to make it?" Alistair asked.

"Usually, we pick one candidate from each day," was the message from the organizers. "Of course, there can be exceptions. On some days, we will not pick anybody at all. In very rare cases, two or more people could be selected from a particular day. It all depends. Just do your absolute best—this is the only way to improve your chances."

The first step was a hundred-question multiple choice test. It was a lethal combination of GRE and GMAT and included questions on mathematics, geometry, logic skills, grammar, and other areas.

The candidates were then split in to two groups. The first group was doing the panel interview, the second— the group case study. In the afternoon, the tasks would reverse.

Anna was part of the group doing the case study in the morning. The case featured a developing country struggling with a wide range of developmental issues. At the outset, everyone was quiet, turning the pages back and forth, glancing at each other. Nobody was ready to take the first step.

"Okay, guys," Anna broke the silence. "We have to deliver a presentation to the President of the country on various avenues for stimulating economic growth. Let's split the responsibilities. I'll come up with some ideas on development of the oil sector and protecting the environment as I am quite familiar with these topics from my work. Alistair, you are an agriculture specialist, right? Can you prepare a few recommendations in the area to share with the group?"

"Sure." Alistair readily picked up a pen and waved it proudly like it was a musketeer's sword.

Other team members received similar tasks. In no time, everyone came up with a bunch of excellent suggestions which Anna grouped into a nice summary document. She then made a presentation to the judges.

Finally, all the team members were released for lunch and instructed to come back for the panel interviews.

Freedom! Anna went flying out of the conference room. All in all, she had done well in the first half of the group interviews. Now it was time to check out the Polaris cafeteria and get a good lunch.

She strolled around the large and luxurious cafeteria, sticking her neck out and squeezing between the people to better see what was on offer. Soon, her tray was full of 'brain' food: fatty fish (salmon, tuna, and sardines), sautéed broccoli, chicken curry dish, a bowl of blueberries, a dark chocolate bar, and a big cup of coffee.

Pumpkin seeds, which were supposedly rich in key nutrients for brain power, were nowhere to be found. Fortunately she brought a box of them from home.

Anna walked towards the checkout counter carefully and slowly with her heavy load. From one moment to the next, she slipped, barely managing to hold her balance. At least her tennis skills were helpful in something.

Jean, the French guy she'd met earlier, happened to be buying lunch at the same time. For a minute, he stood in front of the checkout counter, watching Anna with her lunch tray.

"*Bonjour*! Do you need any help?" he asked in his super sweet French accent.

"Oh, I am fine." Anna blushed. "Feel free to join me for lunch if you want."

"That would be great." Jean paid for his lunch and joined her. His tray included just a small salad and a small plate of scallops in some white sauce. "I hate eating alone."

As they sat down at the table, Anna cautiously glanced at Jean. With a straight and prominent nose, tan skin, ocean blue eyes and well-defined high cheekbones, his face was extremely attractive. He projected sophistication and professionalism. But Jean's smile was the most memorable—dazzling, bright, irresistible. Every time he smiled at her, cute dimples appeared in the corners of his mouth. At one point during lunch, Jean took off his jacket and Anna held her breath—he was very athletic, with his muscles straining against the fabric of his perfectly starched shirt.

"So, what's the deal with all the food?" Jean asked, pointing at the feast which Anna had in front of her.

"Oh, this food will just help to boost my brain power before the interview," Anna explained and straightened in her chair. She wanted to appear as attractive as possible to Jean. "I did some research. Don't worry, I don't eat like that every day. Our family would go bankrupt."

"Interesting idea. Hope that helps. You know, my heart almost sank when I saw you slipping with that loaded tray. If you actually dropped it, I would have needed to help you clean up, and that would take an hour given how much stuff you have there!"

"Hah, do not worry. I have good balance. See, everything worked out."

"So, you are from Ukraine, right? Is this your first time in the States?"

"Oh, not at all. I am actually quite familiar with the area." Anna gave Jean a charming smile. Good thing he asked this question. She could now tell him she was not some country bumpkin and had spent a few years in the States before.

"I had gotten a full scholarship to attend university here in Washington. My parents also lived here for a few years. My Dad held a three-year contract with a local TV station and my mom tagged along. It was a bit of a windfall for our family those couple of years. Later we tried to stay, but nothing was working out. Until this interview. How about you?"

"I was born and raised in Paris," Jean said. "I've never lived in D.C., but visited a few times in the past— my older brother moved here some time ago. I currently work for a small NGO on projects in Libya, Syria, and Afghanistan."

"How are you not afraid to travel to different hot spots?" Anna asked with a lot of interest. "This can be quite dangerous."

"I want to be right where people need me most," Jean confessed. "I don't think about the risk too much. Life is dangerous enough in any city—just browse through Washington D.C. crime reports… A few times, my life was in real jeopardy, but luckily, I am still here having lunch with you."

"Really? What happened?" Anna asked, curious.

"The closest call was when I was working in Uganda a few years ago. One of my government counterparts, Amos Gaye, and I accidentally uncovered a large-scale corruption scheme in the transport sector which benefited several high-ranking officials. As we were investigating, Amos got killed and there was an attempt to assassinate me the very next day."

Anna's eyes widened. "Unbelievable! You did not get hurt, right?"

"I was very lucky. The bullet only grazed my shoulder and I managed to escape. All the officials involved are now in jail. Another close call was in Damascus, a year later. Our NGO team was going to a meeting with government officials and there was a huge explosion on the road we usually took, only ten minutes before we got there. Had we been delayed on the road, who knows what would have happened. Most recently, I was trying to fly out of Tripoli right at that time the rocket assault on the airport began. I was fortunate to escape unwounded… So far, things have been working out for me, you see."

"I am so happy that you are okay!" exclaimed Anna, clasping her hands. She had always admired courageous men like Jean—those who were willing to give up their lives to protect others.

She imagined Jean walking down the streets of Damascus or Aleppo, looking at all the devastation. Especially heartbreaking would be to observe the people; their lives destroyed and dreams crushed.

It was such tremendous luck that she had been born and raised in a beautiful country where peace and democracy reigned. Several times when Ukrainians felt that their liberties were infringed upon they came out to protest and changed the course of history. Unfortunately, Ukraine started facing a lot of challenges when Russia annexed the Crimean Peninsula and also began to instigate a separatist movement in the East of Ukraine. It was a while back—at that time, Anna was still in high school. Luckily, things were peaceful in other parts of Ukraine.

Jean sounded perfect. But she wondered whether he was environmentally cognizant or not.

"My dream is to work on 'green' projects here at Polaris," Jean said. "I would do anything to help our planet and stabilize the climate. You might have heard about the Mekdela Solar Park in Ethiopia which Polaris recently helped to establish. This is an astonishing achievement. I hope one day I can also do something similar."

"Of course I heard about Mekdela!" exclaimed Anna. "It was all over the news. I am totally infatuated with everything 'green' myself. We need to act urgently to stabilize the climate and save our planet. I do everything I possibly can to help the situation. I tried going zero-plastic, so far I have not succeeded, but I got very close."

"Oh, so you are the same 'green' freak as me." Jean laughed. "I have already been able to go zero-plastic, not without challenges, of course. I will teach you some day. And who knows, maybe in the future we will be working on a 'green' project here at Polaris together?"

"Oh, I would love that! We need to do something

really big."

Jean suddenly looked at his watch. "Anna, I hate to bring it to your attention, but we have to leave right away or we will be late and kicked out of the interviews. Then we will definitely never pursue any 'green' projects together. It is almost two o'clock!"

"Oh, shoot!" Anna quickly ate a few final pumpkin seeds from her box. They walked back together from the cafeteria.

"Okay, I'm off to do the case study, and you need to go to the panel interview. If you'd like, we can meet in the lobby after everything is over? Then we can chat some more," Jean said softly and gave Anna an air kiss, although it felt like the kiss landed on her lips.

****

Her heart was pounding fast as Anna approached the panel interview room. *No more distractions, I need to get this right. This is the final—just like Mom said. I have only one chance to get the slot.*

The panel interview was the most important part of the day. Here, all the candidates were tested for in-depth technical knowledge in their area of expertise by five top experts in their field.

Every candidate was expected to answer ten questions. The untold rule of Polaris interviews was that in order to have a chance to be selected for the program, every question had to be answered correctly. One mistake, and you could be certain that the offer to join would never come to you.

"Good afternoon, Ms. Levenko. Please take a seat. I hope you prepared well." The panel of interviewers— three middle-aged women and two older men—looked a lot like a kettle of nasty hawks.

"Yes, I'm very well-prepared," Anna said, her voice calm and confident. Her success at the case study and the multiple-choice test stages had her riding on a high.

"Well, let's find out, shall we?" the head of the panel noted with a cunning smile. "You might have seen a couple of candidates before you ran out of the room in tears. We hope you're not as faint-hearted."

Somebody ran out in tears? Anna's heart sank. These candidates were the cream of the crop! If *they* didn't know the answers, how could she be expected to know? Her confidence suddenly deflated. She now looked shyly at the panel, tucking her legs and raising her shoulders.

The head of the panel smiled even wider. "All right, let's begin. I will ask you ten questions. Your job is to answer all of them to the best of your ability. Be prepared to have a discussion with the members of the panel when we want to clarify something in your answer."

"Okay." Anna blushed and squeezed her fists under the table.

"Question one: Digital finance in developing countries. Please give us some examples of countries which have embraced such technologies. What are some pros and cons of digital finance?"

Anna smiled softly. *This* topic she was very familiar with. She'd even prepared a research paper back in college on digital finance.

She cleared her throat. "In my view, the use of digital finance in developing countries is very important. This channel allows to cost-effectively reach poor people, especially those living in rural areas, who were previously not targeted by banks. Thanks to mobile money, everyone now has access to technology. People can transfer money to each other, make payments for services, like school fees for their children, take out loans—even if they live in a remote village in Africa. They don't need to take a two-day trip to the closest bank. In 'pay-as-you-go' schemes, people can even pay with their mobile phone for use of solar power to light up their homes. If they stop making monthly payments, the switch goes off and they cannot use their solar panel till they start paying again. Pretty cool technology."

"These are some nice examples you provided. What nations are some of the leaders in mobile money?" one of the panelists asked.

"Many countries have embraced these technologies," Anna said. "China is the global leader, but some countries in Africa are also at the forefront of these initiatives. The whole world knows the success of mobile money in Kenya. I read in an article that the value of mobile money operations transacted there in a year was fifty billion dollars. This is extremely impressive. Ghana is another country which is catching up. They're now the fastest growing mobile market in Africa. Thanks to these initiatives, financial inclusion in Africa has significantly deepened in the recent years, improving lives of the poor."

"Do you think this 'mobile revolution' only brings benefits? Are there any risks?" the head of the panel intervened.

"Of course, many risks exist." Anna nodded. "For example, some providers could be fraudulent and steal consumers' money. Or the digital lenders could charge interest rates way above market, and people wouldn't know. It's important to educate consumers on the possible risks, and also the regulator of mobile money operations needs to be enabled strong oversight, and step in when needed."

The questions which followed were a piece of cake for Anna. She felt like she was standing in the middle of the tennis court and, as her opponents on the other side kept hitting tennis balls at her, she managed to hit them back immediately with even more power than their strokes came with. Left, right, left, right… She was winning so effortlessly.

But suddenly the last ball came, and Anna stumbled.

"Green taxonomy—objectives, users, design considerations," the head of the panel announced. "Does the one-size-fits-all approach work?"

Green what? Anna was frantically trying to search in her memory for any possible information on this subject. But she had nothing to say.

"Any ideas on the last question? You did so well on all the earlier ones." the head of the panel looked at Anna almost sympathetically. He no longer appeared beady eyed. He was actually a nice man, from what Anna could tell, trying to give her more time to think.

"Unfortunately, nothing comes to mind." Anna shrugged, a cold sweat rising on her skin. Had she flunk all the other questions, she wouldn't have cared as much. But she'd done so well—up till the last question. For a brief moment, the memories of her last match at the Indian Wells flashed in front of her. Again, she'd come so close to changing her life and becoming a success. And again, the door was shutting right in front of her nose. No matter what she did, somehow Uncle Stepan's shop was the only place for her.

Anna looked at the panel hesitantly. What was she supposed to do now that it was all over? Pick up her handbag and say good bye? Or were they supposed to close the interview with some final words?

"It's a shame." The head of the panel shook his head. "For some reason, I have a feeling that you know the answer: think *green* projects."

An alarm went off in Anna's brain. *Of course*, this question was related to her favorite topic, green finance! She suddenly found the answer on the tip of her tongue.

"I'm really sorry, I didn't understand the question at first. Green taxonomy is a classification system, a list of projects which would be considered environmentally sustainable in a particular country. The solar park Polaris built in Ethiopia would be classified as a 'green' project. When it comes to green taxonomy, one size doesn't fit all. Every country will develop one depending on their goals and needs."

Anna looked at the panel and, to her dazed delight, found them nodding and satisfied with her answer. What a relief! She still had a chance.

As she was leaving the interview room, she turned her phone back on and it started ringing immediately. Anna pulled it out of the handbag. It was her friend Katie video calling her.

"Hi Katie, what's up?" Anna asked cheerfully. Katie was probably calling to find out how the interviews went.

"Anna, help! It's an emergency! I've been calling you for the last hour," Katie shouted, sounding slightly hysterical. Her usual sweet smile was gone and her face looked distorted with pain.

"Calm down, Katie, what is going on?"

"It's Freddie! Something's wrong with him! I just came home from work. For some reason, I sensed that something was happening and left early to check on him.

Freddie seems so lethargic and also has these ugly gray spots all over him. I think it's all over."

"Katie, don't panic. It might still be okay. Tree frogs are nocturnal animals, so we would not expect Freddie to be active in the daytime. Maybe it is nothing serious. You should go to the vet."

"A vet? I have no idea where a vet is for these types of animals. And it's freezing outside. The cold temperature will definitely kill him."

"You have a point. It is better to keep him indoors. Okay, let me come over. Just text me your address."

Twenty minutes later, Anna was already at Katie's condo at Logan Circle, examining the unfortunate patient, while Katie was laying on the sofa. Freddie sat motionless in his glass terrarium staring at the visitor with his bizarre red eyes with vertical black pupils. Katie was right—Freddie's smooth body, which was expected to be bright green, was covered with some grayish spots. Yikes.

"Well, Katie," Anna said finally after carefully inspecting Freddie's terrarium, "I think it is pretty clear what is going on. Have you been washing Freddie's enclosure?"

"Washing? Not really. Do I need to? It seems fine to me. I mean, it's not like the frog cares."

"No, it does not look fine, it is actually pretty filthy. I am ninety-nine percent sure that what Freddie has is called oodinium. It's a rather common disease among the tree-frogs, and it is caused by dirty conditions in their cage. The spots will go away if you put Freddie in distilled water and thoroughly clean his habitat. But let's also consult with a vet, just to be sure."

"Where will we find a vet?"

"Let's just talk to one online. I don't think we need to take Freddie anywhere, judging from what I see."

The online appointment was booked, and Anna's diagnosis confirmed by the vet.

"Thank you Anna," Katie said. "You should be a vet yourself. You're really good at this."

"It must come from my late Grandpa. He apparently was an extremely skillful vet, famous not only in Ukraine but all over the Soviet Union. He had always been called to various zoos. I don't know how Grandpa did it though… I would not be able to do this as a profession. I had volunteered at the vet clinic when I was still in high school, and I came back home in tears literally every day! That's why I picked economics instead."

"Speaking about professions, forgot to ask you. How did the interview go?" Katie suddenly remembered. "Sorry I didn't ask earlier. I bet you charmed the socks off everyone? You're so brilliant, sister."

"Oh, Katie, it went great!" Anna shrieked excitedly. "It was definitely my day. I did fantastic at the case study, then I met this great guy, and then I had an excellent interview."

"A guy? Which guy? You met somebody at the interviews?"

"Yes, a Frenchman, his name is Jean. Really, really handsome and super accomplished. One of those guys who wants to change the world. We had lunch together, and I did not want it to end… I have no idea whether he liked me as much as I liked him, but I hope he did. He suggested to go out tonight and I agreed, of course—OH NO!"

Anna never had the chance to talk to Jean after the interview, or even get his contact information. She quickly looked at her watch. It was now past eight. The chances of finding Jean were slim, but she needed to give it a shot.

She rushed outside and jumped into the first red cab passing by.

"Mr. Washington, Mr. Washington!" Anna yelled, as she ran into the empty Polaris lobby.

The old guard, who was dozing off at his desk, opened his tired eyes. "Anna Levenko, what are you doing here? The interviews are all over. Everyone left a while ago."

"Yes, I know, but there was somebody waiting for me… A blond-haired guy…Tall, good-looking…" Anna was still trying to catch her breath.

"Oh, you already found yourself a date. Good for you," Mr. Washington said calmly and gave her a look of approval.

"Not quite. This guy at our interviews asked me to meet him in the lobby. And I missed him. Now I don't know how to find him. You've gotta help me!"

Mr. Washington looked at Anna sheepishly. "Yes, a blond guy did ask me about an hour ago if I had seen some Ukrainian girl with the long wavy hair… I said no. I thought he meant someone else. He kept lingering around the lobby for quite some time."

"Right… Thanks Mr. Washington." Anna turned around and started slowly walking away, dragging her handbag behind her like a little dog on a leash. Then she turned back and asked him, "Did he looked disappointed that he didn't find me?"

"If it makes you feel better, yes. He clearly looked upset."

Chapter 6. Emily at Home, at Work and in Love

Washington, D.C.

"Emily, I greatly appreciate your time and work on the report. However, I found your contribution... weak and disappointing." Miguel Vasquez, principal economist, looked straight at Emily as she sat across from him in a small conference room. He could have found some less insulting words, but he clearly didn't make an attempt to sugar-coat anything.

"If you'd like, feel free to revise your chapter. I have written a lot of comments which could help improve it. However, I'm not quite sure you have the right skills to do the revisions. Not like you're going to learn overnight."

Emily's face became ghost-pale. All of a sudden, tears burned in her eyes, slowly slipping down her cheek. She'd been expecting to hear nothing short of praise for her research during this meeting! How could Miguel speak in such a manner about the great work she did?

She lowered her eyes and started glancing through the pages of case studies she had so diligently prepared. They were so well-researched, so well-written. She'd spent several weeks on this task, working late every night. She knew how vital this report was. Senior management was awaiting it, and there would be huge media coverage on it.

"I'll revise it," Emily said quietly, although everything inside her was screaming. Her lip wouldn't stop quivering. "Sorry this is not what you were looking for."

"All right." Miguel nodded. "But hurry. I need to see the new version tomorrow at the latest. I am thinking of replacing you with someone else on this, in case your work is still not up to my standard."

"Replace me? With who?" Emily gasped for air.

"It doesn't really matter, but we have a very good new Global Associate in the unit, I'm sure she'd do a marvelous job. She is already working on several important reports but apparently she has room to take even more. Very bright young lady who holds a PhD from a top school. I'd love to have her on my team. In any case, if you want to revise, go ahead and send it to me by no later than tomorrow. Now, I have to go to another meeting. Call me if you have any questions about my comments. I'll be back in the office after lunch. *Adios*!"

A new Global Associate. Right. Emily should have guessed. Everyone at Polaris was just infatuated by people who carried the fancy title of a Global Associate. They were the most privileged group. All the best projects went to them. All the staff wanted them on their team. Nobody would tell them that their contribution was "weak and disappointing." That's for sure.

Emily would have given up a kidney to get accepted into the elite program. But it was out of reach for her. No matter how many times she'd applied, all she received was a standard rejection response.

She'd never made it even to the interview stage. Every year, she looked with envy at the incoming Global

Associates class and wondered: *Why didn't they pick me? I would be the best Global Associate they could have here—the most hard-working, intelligent, and dedicated.*

Emily ran into her office, threw the report on her desk, and slammed the door shut so hard that she was fairly sure the whole building hummed. Her blood was boiling and she felt moments away from exploding. She leaned over her desk and sat motionless for a few minutes, trying to think some positive thoughts, like her last vacation in Maui, and look at the portrait of Fofo. The tension finally began to fade and she gradually regained her composure.

A tall smiling lady in an exquisite light-blue pantsuit softly opened the door and stuck her head inside Emily's office. "Emily, hey, would you like to go for lunch?"

"I don't know." Emily let out a heavy sigh. "Look, Linda, I'm not in the best of mood. I just got comments from Miguel on my report chapter. He totally hated my contribution. You have no idea how much effort I had put into this!"

"Miguel Vasquez? Oh come on, everyone knows that nothing ever pleases him." Linda laughed. "He only wants to show his superiority, that's all. He's only recently been promoted to principal economist, even though he's been working here for decades and is well into his fifties. I hear that he made presentations of some disappointing research papers at several conferences. Everything he said was old news. Nobody wants to work for Miguel, and he is desperately trying to attract attention to himself in any way he can."

"Well, he told me he'd replace me with some super-duper brilliant Global Associate," Emily grumbled, fiddling with her report. "Apparently, she wants to work for him."

"Oh, that's what got you? I know you applied to that program. But you already have a job here at Polaris, that's all that matters now."

"Well, that's true. I'm still upset though. If I do a good job, I want to be recognized, not humiliated... By the way, how was your trip to Malaysia for your healthcare project? You just came back yesterday, right?"

"This morning to be precise." Linda winked. "I had to rush to the office from the airport because we had a review meeting scheduled. The meeting went well, the management allocated $150 million for the construction of several rural hospitals and the development of a smart tracking system for the distribution of equipment and medicines. Such a pleasant surprise. I thought we'd only get half that, if anything at all... Also, some donors I had approached earlier decided to jump on the bandwagon. This is going to be a huge! I could tell you more at lunch... But you're still not in the mood?"

Emily perked up. "Now I am." If it had been anybody else, she would have definitely declined the lunch invitation, but how could she miss an opportunity to learn from an experienced team leader like Linda Bloom? She was the top healthcare expert at Polaris, with at least thirty large projects under her belt. All her research papers were groundbreaking and were quoted over and over again. Government counterparts adored her and considered it an honor if she agreed to lead a program in their country. She had a magic touch, no question about that.

"Just give me fifteen minutes," Emily asked. "I'll check my emails and then stop by your office."

She quickly glanced through her emails, not finding anything important. Most of the messages were invitations to various learning events and international conferences. Hundreds of them came in each day, as Polaris greatly valued knowledge sharing and encouraged all the staff to participate in these types of events.

Emily fixed her blond locks, grabbed her bag, and was right about to leave when her cell started ringing. She glanced at the screen.

What the heck? The call was from Anna Levenko. By now, it has been two weeks since Emily had seen her in Washington. She probably had her interview and wanted to chat about what a disaster it was!

Emily's mood instantly improved. She eagerly picked up the call, put it on speaker, and spoke with a cheerful voice. "Hey Anna! You in Kyiv already? Interview went okay?"

Of course, now she'd hear a gloomy voice on the other end of the line, maybe some sobbing, and get a full flavor of how all of Anna's dreams had been crushed forever. They would commiserate together about how impossible it was to get into the Global Associates program and how folks from the Ivy League schools took up all the spots.

"Thanks for asking Emily! I think I did quite well and got all the questions at the panel interview right," Anna replied joyfully. "The case study and the multiple-choice test were not too difficult either. It seems I have a real chance to get in."

The smile immediately slid off Emily's face. Anna did well? But… She was supposed to fail miserably at the interview!

Valeriya Goffe

True, Anna had always gotten good grades back in business school and graduated with honors, but somehow Emily never believed that these were legitimate. Someone who was so focused on sports for a large chunk of their lives could not just become a star business student. Emily never considered Anna a competitor in business school. For that reason, they got along quite well. Anna was easy-going, kind, good-looking, harmless—a good friend to have and go to various school parties with.

Emily did not think it was remotely possible for her and Anna to work in the same organization. But now it seemed she might have completely underestimated her college friend. If Anna felt that she got all the questions right, she probably had. That meant she was much better than Emily ever imagined. Better than Emily herself...

Emily immediately pictured Anna prancing around the Polaris offices with her long luxurious hair, charming all the management, and taking over Emily's projects just because she was part of the elite program.

"Oh, great," Emily finally squeezed out. "Hope you get the job."

"Yes, but I want to ask you a big favor in the meantime. I'm not sure if you can help, but just in case you hear something. That is why I am calling."

"I'm listening." Emily perked up. "What is it?"

"Well, I happened to meet a really nice guy at the interviews, a Frenchman, his name is Jean. I liked him a lot. And imagine, I did not get his last name or any other information! Just in case you hear something about him, do let me know. It is a bit of a stretch, but you are the only one I know at Polaris, so I thought I would ask you."

It did not take Emily long to put two and two. A

couple of days ago, she went out with her sister, Lauren, Lauren's fiancé Arnaud Rolland, and his brother Jean, to dinner at a popular Spanish restaurant. During the dinner, Jean had been talking about "the Ukrainian girl" he met at the interviews. At the time, Emily had ignored the comment. But now it was clear that Jean was talking about *Anna.*

"What's Jean like?" Emily asked carefully.

"Blond, blue eyes, very good looking," Anna explained quickly. "Works on projects in various war-torn countries."

Yes, beyond any doubt, it was Jean Rolland she was speaking about. He was still in Washington, and Emily could have easily put Anna in touch with him. She herself had no particular interest in Jean, but did she want to help Anna?

Emily thought about it for a few seconds and the answer came naturally. "No, unfortunately, I don't know anything about Jean. Never heard of him. If I come across him here at Polaris, I'll let you know right away."

"Thanks so much, Emily! I owe you. Please give me a call at any time, and hopefully I will see you in the Fall. That is, if I do get into the program. It would be so great to work together. I will keep you posted."

"Yes, by all means, please do," Emily said dryly and hung up the phone. By now, Anna Levenko was really getting on her nerves. It was bad enough that Emily was about to be replaced on the team by some lousy Global Associate she didn't know. But having Anna, her former classmate, the *Ukrainian*, in the Global Associate program? That would not do.

Come to think of it, Jean *was* a rather attractive guy. Maybe he merited another look?

Of course, getting Arnaud out of her head was not going to be easy. Emily had first met him a few months back at a reception her father hosted in their mansion to honor the incoming Emerald Hotels & Resorts executives...

****

In order to please her father, she wanted to briefly show her face, and later disappear quietly, the way she had done many times. However, when her eyes landed on Arnaud, standing in the middle of the room, she did not want to go anywhere. He was tall and handsome, surrounded by a flock of smiling ladies, but clearly indifferent to their charm.

Before Emily made up her mind to approach Arnaud, her dad emerged and touched her on the elbow. "That is Arnaud Rolland, our new head of strategy. He's a magnet for all the ladies. I even see your mother standing there talking to him."

"Yes. I happen to find him quite attractive. Any problem with that?" Emily asked, unsure where this was leading.

"No problem. Though, Arnaud would be perfect for your sister. They met a few days ago and, of course, she is completely smitten by him. He is such a handsome fellow. They are going on a date tomorrow. Please do not interfere."

"I seriously doubt a guy like that could ever be interested in Lauren. He is way out of her league."

"Well, we will see about that. Please give them a chance. That's all I am asking. You can have any guy you want. Just leave this one for Lauren. I am worried that with slim dating options, she will fall for someone... less desirable."

"Fine, Dad, I don't really care. Lauren can have Arnaud if she wants," Emily said contemptuously. Poor Lauren was running out of chances to ever get married. This relationship was not going to last. The most Lauren could hope for was a couple of dates, max.

****

But as it turned out later, Emily did care. She still could not get Arnaud's image out of her mind—his gaze, his indulgent smile, his seductive lips. To make matters worse, Arnaud and Lauren miraculously managed to hit it off. They were inseparable, and Emily had to endure watching them at various family events, sitting side by side and laughing at each other's jokes.

It was high time for Emily to move on. And why not do that with Arnaud's younger brother, who looked a lot like him? They had a nice enough conversation while at the restaurant. It was pretty clear that Jean would be accepted into the Global Associates program and soon move to Washington.

True, Jean seemed quite interested in Anna, but that wouldn't last. Out of sight, out of mind. Girls like Anna were a dime a dozen. Girls like Emily, on the other hand, were as rare as Myanmar rubies. No guy was able to resist her charms.

"Time to give Jean a call while he is still here in D.C.," Emily decided, talking to herself as she looked around her office. "Sorry Anna, you might not make it into the program after all, so no hard feelings."

Chapter 7. The Family Affairs

Kyiv, Ukraine

Maria adored spring, and this year it was even more gorgeous than she remembered. Just a mere week ago, the sky was still dark gray, heavy clouds crawling around it like giant spiders, while the ground was covered by an impenetrable layer of snow and ice. But all of a sudden, the bright sun cautiously peaked through the clouds, the frosty wind warmed, and flocks of happy, carefree birds appeared, chirping loudly. Soon enough, the ice melted, brand-new bright green leaves proudly crowned the bare trees, and the happy messengers of spring—chicken-yellow daffodils and deep-purple crocuses—blossomed all around.

Maria's birthday was on May fifth, and, just like previous years, a diverse group of family and friends gathered at the Levenko family *dacha* to celebrate this wonderful occasion. The dacha was situated in the *Pushcha Vodytsia* area in the outskirts of Kyiv.

Maria's heart skipped a bit as she watched her guests arrive and her garden gradually fill up with joy and laughter.

"*Zdoroven'ki buly!*"

"*Zdrastujte!*"

"*Dobrogo vechora!*"

The first ones to arrive were Anna, her parents

Olena and Ivan, as well as the family dogs.

"Look at these beautiful girls!" Maria clapped her hands, as she watched Lapa and Zirka, outfitted in party hats and capes, jump out of the car and immediately start running around the garden. This would be her first birthday with the furry guests. What a wonderful addition to the family!

Soon after, Dima Kudermet walked in, together with his father. Unlike Lapa and Zirka, the pair were "regulars." Maria saw them at every single party of hers ever since Anna and Dima started dating back in high school. Anna had quickly broken it off with Dima but he never left the family. Was he still romantically interested in Anna? Maria never could figure Dima out. Relationships of young people these days were too complicated for her.

A large group showed up next, descending from a black Range Rover. Ivan's brother Stepan, Stepan's wife Motria, and daughter Sveta with her new fiancé, the big-time politician.

Oh no, not Mr. Banduchenko again! He was on Maria's black list. Last year, without thinking, she'd placed him next to the big plate of sandwiches with red and black caviar. These were very expensive sandwiches, a highlight of the party. She had been saving her pension to buy several cans of red and black caviar. And what did Mr. Banduchenko do? The cheat wolfed down all of her delicious sandwiches in the space of five minutes! Not a single one was left for her other guests. A disaster. When Maria confronted him, he just blinked his eyes innocently.

Naturally, nothing good could be expected from a "turncoat." Mr. Banduchenko had previously worked in the pro-Russian government of the ill-famed dictator Viktor Yanukovych. After his regime was overthrown, Mr. Banduchenko suddenly became a supporter of pro-Western policies. She didn't trust him.

A few neighbors, old friends from college, and former co-workers at the pediatric hospital then trickled in. Maria's cousin Tolik was the last one to arrive. The assembly was now complete.

All the guests, dressed in their most festive vyshyvankas, gathered in the alcove at a large table covered with grape vines. She sat at the head of the table, surrounded by gorgeous flowers, smiling widely, enjoying the nice weather and excellent food and chatting with everyone.

Without any delay, the guests started munching on all of the great Ukrainian birthday party dishes. The overall favorite was the famous *Olivier* salad, which was made from mayonnaise, peas, carrots, chicken, and pickles. The *Mimoza* salad made with fake crab sticks and cheese was also popular as were the delicious *varenyky* (dumplings with meat, cabbage, and potato). In addition, the buffet also included cold boiled pork, ham, sandwiches with red and black caviar, sardines, smoked salmon, other delicacies.

"Who prepared all of these delicious dishes?" asked Leonid, one of Maria's former co-workers. "I bet they did not come from a restaurant."

"My granddaughter Anna prepared most of the dishes," Maria said proudly. "Olena and I made the rest. Our family prides ourselves for never ordering catering for the birthday parties. Everything is fresh and authentic and based on our favorite recipes."

Of course, no Ukrainian birthday party could take

place without large quantities of *horilka* and other alcoholic drinks. These were very useful in prompting creative toasts and also greatly improving singing abilities, especially of romantic Ukrainian songs. The *bandura* music, popular among Ukrainians, was readily available at the party and greatly amused all of the guests. Tolik had fully mastered this Ukrainian folk instrument. On several occasions he presented his broad repertoire to the audience with a lot of passion and creativity, and received thunderous applause.

It was soon time to start serving the main course. Maria got up and walked into the house in order to heat up the mashed potatoes, grilled vegetables, fish, and chicken, prepared that morning. Anna followed her.

It was warm and cozy inside. A little bit dark and very quiet. Peaceful. There was no elaborate furniture in the slightly constrained space. The rooms permanently smelled of apples and berries, regardless of the season. There were no modern conveniences like a TV or a computer. The family had been long suggesting Maria to tear down this old house and build a new modern one, but she'd never agree to that. She wanted everything here to remain the same as it was fifty years ago. Back when she was young, happy, and hopeful—at least for a brief moment.

This dacha once belonged to Solomon, her late husband. He'd started out with just a large plot of land, but soon enough, he put up a simple house and a barn where he kept various gardening instruments, as well as planted trees and berry bushes. Where he had gotten all the energy and the know-how, Maria had no idea.

Well, that was just Solomon. He was good at everything. There was nothing he could not tackle. Not only a skillful vet, famous all over the Soviet Union, but he spoke several foreign languages and was well-versed in history, art, and culture.

Until this day, Maria had not met anyone who could surpass Solomon in kindness and intelligence. He was the star of every party, even without trying. No matter where he went, he stood out. Whenever he opened his mouth, everyone listened with a lot of attention. There had been something about him which she never managed to get her finger on.

Ever since Maria retired, the dacha had become her refuge. Getting here was far from easy—Maria did not drive and she usually spent two or more hours commuting, sometimes forced to wait for a bus under the hot sun, rain, or snow. But it was well worth it.

"Grandma, you don't really need to do anything," Anna said, pulling Maria from her musings. "You just need to sit and rest, chat with the people. I'll bring all the dishes to the guests myself. This is your party. Why do you insist on doing so much every time? Mom and I are perfectly capable."

"It's okay, Anna. I really enjoy getting everything ready for the party. You know, it's my absolute favorite time of the year—being around everyone I love and treasure. Well, *almost* everyone."

Of course, one person had not been with them for many years. But she never forgot him. Not even for a second. It seemed like an eternity had passed, yet Maria could still hear his voice and his footsteps from time to time. Sometimes she saw him in her dreams.

"You are thinking about Grandpa Solomon, right?" Anna left the dishes alone and sat down next to Maria.

"Of course, I am… Always. You know, every day

you look more and more like him. You have the same smile, the same eyes and nose. Olena looks more like me, but you, you remind me so much of your grandpa. He was also tall and strong, just like you. It's impossible not to think of him when you are around."

"My heart breaks every time I think of you losing Grandpa. You must have been so devastated." Anna looked into Maria's eyes with a lot of tenderness and sympathy.

"Completely. It was the most horrible day of my life," Maria said, her lower lip trembling and her body vibrating with pain.

She had a feeling that something bad was going to happen that day, already five decades ago. When she'd been walking back home from the store in the afternoon, a coal black cat ran right in front of her. She stood there for a few minutes. Normally, she would have found another path but she saw no other way to go. *It's going to be okay*—she'd whispered to herself, as she kept on walking. But deep in her heart, she'd known that trouble was already brewing.

"Solomon did not arrive home from the animal hospital that evening. I was worried. He often worked late, but not that late… My heart told me something must have happened. Finally, at two in the morning, I got a call that Solomon was in the hospital. He had been in a car crash! Apparently, he was still able to say a few words when the paramedics found him. He asked them to get me as soon as possible, he had to tell me something incredibly important about his family. 'Hurry up, please,' the voice begged on the phone, 'your husband is very weak, and we don't know if he will live much longer…'"

"What could be so important?" Anna asked, breathing through the terrible anxiety building in her chest. "It's the first time I heard the full story. We've rarely talk about Grandpa, you know... Mom always gets so upset when the subject gets brought up, and we stop right away."

"Yes, that's true." Maria nodded her head. "A deep wound glows in your mother's heart; it never healed... Well, to this day, I have no idea what Solomon wanted to tell me. I frantically tried to find a car to take me to the hospital. Your grandpa had a Volga, and we didn't have any other cars in the family. I tried calling some friends and relatives. Nobody was picking up in the middle of the night! Eventually one person agreed to take me. We rushed to the hospital. I was praying the whole time. It was late by the time we finally reached the hospital. I ran into Solomon's room, but he had just passed away. Just minutes before I arrived."

Maria and Anna sat for a minute in silence. Maria's soul was drained, as if she had lost Solomon all over again. But, at the same time, she was relieved. Tonight, on her seventy-third birthday, she felt a strong urge to share these sad memories with someone.

"Grandma, I wonder why you never tried to meet grandpa's family?" Anna asked quietly. "Even after he passed away, they would probably want to get to know us? Imagine how interesting it would have been to travel to Africa and see our other relatives."

"I did not have any contacts for them, unfortunately," Maria replied sadly. How easy things would have been, had Solomon lived in the current times! But back in the seventies, no Internet existed. Finding people living in another country was very difficult. In another continent—impossible. Some of the African countries might have had embassies somewhere in the Soviet Union, but none of them were in the Ukrainian republic.

"Solomon came to study veterinary medicine in Kyiv and settled here. He did not visit his family in Africa for a while. Apparently, there was some estrangement… But eventually, he made a decision to move back. He said it would be better for me and your mother… Solomon didn't mention any names of his relatives other than his younger sister, Gloria. She was the one who he was really looking forward to seeing."

"Gloria? What a beautiful name," Anna said in delight.

"Indeed, a gorgeous name. Gloria Malekano!" Grandma said proudly. "This was the last name of their family… Gloria had sent a letter to Solomon not long before his death. He had showed it to me. Her handwriting was as beautiful as her face! She had even put a few dried-up clove buds inside the envelope. She had been excited to meet us all."

"Do you still have the letter?" Anna checked.

"I wish! It had Gloria's address on it, you know… I looked really hard, but never managed to find it among Solomon's things. I still have Gloria's picture, however. The one Solomon used to keep in his office, where he spent most of his time. Do you want to see what she looked like?"

"Yes!"

Maria went into the living room and opened one of the wooden drawers where she kept important things. She pulled out a black and white photo in a metal frame and carefully wiped a thin layer of dust from the glass with the palm of her hand. In the photo, a thin and cheerful girl was laughing. Her long wavy hair was cascading over her shoulders and her white teeth were shining like moonstones in the bright sun. She had large almond-shaped eyes, flawless skin, and perfectly sculpted features. The photo was taken on the terrace of a large house, with some palm trees in the back.

Anna gently took the picture in her hands and looked at it very carefully. Her eyes widened instantly. "Gloria looks a lot like… me?"

"That's right. If only we could have met… But unfortunately, I don't have any clue how to find Solomon's family. I don't even know which country they lived in! Solomon was a very private person and shared little about his time before. It wasn't a big deal for me— I loved him and trusted him no matter what. I just had no idea our love story would be over in a flash."

"I'm so sorry, Grandma." Anna's eyes glittered with tears. "You deserve all the happiness in the world."

"Well, I *was* happy, Anna—even if for a short time… But the good news is, nothing prevents me from dreaming. Every day, I dream about beautiful Africa— the land of eternal summer and everlasting youth, somewhere really far away, at the end of the rainbow. I walk along the golden beach holding Solomon's hand, we dive in the clear ocean waters and kiss under the swaying palm trees. We are young, beautiful, and carefree. It's magic."

Maria slowly got up from the chair and glanced at the stove where the main courses were heating up. "All right, enough sad stories for one day. I think everything is ready. Let's put our smiles back on and return to the party."

"Okay." Anna put her arms around Grandma. "Let's go back to the guests. They are waiting for their lovely birthday girl."

Chapter 8. The Luck of Chervona Ruta

Kyiv, Ukraine

Anna opened the store right at nine. A few customers at the Svyatoshyn market were already starting to gather around it.

The day went on as it always had. Babusias complaining about the high prices on soap and demanding steep discounts, young mothers buying loads of diapers, middle-aged ladies looking for some premium brands of shampoo, perfume, and nail polish which would instantly transform them into runway models or movie stars. Several teenagers came in to buy some chewing gum, but in reality they wanted to have a good look at Anna.

At one point, Baba Kateryna came for a chat. Despite being competitors, she'd eventually warmed up to Anna and frequented the store, especially at lunchtime. "So, any news from America?" she asked her daily question. Of course, she was well aware that Anna flew to an interview with some company in Washington D.C. A substitute salesperson with a big mouth had worked at the Chervona Ruta store for a week.

"Unfortunately, no," Anna said frankly. "I have not received any call or email from HR."

"Hah. That's what I expected. In any event, nothing for you to see in that America. All they have are narcotics, protests, and shootings." Baba Kateryna was the most violent critic of the Western world. In her expert opinion, nothing worked there, and it would collapse in no time. In contrast, Ukraine was the center of the world and the Svyatoshyn market was the epicenter of all the action in Kyiv.

"Well, Baba Kateryna, many young people found great opportunities in America. I also wanted to try. But it seems I didn't succeed, so I will be staying in Ukraine."

"Very good. Oh, listen, I saw the interview with Mr. Banduchenko last night. What a handsome, intelligent man! Mighty eagle, powerful falcon. My heartthrob. His sparkly eyes and handlebar moustache give me goose bumps. Apparently, he is planning ambitious renovations for our market. Imagine… he will put in some new toilets, a better roof for the vegetable pavilion, and even repair the road!"

"How nice of him." Anna rolled her eyes. Mr. Banduchenko was always implicated in some corruption schemes. He never did anything unless it somehow benefitted him. With the market improvements, he was probably looking to acquire more votes of ignorant people like Baba Kateryna. And he would undoubtedly get substantial kickbacks from the companies doing the improvements.

"If only I were thirty years younger, I would definitely try to steal this splendid man from your cousin," Baba Kateryna continued excitedly. "You know, back in the day, I had a lot of success with the men."

"Oh Baba Kateryna, I have no doubt about that. You are still very attractive. Did you see how Did Vasya is looking at you? I think he even started putting on cologne to impress you."

Baba Kateryna nodded her head in approval. "Yes, he keeps coming by to chat. You are right, there might be something there. I am not sure I like his name, Vasya, sounds just like my cat Vasya. But it is okay. I could have a cat Vasya and a husband Vasya, right? Let me stop by casually and go see what he is doing."

Baba Kateryna checked how she looked in Anna's mirror, adjusted her headscarf, walked out of the Chervona Ruta store, and confidently headed to the "Rybalka" (Fisherman) shop a few stores down. Although Did Vasya was obviously not as attractive as Mr. Banduchenko, he was still a good enough catch. Anna smiled as she watched Baba Kateryna disappear around the corner.

Right at noon, Anna checked out the final customers and closed the shop so that she could have the lunch she'd brought. At lunch time she usually read some economic books and magazines in order to be up to speed with all the latest developments in the market. She had organized a little shelf in the corner for all her items. Today, however, all her past efforts seemed completely useless.

Why did she need to know about the latest trends in the venture capital investments, for example, if she was going to work at Uncle Stepan's shop for the next thirty years? It seemed a much better idea to brush up her skills in cost accounting—maybe she could eventually start helping Uncle Stepan on the finance side. This wasn't the most exciting job prospect, but at least it would be some professional growth. Better than nothing at all.

At the end of the day, with only five minutes before

closing, Anna was attending to her last customer, Uncle Opanas. He was buying an electric tea kettle. She fidgeted behind the counter. *This will take forever! Uncle Opanas never spends less than an hour on pricey purchases like this.*

After twenty minutes of analysis of various options, Uncle Opanas seemingly settled on one tea kettle, but still needed more time to review the user manual and make his final decision.

Right at that moment, Anna's phone suddenly rang. She motioned to Uncle Opanas to continue reading the manual on his own and picked up the phone.

"Hello, this is Michelle Miller," a calm and pleasant voice announced. "Can I speak to Anna Levenko, please?"

Michelle Miller?
Michelle Miller!

Of course, Anna would never forget that name. It was so firmly embedded in her memory ever since she was sent an invitation to the interviews.

Holy crap, the Polaris HR was finally calling! There had to be good news. Nothing else was acceptable.

Anna just opened her mouth to say: *Yes, it's me! Tell me, tell me!* when uncle Opanas interrupted. "Anna, I think this tea kettle is no good. The user manual is so complicated. Plus it is way too expensive. I want to see the other kettle we were looking at earlier. Can you get it for me from the shelf again?"

"Oh, Uncle Opanas, please, let me listen to the call!" Anna pleaded. "This is something important. It's actually related to my past trip to America, remember? I will be right with you."

"What can be more important than the tea kettle?"

asked a bewildered Uncle Opanas. "I will wait, okay. But not too long."

Anna returned to her call.

Was the lady still on the line? *Please let her still be on the line!*

"Yes, yes, hello, this is me… This is Anna Levenko speaking! Sorry, I had a bit of a problem before… I'm listening now!" Anna yelled on the phone and then held her breath.

Please, please, please.

"No problem, Anna," the sweet voice said calmly. "I wanted to congratulate you and let you know that you have been accepted into the Global Associates Program. We will be sending you an email with all the details later today, so just make sure you do not miss it. You need to urgently review and sign your employment contract."

"Thank you, thank you!" Anna was already making a silent victory dance around the store while Uncle Opanas watched on in astonishment. "I will be waiting for the documents to sign. Good bye!"

Anna finally stopped her dance and looked around the Chervona Ruta store and at the red face of Uncle Opanas. Suddenly, all of this no longer mattered. Her life was about to change.

"Uncle Opanas, you can have any tea kettle you want," Anna declared generously. "It is on the house. Come to think of it, take both of those you were looking at! You earned them, since it was you who got me to the airport on time."

She handed the two tea kettles to the astounded minibus driver. This was the last sale she would make at the Chervona Ruta store. She was sure of it.

****

"Mom, are you sitting down?" her daughter Anna asked cheerfully on the phone.

"Sweetie, I'm still busy with the class. I'll call you back in ten minutes, okay?"

Olena quickly stuck her cell back in the pocket of her spandex sport jacket. She was definitely not sitting down. She was standing in the middle of the tennis court with a giant tennis basket, feeding balls to the clumsy teenage twins, Masha and Dasha, who she had been training for the last two years.

Masha and Dasha were daughters of a renowned pediatric surgeon and their father generously funded their semi-weekly tennis lessons. They were no rising tennis stars, but who said everyone had to be? Olena was done with tennis stars. Once and for all. "Done" was really an understatement.

After Anna's tragedy at the Indian Wells, Olena had spent two years going to a therapist. She had nightmares every night. As soon as she went to sleep, she would wake up in a cold sweat, still hearing Anna screaming with pain on the court. At one point, Olena even started sensing that her own shoulder was burning with pain. Guilt suffocated her and drove her insane each moment of the day.

Therapy—and time—seemed to help.

Olena's guilt had not completely gone away, but it no longer infused her whole. It crawled down Olena's heart and quietly settled there. From time to time she felt its sharp claws pinch the heart, but then it let go.

The best cure for Olena was Anna's eventual recovery. Seeing Anna do her favorite activities again brought tears of joy to Olena's eyes. Eventually, Olena made her way back to coaching as she was doing today.

But now she focused on players who would never make it to the big stage.

Masha finally hit the last ball—again into the net. Both she and her sister quickly picked up all the balls and then ran up to the net, their high pony-tails jumping up and down.

"Are we done, Aunt Olena?"

"Yes, thanks girls, this is all for today," Olena said warmly. "You did great. Please continue working on your fitness. You know that this is a must. On Thursday we will be practicing your volleys and overheads."

Now was a good time to call Anna back. She should have just finished her day at the Chervona Ruta.

Olena casually sat down at one of the plastic chairs standing on the side of the court and dialed her daughter's number. "Anna, it's me. The class is all done. What's going on?"

"Mom, you won't believe. I got into Polaris!"

"You got where?"

"Polaris, Mom. *Polaris*!" Anna squealed in delight. Her voice was so loud, full of so much joy. Olena loved this voice. The last time she'd heard it was many years ago. Back when Anna had gotten into the quarters of Indian Wells. "They just called. I got into the program, Mom!"

The phone almost fell out of Olena's trembling hands. For a brief moment, she just sat in her chair motionless. Then, the tears started flowing. One after the other, they hung on Olena's thick eyelashes and later dropped on her cheeks. She could not stop them.

Against all odds, *her daughter* got into one of the most sought-after programs in the world. The judges picked her Anna! Her sweet, beautiful, brilliant Anna.

"Anna, this is so wonderful," Olena whispered, sobbing. "You are finally on top of the world—this seems like a dream come true."

"Mom, please, there is no need to cry! This is supposed to be happy news! All of my hard work finally paid off."

"I know, I know… I *am* happy. I just did not know you would ever get into the winners' circle again, after everything what happened, that's all…"

Olena closed her eyes. She was back at their tiny hotel room at the Indian Wells, sitting next to Anna's bed, slowly stroking her hair. Trying to make her pain go away. Thinking that life would never be the same, for both of them. Anna had never said a cross word to Olena after that fatal match. She was just a child. Too kind and innocent for blaming anyone in the disaster which happened to her.

Olena had wanted Anna to yell at her. They would have had a fight, and it would be easier to get over what happened. But instead, her sweet daughter just laid there on the bed clutching her worn-out teddy bear.

Everyone in the family blamed Olena. She was supposed to keep Anna out of trouble. And she hadn't. Up till this day, Olena wondered herself why she had made that choice. Why she'd let Anna play through the injury.

What was she supposed to think when Anna told her about the sore shoulder that day? *It's nothing. It will go away. It's probably just jitters before the important match.*

Today, Anna was starting a new chapter of her life. A great company. A great city. Olena wished with all her heart that her daughter would be successful in her pursuit for happiness. Of course, Anna would do fantastic at Polaris, just like she did at everything else. She'd get promoted quickly and be respected by her colleagues. She'd meet a wonderful guy and get married in no time.

"All right, no more tears. Let's celebrate! We are going to invite all of our close friends and relatives to our apartment tomorrow," Olena suggested in a much happier tone. "We can have a nice party to applaud your achievement."

"Yes, Mom, I like this much better! I can't wait to see everyone's astonished faces tomorrow."

****

Anna felt her chest filling up with the greatest pride she had felt in years. One by one, her guests came in and congratulated her as if she had won a Nobel prize:

"Congratulations!"

"What a wonderful achievement!"

"Unbelievable! I never doubted your intellect and perseverance!"

"Good luck in the United States!"

Now she was the most famous relative in the family. Everyone was staring at Anna as if she'd suddenly grown a second head. She was now a new breed of person, someone to be respected and admired.

"I think your aunt Motria looks quite envious," her mother commented to Anna quietly. "She did not say much when she came. And she is parading all her jewels. She glitters like a *maharaja* now. As if anybody here cares."

"I bet she is so jealous, her face is just about to crack." Anna glanced in Aunt Motria's direction and bit back a laugh. "It's always been '*Sveta this, Sveta that*' and '*Ahh, poor Anna*'"—*sigh*—"But now Sveta doesn't really have much to show compared to me. Hey, did you invite Mr. Banduchenko? I thought he wouldn't be here. I hate him." Anna pointed at the red-faced Mr. Banduchenko standing in the middle of the room with a beer mug, explaining something to Uncle Tolik.

"Of course I didn't invite him." Olena rolled her eyes. "He just tagged along with Sveta. They are now engaged, remember? The guy just cannot miss a chance to celebrate and drink lots of beer and horilka. I can assure you he doesn't even know what Polaris is. But he is the first one in line to get a drink and then brag on TV how he is working to strengthen ties with the U.S."

Lapa and Zirka could not hide their excitement. The family dogs fed on the energy surrounding them and kept jumping up and down from the sofa and doing somersaults, barking non-stop. Something great was happening, and they always wanted to be part of everything great.

Anna patted her furry friends. "Girls, it is going to be tricky to move you to the United States. It will be a whole new experience for you! But I am sure you will do just fine."

Olena looked at Anna skeptically. "You are not thinking of bringing them right away, are you?"

"Sure, why not?"

"It would be a terrible idea. You need to find a place to live, organize everything, start your job… They will just get in your way. First you settle down, then you can bring over these… freeloaders."

Lapa and Zirka stopped their summersaults and perked their ears up.

"Mom has a point," Anna said sadly, still watching her furry friends. "We should wait a couple of months, and then you can come and live with me. I will make sure everything is perfectly organized for you, and then you will arrive and live there as royalty. Great food, long weekend hikes, new friends. I promise."

The conversation shifted to other topics. Of great interest to all the relatives was the size of the paycheck Anna was expected to take home. She preferred not to reveal this sensitive information to everyone, but her mother was of a different opinion.

Olena, sitting at the desk with her glasses down her nose and calculator in her hand, announced that Anna's annual salary would be over four million Ukrainian hryvnia—more than the whole family were earning all together. Of course, life was much more expensive in the U.S., but she'd suddenly become the big earner.

"Anechka, would you be interested in some investment opportunities?" Uncle Stepan suddenly asked.

"I have not thought about that yet, Uncle Stepan." Anna blinked her eyes innocently. "Maybe at some point. You know, my job only starts in September, and I'll have a lot of upfront expenses. What do you have in mind?"

"Well, I have a lot of ideas for expanding my business, in case you would ever want to go in as a partner, we could discuss them. I was thinking of opening an online pastry shop—various Ukrainian and international delicacies for upscale clientele delivered to their door. Dima could help us promote it through his social media channel. Also, possibly a travel agency. And again, Dima could promote us, this time through his blog."

"Both sounds like interesting ideas. Definitely

worth considering," Anna said.

Olena perked up. "Let's talk about this in six months' time," Olena suggested. "We will then have a better idea of Anna's finances and how much she can invest. But it would be a good idea for us to become partners." Uncle Stepan and her mother continued talking, leaving Anna alone for a moment.

"Anna, maybe I can come to visit you in the U.S. sometime?" Sveta asked quietly, suddenly standing beside Anna. "We could do some things together."

Anna looked at Sveta suspiciously. She and her cousin had never been close, even though neither of them had any siblings and both were of a similar age. But they were such different people. Anna had more in common with Katie, who came from a completely different background, than with Sveta who grew up right next door to her.

This was the first time Sveta actually reached out to participate in some activity Anna was involved in. Well, maybe something good would come out of it… "Of course. It would be great to have you in Washington. I'll show you around."

"Sveta, don't be crazy," interjected Aunt Motria. "Anna is going to the United States for an important job. What are *you* planning to do there?"

"I don't know yet. I could find a job, too."

"I seriously doubt that." Motria wrinkled her long nose. "Also, you're getting married soon. Let's not forget. But of course, you can visit your successful cousin. Once she settles down, obviously."

Olena then caught everyone's attention as she made an important announcement. "*Panove*, and did you know that Anna will be the *first Ukrainian ever* to land a job with Polaris?"

All the guests, who were by then dozing off after a fulfilling meal, suddenly perked up. Everyone's faces instantly became serious and attentive. All eyes were on Anna.

"Well, this a lot of pressure on you, Anna!" Uncle Tolik finally spoke up, getting up from his chair. "You will now have to enlighten everyone in your organization and make sure they know what Ukraine is like. You thought you got a big job? Now you got an even bigger job in front of you! Hope you're up for it."

"Of course, Uncle Tolik. I will do my best to ensure that everyone at Polaris learns about Ukraine," Anna said confidently.

Uncle Tolik was one of the greatest Ukrainian patriots Anna knew. He had taken an active part in the Orange revolution which happened in the early 2000s to protest against the presidential elections marred by corruption. A decade later, he was an active participant of a similar event—the Euromaidan (Independence Square) revolution of 2014, when protesters exiled Viktor Yanukovych, a corrupt President, and overthrew the Ukrainian government. Following the Euromaidan, Tolik spent some time working at the National Anti-Corruption Bureau, until returning to his regular engineering job at the aircraft plant "Antonov" a few years ago.

"Very true," Olena echoed Uncle Tolik's statement. "When we lived in the States for a few years, I quickly learned that not too many people knew about Ukraine. I had to educate them on our rich culture and literature." She glanced with a lot of tenderness at the bookshelves standing in the Levenko living room, housing the works of her beloved Taras Shevchenko, Vasyl Stus, Ivan Nechuy-Levyzky, Mykola Bazhan, Lesya Ukrainka…

"Okay, Anna, here are a few tips for your Polaris job." Tolik cleared his throat. "First and foremost, I suggest that you bring a Ukrainian flag to the office."

Anna nodded, as she proudly glanced at the freedom blue and the sunshine yellow colors of the Ukrainian flag in their living room. Similar to many Ukrainians, the Levenkos had large-sized Ukrainian flags on prominent display at both their apartment and their dacha, while small flags were placed strategically in some flower pots and pen holders. "Should I bring a big or a small flag to the office? What do you think?"

"Let's get a really big one," Ivan suggested without hesitation. "You can hang it on the wall in your office."

"Also, I would suggest you bring a portrait of Yulia Tymoshenko," Tolik continued. "Everyone needs to know who the leader of the All-Ukrainian Union 'Fatherland' is and how she was a political prisoner of the cruel Yanukovych regime. And, of course, make sure you wear vyshyvankas. How many are you taking?"

"I don't know, maybe ten?"

"That's not enough," Tolik objected.

"Tolik is right. You need at least twenty," Olena chimed in. "We'll buy some new ones this week. You'll wear different vyshyvankas for different occasions. For the first day in the office, you'll also need to wear a Ukrainian *vinok* with flowers and ribbons."

"Is this really necessary?" Anna asked anxiously, picturing herself entering the Polaris offices with a bright Ukrainian wreath on her head. "It might be a bit much. People at Polaris might take our patriotism the wrong way."

"I wouldn't worry about it," Olena said. "It is only normal that we want to promote our culture."

"*Donechko*," her father noted using the Ukrainian word for daughter. "Please keep in mind that you will be representing our country. You have a debt to your motherland. This is not just about you now. It's about the whole Ukraine. You'll be the first Ukrainian at Polaris, so there are no shortcuts. You need to make sure everyone learns about our home country."

"One of my friends is a *Cossack* descendant," Uncle Stepan chimed in. "His son wore a Cossack costume to his first day at a prominent law firm in Chicago. Everyone was impressed. He got promoted to partner in no time."

"Fine." Anna finally gave in. "I will double-check with my friend Emily who already works there, just to make sure this will be okay with the company."

Chapter 9. The Return with Fanfare

Washington, D.C.

"Hello, Washington. I've missed you," Anna whispered as her airplane softly touched the runway. Light rain streaks glowed on her window like tears on a pale cheek, the sky dark and gray behind.

Anna laughed and cried at the same time. Her career was about to begin at one of the most prestigious companies in the world. Hopefully, the guy of her dreams made it through the interviews as well and they'd be in the same program, doing some "green" project together. Yet her entire family was back in Ukraine. They would see each other, of course, maybe for some holidays and during the summer vacation. But it would never ever be the same.

Hopefully, I made the right decision moving here. Anna took a deep breath, picked up her suitcase, and headed for the shuttle together with the other passengers. She quickly mixed in with the crowd. Millions of people like her arrived in the United States each day, in search of a better fortune, leaving everything dear to their hearts behind in their native lands.

It felt as if Washington welcomed Anna back with open arms. She quickly settled in. She rented a two-bedroom condo in a lovely housing complex close to the Tenleytown metro station. Soon after moving in, Anna spotted her new neighbors—a gay couple living on the same floor with her. Pablo worked as a real estate agent and Ben as a lawyer at a prominent D.C. law firm. They had recently married in California.

"And who might you be?" Anna exclaimed, as a cute basset hound with long droopy ears and meditative eyes approached her slowly. She missed her furry friends, and this cutie could provide a good temporary diversion.

"Please meet Sausage," Pablo said cheerfully. "If you'd like to know more about him, you can follow him on social media. We've put up plenty of funny photos there."

"I should probably open an account for Lapa and Zirka when they get here." Anna patted Sausage's floppy ears. "I have two dogs coming to live with me in a few months."

"Fantastic! Did you hear that, Sausage?" Pablo jumped up. "Two pretty furry girls are coming to live next door! It is going to be totally awesome! You can all take walks and hang out together."

"Get ready to have your heart broken," Ben added.

****

New job to pay the bills, new apartment, new to her car… Everything was looking good. Now it was finally time to give her old friend Emily a call.

Anna felt her throat get a little dry—and her fingers a little sweaty—as she hesitated dialing Emily's number. She had called Katie earlier, and spent at least an hour listening to Katie's praise of her intellectual abilities. Good old Katie. With her, there was never anything to worry about.

On the other hand, Emily was quite moody. She

never knew which Emily she'd run into on a given day. Normally, Anna didn't care, but today, Emily's friendship was more important to her than ever.

Who else would advise Anna how to handle herself at Polaris, where to look for information, how to work on various projects? Emily knew Polaris inside and out. She would be a lifesaver for Anna, who was coming straight from Ukraine with zero experience at a Western company, and *lying* her way into the job on top of everything. Without Emily's help, Anna's ship would definitely sink before reaching the harbor. No doubt.

RING.

RING.

Emily picked up right away.

"Hello!" Anna yelled happily. "Emily, it's me! Guess where I'm calling you from? Hint: somebody got accepted into the Global Associates Program."

No answer followed. She looked at her phone. Ah, for some strange reason, the call got dropped. Well, maybe coverage was not very good in her new kitchen.

Anna walked into the living room and dialed Emily's number again. This time the line was busy. Anna kept calling for good fifteen minutes till Emily finally picked up.

"Hey Emily, something strange is going on with my phone… Sorry about that. Anyways, I'm back in Washington, starting the job with Polaris this fall, can you imagine?"

"Congratulations." Emily's voice sounded muffled.

"Let's meet up sometime soon?" Anna asked hopefully. "I'd love to get some advice from you about how to best start my career at Polaris. You already have several years of experience. And it will be great to just catch up on everything."

"Real sorry, Anna, but looks like I won't be in Washington for the next two weeks," Emily said. "I am on a business trip now, and then I'll be taking some time off for vacation."

"O-o-oh..." Anna exhaled and almost dropped her phone in disappointment. Of course, this was summertime, when all the hard-working people would be taking vacations. "All right. I guess we'll have plenty of opportunities to chat when I start working in September... Wanted to ask you one thing before I forget—my parents suggested that I bring a Ukrainian flag and some other Ukrainian things to the office, and possibly wear a national dress for the first day. You know, in Ukraine everyone is so patriotic. Is it okay for Polaris, or too much?"

"Of course, Anna, that's a wonderful idea! Yes, by all means, bring as much Ukrainian stuff as you can," Emily replied cheerfully. "I have seen many colleagues with their national flags in their offices, and I regularly watch people in various national costumes walking down the hallways, showcasing their culture. You'll fit right in."

"Oh good." Anna sighed with relief. "Thanks a lot and have a good vacation! See you at Polaris."

****

Along with the packet of paperwork to fill out, Anna received a surprising email from the Human Resources that she was now eligible to join the Clear Spring Country Club located in Montgomery County, Maryland, for a small monthly fee.

Anna looked at the email suspiciously. *What's even a country club?*

She quickly texted her mom:

Anna—*Mom, what do you think of me joining the Polaris country club? Waste of money, right? We don't even have country clubs in Ukraine—*

Olena—*Oh, come on! Money's not an issue here—*

Anna—*I just don't want to pay for something which is useless. Normal people in Ukraine entertain themselves at family dachas and public parks. Why pay?—*

Olena—*Well, I happen to know what a country club is. It's a place where you meet and hang out with the right people—*

Anna—*Okay, I'll think about it—*

Olena—*Nothing to think about. This is a golden opportunity to meet some handsome Polaris executive! Or at least find some friends and possibly mentors for yourself—*

Anna—*Fine. I'll go check it out with Katie and Dima on the weekend—*

Olena—*Dima's in D.C.? I didn't know—*

Anna—*Yes, he's here for a week. He always finds hotels willing to give him free stays—*

A warm and sunny Saturday morning, almost a week later, turned out to be the perfect time to visit the so-called Polaris club. Anna drove her new car, picking up Katie and Dima.

"Anna, I hope you did well in the driving school," Dima commented. "I think you are swinging a little bit too much from one side of the road to the other. Please be careful—you have some important passengers here."

"I am doing my best, Dimochka. Feel free to walk if you'd like," Anna responded through gritted teeth. Of course, Dima spotted the "New Driver" yellow sticker

on her car. Back in Ukraine, Anna never had the means
to buy a car, but here in D.C. it was a necessity. One of
the first things she had done this summer was enroll in
driving school.

The way to the country club was not easy to conquer
for a new driver at all. With its multiple lanes, bicyclists,
curvy roads, and impatient drivers honking their horns at
Anna's slow car, it was actually quite a challenge.

"Anna, I think it might be time for you to buy a place
here," Dima declared as they were driving past the large
and beautiful mansions in Potomac. "This is
unbelievable, just look at these estates!"

"Dima, it will take me a long time to buy a place like
you are imagining. I got an entry level job, and I am not
in investment banking, you know. We don't get hefty
bonuses, just a decent base salary to live on."

The three friends continued driving along River
Road, lined with mansions. Extravagant Porches,
Corvettes, Bentleys, various antique cars, and even a
Ferrari and a Rolls Royce passed them on the road.

At one point, they were passing by what appeared to
be a villa on a hill. Anna slowed down. "Please pay
attention everyone," she said to Dima and Katie, "This is
Emily's house on the left. Remember, Katie?"

"Oh yes!" Katie yelled. "Shall we stop for a visit?"

"Oh sure." Anna giggled. "Let's stop and say,
'Remember us? We were here a couple of years ago and
really enjoyed your party, but then you never invited us
back. So, we decided to stop by to see if maybe our
invitations had been lost in the mail. Here we are. Did
you miss us, ha-ha?'" She still vividly remembered that
New Year's Eve party at Emily's parents' house. Well,
it wasn't even a house. Emily's family lived in nothing

short of a jaw-dropping estate. An enormous gray mansion on a big green hill, with a snow-white fountain out front, ten bedrooms and uncountable other rooms, a heated indoor pool, a tennis court. That kind of thing. Mind-boggling for somebody like Anna who had grown up in a one-bedroom apartment.

****

Anna and Katie got out of their taxi and timidly walked through the door. At the outset, they caught a sight of Emily in an exquisite pink ball gown and a show-stopping tiara. Oh good! Hopefully, she would show them around and clue them in on what was going on.

"Hey, Emily, where should we…" Katie began. But no luck—Emily only briefly waved to them and quickly disappeared in the vast sea of exquisitely dressed guests.

Anna and Katie remained on their own to plunge into this unfamiliar territory.

"We don't quite belong here," Anna remarked. "But I figure, let's just walk around and explore."

The living room was enchanting: a tall spruce tree stood in the center, covered by marvelous ornaments from all parts of the world. The pair hugged the walls as they made their way around the room.

"Look at the paintings, Katie! I bet this gorgeous birch forest is painted by Ivan Shishkin, one of my favorite landscape painters."

"Paintings are lovely! But make sure to pay attention to the crowd." Katie had a serious face as they walked. "I already spotted a couple of well-known journalists, writers, and politicians. Oh, I think I see Emily's parents! They are standing right over there, together with her older sister Lauren. I just saw a few people come up to them and chat casually."

"Do you think they'll want to talk to us? Emily already blew us off…"

Anna took a few seconds just to observe the Roberts family from afar. What kind of people were they? Margaret, and Charles Roberts, must have come from a lot of money to have a mansion like this.

Mrs. Roberts was blond like Emily, in her late forties, impeccably dressed in a very elegant black pantsuit covered by tiny crystals. She looked a bit bored, with her gaze wondering aimlessly across the room. Mr. Roberts seemed a few years older than his wife, very tall and rather handsome, dressed in a tux. Unlike his wife, he appeared to enjoy the party and warmly greeted the bigwigs who kept streaming through the door.

Lauren appeared rather plain between the pair, quite a contrast to the ravishing Emily. Lauren was wearing some strange dark blue tunica with flats, which looked quite out of place at such a grand party. She was also much older, in her early thirties.

"Ladies, how wonderful to meet you!" Lauren exclaimed when Anna and Katie finally introduced themselves. "Emily told me a few of her classmates were coming, but she didn't point anyone out to me… I've been dying to meet you. Are you enjoying the party?"

"Extremely," Anna replied, delighted. At least they got a warm reception from somebody in the family. Lauren was so sweet and genuine. "This is the first time I have visited a beautiful home like this."

"Welcome." Mr. Roberts extended his hand and looked Anna over from head to feet. "I sense an accent. Where are you from?"

"Ukraine," Anna said quietly. In all likelihood, nobody here would know anything about her home country.

"Oh, how wonderful!" Lauren's eyes immediately lit up. "What an incredible coincidence! I was just watching this brilliant documentary about the Kyiv Pechersk Lavra. It's a famous Ukrainian monastery of the caves built in the eleventh century. It's been designated as a UNESCO World Heritage site," she explained to her parents.

"That's impressive," Mrs. Roberts squeezed out. Her wandering gaze focused on Anna for a brief second. And then shifted once more.

Lauren pulled out her phone and started showing the Kyiv Pechersk Lavra pictures to her parents. Whether they were impressed or not, it was really a nice gesture on Lauren's part.

At this point, a good strategy was to thank the hosts for the invitation, smile widely, and go talk to somebody else.

"And what do you do, Mr. Roberts?" Katie suddenly asked in a squeaky voice.

Anna gave Katie a subtle nudge with an elbow. She glanced back at Anna like she had no care in the world: *Relax! Everything's under control.*

"I'm an executive at the Emerald Hotels and Resorts chain," Mr. Roberts replied succinctly.

"Business must be going really well," Katie mused. "This seems quite an impressive mansion you've got in here. Maybe I should look into the hospitality career myself. My GPA isn't a 4.0, but I have good potential, as my parents say. You have any openings?"

"You can review our career website," Mr. Roberts said dryly and turned away, as a distinguished white-haired man approached him.

Surprise, surprise, Roberts family invitations never came for the following years. Neither for Anna nor for Katie.

****

The sign "Clear Spring" marked the entrance to the property. Anna navigated the narrow road before finally reaching a large white clubhouse with a beautiful garden around it.

Katie and Dima waited outside while Anna went to find somebody from administration to discuss her membership. It didn't take long—a couple minutes later she walked out with a membership director, ready to show her around.

It turned out that this time, Olena was absolutely right—Clear Spring was definitely worth joining. The club had an eighteen-hole golf course, fifteen outdoor tennis courts, a tennis bubble with five indoor courts, a soccer field, a basketball court, three outdoor swimming pools, a playground for kids, and two restaurants. All the people in the club were well dressed.

"What an awesome resort!" Dima exclaimed in total delight, as he was taking pictures of all the facilities and patrons passing by. "I do not think you could do any better, Anna. I am going to write about this club on my blog tonight. Let's go check out the tennis center over there? A large crowd is cheering loudly. I think some tournament is going on."

Anna's heart skipped a beat as she approached the tennis center. Once a tennis player, always a tennis player.

For a brief moment, her mind took Anna to the beloved tennis center in Kyiv—"Antej," where she had been training. There she was, walking proudly through the magic gates, catching soft golden sunbeams on her face, exchanging a few cheerful words with other players and coaches, and finally stepping on to the red clay court—her personal red carpet. Sparkles started to fly as soon as she touched the ball with her racket. Her eyes shone brighter than diamonds and heart filled up with a tremendous thrill, ready to jump out of her chest. Every shot was a masterpiece, carefully developed and executed.

Antej tennis courts were always full of life, but they especially lit up during the annual city tournament. Hundreds of hopeful juniors walked around with their tennis bags, waiting for their matches. Every time, Anna's head spun with excitement when she looked at the white sheets of paper pinned to the wall of the administration, announcing the draw. Who would be her first opponent? In what quarter of the draw did her main competitors end up?

"Hey, earth to Anna," Katie suddenly yelled. "Come on, let's go check who's playing! Maybe we'll get to see some tennis stars?"

Rather than a tournament, all the loud cheering was at just one court where a young blond girl, probably eight or nine years old, dressed all in pink, was playing against two older boys. Everyone in the crowd surrounding the court was taking photos and videos with a lot of excitement. Anna and her friends stood there confused.

"Excuse me, ma'am, who are these kids?" Katie finally decided to ask a tall and skinny lady wearing big sunglasses.

She gave Katie a surprised smile. "You guys new here?"

"Yes," Katie confessed, glancing back at Dima and

Anna.

Anna shook her head. She no longer followed junior tennis. And she definitely wouldn't know anyone in the ten and under category.

Dima then looked at the players more attentively, squinting his eyes, and suddenly blurted in a low voice, "Wait a minute. Is that… Erica Jameson?"

The lady nodded her head lightly and smiled again, while Anna gave Dima a puzzled look. Why would he know any young tennis players?

"Erica is a social media sensation!" Dima was almost spitting with excitement. "If I managed somehow to use Erica's influence to promote my channel and blog, it could help to boost my following. Being friends with a celebrity equals more clicks, likes, and more traffic on my social media channels. The question is, how to approach her…"

Erica continued hitting balls to her two partners, oblivious to everything going on around her. Dima kept fidgeting in his seat, powerless to attract her attention.

"Interesting how times have changed," Anna said to Katie as they got comfortable in the stands. "Back when I was these kids' age, social media wasn't yet such a big deal. I had won the Wimbledon junior title and almost got into the top one-hundred best tennis players in the world, but I didn't make much money to speak of. I actually *lost* all my family's money. I was one step away from signing a contract with a high-profile agent. But now kids can become Internet sensations in a blink of an eye. They don't need to sign a contract with the top tennis agency."

"You won Wimbledon junior title?" the lady in the big sunglasses suddenly looked at Anna, scrutinizing her from head to toe.

"Yes, some years back." Anna shrugged. Who cared about that now. It was ancient history.

"I think I know who you are," the lady said slowly. "You've gotta be…Anna Levenko, no?"

Anna's and Katie's eyebrows lifted incrementally. They exchanged puzzled looks. *How did she know Anna's name?*

"Well, you definitely don't remember us, but you gave your autograph to me and my daughter when you played at the Indian Wells that year, a long time ago," she declared. "I'm Teresa. My daughter Erica was just a toddler back then, so you probably don't recognize her. But you look pretty much the same."

Of course! It would have been one of the last autographs Anna ever gave out in her tennis career… she suddenly felt a lump in her throat. Many years had passed since that dreadful day. It was still as fresh as ever.

"I… I think I remember you both too," Anna said, trying to fight the strong emotions brewing in her soul. How could she ever forget Erica, a miracle child cured of cancer? That day when Anna met them at the Indian Wells, Erica's face was strikingly pale, eyes full of sadness. Her mother had to carry her or push her in the stroller as she was too frail to walk. What a relief it was to see her now, years later. She was so tall and strong, her rosy cheeks glowing with health!

"It looks like Erica completely recovered?" Anna asked excitedly.

"Yes, she sure did!" Teresa nodded, her eyes full of joy. "The experimental treatment she received at the children's hospital… it was a miracle. Now she is one of the most athletic kids —who could have guessed that? The social media quickly picked up on her story—and the rest you could say is history." Teresa nodded in the direction of spectators. "It's very nice, of course, but I would have much preferred Erica to be just an ordinary kid. Healthy and happy. We didn't need this fame."

"Well, I guess it was just meant to be this way. Now she has a great tennis career in front of her! Unfortunately, mine was cut short."

"We were at your last match!" Teresa said eagerly, "I prayed you would return to the court after the medical timeout and win those last two points and the match. But then we saw an announcement that you wanted to change career. I still secretly hoped that you'd come back to tennis. You had so much talent! What happened after the Indian Wells?"

"Well, a lot of things happened," Anna said, trying to figure out how to sum up her last six years—the good, the bad, the ugly. Normally, she wouldn't share such details with a person she just met. But Teresa wasn't a stranger to her. Not at all. Many years ago, she was Anna's fan. They shared an unbreakable bond. "I went back to Ukraine. Eventually, I had an operation on my shoulder. We didn't have enough money to go to an expensive clinic and did it at a public hospital. The operation wasn't very successful. My shoulder felt better but was still very stiff, even months after the operation. I could still play sports, just for fun—but playing competitive tennis was no longer an option. In the end, I decided to enroll in business school and now I made it into the Global Associates Program at Polaris. So that's kind of my story."

"Wow! I'm glad you did not give up after your

tennis career didn't work out, and instead reinvented yourself. That's what real champions do. Polaris is a great place for young and ambitious people like you. I work there too and can give you a lot of advice… Erica! Come here, sweetie!" Teresa suddenly yelled out. "I think you've had enough practice today. Plus, I have someone for you to meet."

And just like that, the unapproachable pink social media princess was right there in front of them, shaking hands, giggling, and chatting. Erica trained here at the Clear Spring country club and aspired to hold a junior Wimbledon trophy one day.

"Anna, please, let's play tennis together one of these days!" Erica begged. "I'd love to see your shots and try to improve mine. Mom was telling me you had some wicked backhand with a top spin, right in the corner? Apparently, your opponents had such a tough time returning it."

"Yes, that's true. I can teach you that backhand. You will beat everyone in no time." Anna gave Erica a hug.

"Mom, please give Anna our contact info so that we can stay in touch. We'll need to set something up for next week. Let's play on the clay court, that's my best surface." Erica was all business. So much maturity for a little girl.

Teresa handed Anna her business card: *Teresa Jameson, PhD, Polaris Chief Economist.* While Anna held the card, Dima came up beside her.

"Erica, so nice to meet you! I'm Dima, Anna's *best* friend. Can I help you with anything, sweetheart?" Dima asked in his sugary sweet voice. "How about I carry your tennis balls and rackets to your car? I also wanted to ask you something about your social media channel, if you have a little bit of time."

"Sure," Erica said cheerfully. "Anybody who is Anna's friend is my friend as well."

It did not take Dima long to convince Erica to do some project together in future. He also got a permission to add her as a friend on social media and direct message her. Anna watched all this in a daze, still holding the card. It was the best day ever.

Chapter 10. The First Days in the Office

Tunis, Tunisia & Washington, D.C.

The orientation for Polaris Global Associates was held in Tunis, the sprawling capital of Tunisia on the shores of the Mediterranean Sea. At five in the morning, Anna was laying wide awake in the spacious room of her hotel, listening to the soft sounds of waves, and thinking what the heck she got herself into. She was about to begin working at one of the best companies in the world—her *dream* job—because she lied on the application.

What am I going to say to everyone when they ask about my background? How will I look people in the eye? Everyone else in the class earned their way into the program—except for me.

Anna sat up on the edge of the bed. Her chest felt heavy, as if an elephant sat on it. It was useless trying to go back to sleep.

If only she never responded to that Polaris recruitment ad, she would be still in Ukraine, not worrying about a thing. In all likelihood, some other good, impactful job would have come her way. She'd be happy and free to build her career the way she pleased, without having to look over her shoulder all the time.

But Anna could not erase the past. All she could do now was to keep telling her ridiculous story about the adviser to the Minister of Finance, which made her want to vomit.

"I have nobody else to blame but myself," Anna whispered as she was starting to dress for the orientation. Despite being extremely embarrassed, self-conscious, and ill-at-ease, she'd have to put a bright smile on her face, walk into the room and mingle with other Polaris Global Associates and staff like she had no care in the world. Like she belonged among this elite group.

Anna shyly walked into the conference room with the sign "Polaris orientation" and sat down at the table in the first row, continuously fixing her skirt or hair and nervously looking around. She was the first one to come, but soon enough, the room filled up with other Global Associates. They were all energetic and happy, shaking hands, grabbing coffee or tea, and loudly exchanging their views about Tunis and the hotel they were staying at. Clearly, they didn't have a worry in the world and none of them had spent the previous night stressing about their unethical behavior.

Anna decided to just stay in her seat for the time being and wait till somebody sat down next to her. She glanced through the thick binder which had been placed at her seat; it contained various presentations to be delivered during the training sessions. Wow, a lot of material was going to be covered! The curriculum of the orientation looked very interesting.

In the back of the binder, Anna also found a list of all the Global Associates who were joining Polaris this year.

Anna held her breath. Somebody named "Jean Louis Rolland" from France was on the list!

Could that be *her* Jean? Anna looked around the

room several times, her eyes full of hope, but did not see anyone who looked like him.

All right. It's not the end of the world. Maybe he didn't arrive yet—for example, his flight could be late or cancelled. For now, let's just try to stay calm. Wait a second—could this be... Rosie entering the room right now?

It sure was the charming Rosie—no mistake about that. Anna should have guessed it. Rosie had to get the slot in the program, with her impeccable credentials.

"Anna, you got accepted, too?" Rosie gasped in delight and gave Anna a big hug. "This is fantastic! I'm so happy we're both in the program."

Anna and Rosie sat together and soon were joined by Alex van Greuning—a technology expert from South Africa—and Wendy Stevens—an American agriculture expert. The appearance of Rosie at the orientation definitely calmed Anna down a lot. She finally got enough courage to speak to other Global Associates and felt more at ease.

Now, where was Jean? Two hours of the training passed, and he was nowhere to be found. It was time to start a thorough investigation.

During the break, Anna walked up to the administrative assistant who was the focal point for everything to do with orientation.

"Sally, excuse me please, somebody named Jean Louis Rolland is on the list. Is he in the room? I need to talk to him about something, but I don't see him for some reason," Anna asked, looking at her pleadingly.

"No, he actually is not here. Let me check in my computer what could be the reason..." Sally opened some document and scrolled through her screen. "Mr.

Rolland started his job at Polaris before the rest of the class. He had been sent to an African country, Sierra Leone, for one month to supervise the implementation of a project there, the construction of a primary school for children in some remote village."

Anna's face lit up. That sounded a lot like the Jean she had met! Who else would already start such a challenging project here at Polaris?

"Oh, I see… I-I need to urgently contact Jean. Is it possible to give me his email address?"

"No problem at all!" Sally wrote the email address on the piece of paper and immediately handed it to Anna.

It seemed so easy! Now all Anna needed to do was send Jean a note, and the guy of her dreams would be back in her life. She could do it—she was a young, modern woman who would take her own fortune in her hands. She did not need to wait for Jean to find her—she could make the first step.

But when Anna returned triumphantly to her desk, she suddenly got cold feet. First, what if she were wrong, and the Jean accepted into the program turned out a completely different guy? Jean was such a common name. Millions of people in France were probably named Jean. Sending a note to a stranger and making a fool out of herself was not quite something she wanted to do at the beginning of the program.

Second, even if she convinced herself this was the same Jean she had met, what would she write to him now, eight months later?

Hi Jean, I am Anna from the interviews, remember me? Sorry to contact you so late… We faced a bit of a problem with a frog, Freddie (long story), so I had to run after the interviews. I was thinking about you this whole time and I just got hold of your email address. So, how have you been? You're in Sierra Leone, right? Want to hang out when you get back?

Agh, it all came out completely wrong... Anna pushed her laptop away in disappointment. Clearly, she just needed to wait till they met again, so she could explain everything to Jean. That would probably not take too long. Just a little bit of patience. She'd already waited this long.

Anna put the paper with Jean's email address in her handbag. It was better to stop daydreaming about Jean for now and focus more on the training sessions.

She had imagined that orientation was going to be a walk in the park after passing the grueling interview, but that was the wrong assumption. Theory was one thing, practice was another.

Within the first couple of hours, she was drowning in the various products, services, and procedures which existed at Polaris. What was an investment project in the healthcare sector? How do you structure multi-year technical assistance to the Ministry of Energy? How do you write a completion report for a department strategy? All of this seemed like a foreign language.

Other participants seemed to have a much better grasp of all these concepts. What was their secret? Well, pretty soon it became apparent that there were no secrets. There was just some homework which Anna never completed. Anna did not even think that the email sent last month contained a link to an online training and various supplementary materials which needed to be reviewed and preferably memorized prior to the orientation.

Today was also the day when everyone in the

program got assigned to various Polaris departments where they would begin their career. Right after lunch, most of the associates received emails from their bosses welcoming them to the new departments.

"I'll be covering India!" Alex yelled cheerfully as he opened the email from his boss. "This is super cool. I can't wait to start my new job. How about you, Anna?"

"Let me check. I think the email just came in."

Anna held her breath. What country was she going to cover? It didn't really matter—she was new to Polaris and up for anything—but still, it was exciting to find out. In most likelihood, she'd be assigned to some country close to her background—maybe Europe or Central Asia.

"Hmmm, it's Tanzania for me?" Anna murmured, as she clicked on the email which just came in from somebody named John Walker. This was quite unexpected. But then again, Emily had mentioned that Africa was now one of the priority regions for Polaris. "I've never been to Africa, so it's going to be very interesting to visit."

"Great!" Alex smiled. "Excellent region and country to work on. I'm a bit biased since I'm from South Africa, but you get the point… Rosie, and where are you assigned?"

"I don't know." Rosie looked at her email anxiously. "I just got an email from HR that for some reason, no manager was interested in my profile. Now they need to find a unit to take me… Hope something comes up soon. I don't want to go back home!"

"How strange." Anna shook her head. "With your background, managers should be lining up to hire you. I'm sure this will be resolved soon."

****

Every day of the orientation was packed with a lot of activities till the late evening, so Anna didn't get much chance to enjoy the resort. Finally, on Thursday, the training sessions ended at five. Without thinking twice, Anna headed for a swim.

The beach was rather empty, as most of the patrons of the hotel already had finished their sunbathing by that time. Anna did some swimming and then got comfortable in the beach chair and pulled out the novel she'd brought by Ivan Nechuy-Levyzky, a famous Ukrainian classical writer.

Burlachka, or its English equivalent Factory Girl, described the fate of a young Ukrainian village girl living in the nineteenth century. Five minutes into reading the book, and Anna was immersed into the splendid world of her home country—snow white hatas surrounded by the magnificent gardens full of cherry and pear trees blooming in spring, steep mountains, vast valleys, lakes bounded by willows, and old oak forests.

Suddenly, a loud voice pierced through the silence and tranquility.

"Nice day for the beach, no? Your name is Anna—do I remember correctly?"

Anna turned her head in the direction of the voice and saw one of the managers who did a presentation at her training. What was his name? Lenny Jameson, or something like that. He looked quite different in a swim suit—bright orange trunks—compared to the sophisticated black Armani suit he wore during the presentation. He must have been in his late forties, not too athletic but in a pretty good shape for his age.

Anna put the book down in disappointment. "Hello,

Lenny. Yes, I like the beach a lot. It's pretty nice to have our orientation in a place like Tunis."

"At Polaris we try to hold such orientations in a memorable place every year. Sometimes it is Tunis, other times Istanbul, we have also done it in Rome. We want to make sure the incoming class bonds really well and also remembers this experience for the rest of their career."

Anna nodded. Hopefully, Lenny would now keep on walking so that she could continue reading *Burlachka*. But—alas—he was not going anywhere.

"So, what did you think of my presentation of commodity exchange best practices?" Lenny asked, moving right next to Anna.

In all honesty, Anna did not think much of Lenny's presentation. But for politeness's sake, she could say something neutral. Lenny was clearly fishing for compliments. "I think our class greatly enjoyed your presentation," Anna finally offered, subtly staring at Lenny's putrid orange trunks. An executive of his level should have planned his swimming attire more carefully.

"Glad you liked it. I have worked on various projects in Latin America and Africa. My new program is in India. If you are interested, I could take you on the team. If you like beaches, India is a great place to go. We could visit some incredible ones in Goa. I give you my word that you will learn a lot from these trips."

By now, Anna was pretty sure she did not want to be on his team. A burgeoning sense of unease started brewing in her heart.

"Lenny, this sounds really exciting, but unfortunately I'm already assigned to the Tanzania team. Thanks a lot for such a kind offer though, I greatly appreciate it."

"Any time." Lenny did not give up. "If you'd like, we could meet later tonight and grab a drink at the hotel restaurant. I can tell you more about commodity exchanges and work at Polaris in general. You need to start your career right in order for you to achieve your full potential."

It was time to get out of this conversation. Being caught having drinks with a manager, twenty years her senior, at the *orientation,* would most definitely not be a great start to Anna's career.

"Oh, that would have been wonderful, but I already have an evening meeting with some friends. I need to get going now, or I will be late, but it was great chatting with you."

****

In the morning of her first day in the office, Anna got up very early to make sure everything was in order. Her best-looking *vyshyvanka* and a traditional woven *plakhta* (skirt), check. The vinok of bright red poppies with long flowing ribbons, check. A large Ukrainian yellow-and-blue flag, check. Some small stuff for office decoration—a basket of beautifully decorated *pysankas* (Easter eggs), a couple of *rushnyks* (cloths) embroidered with various red symbols, and some small clay whistle statues. Check. Yulia Tymoshenko portrait. Check. Everything seemed fine. Anna was now ready to make a triumphant entrance into the Polaris building.

She parked at the Polaris garage and walked into the elevator with her head held up high. It was a little bit tricky walking while carrying the flag on her shoulder and an egg basket on the elbow, plus her wreath kept sliding down her head—maybe she should have bought a smaller size—but Anna figured those were just temporary inconveniences. Nothing to worry about.

She joined several good-looking well-dressed Polaris staff in the elevator. Everyone exchanged surprised looks when they saw Anna and one of the gentlemen asked, "Is there some folk dance performance today?"

"Dance performance?" Anna said. "Oh, I do not know. It is actually my first day at work. I would love to go if there is one."

She got off on the tenth floor where her department and her office were expected to be. She walked down the hallway looking for room number 1011. The numbering system was not straightforward, the hallways looked a little bit like a labyrinth, so she ended up walking back and forth several times. The load she was carrying was feeling heavier and heavier, so Anna decided to put all her stuff down for a few minutes and rest.

A few people noticed her maneuvers and came out of their offices to check out what was going on.

"Can we help you?" asked a tall and slender African guy, glancing at the flag on Anna's shoulder with a puzzled look. "You seem to be lost. Where are you heading with all these things?"

"Just searching for my office," Anna explained. "The numbering system here is really weird. I keep walking in circles and still cannot find it."

"Your office? These offices are for Polaris staff only. Not sure who you are and what you will be doing here..." a short Chinese lady in glasses said after taking a good look at the basket with the eggs. "Are you trying to sell arts and crafts? Who let you in?"

By that time, about a dozen staff gathered around

them to see what was happening. Anna noticed that there were people of different nationalities, but nobody was wearing any traditional clothing. In fact, everyone was dressed in dark business suits of the latest fashion, very standardized. All the men had coats and ties on; all the women wore knee-length skirts.

Anna stood there red as a tomato.

"I am a new Global Associate, Anna Levenko," she finally said.

"Oh, you are Anna?" The African guy broke into a big smile. "We have been expecting you! I am Bernard Kaye. Let me show you to your new office. Sorry, we just did not know what you looked like. Guys, everything is fine. It is just our new Global Associate. You can go back to work."

Anna waved to everyone and gave a weak smile. Bernard quickly took her to office number 1011. It was indeed tricky to find. The new office was nice, modern, and spacious.

As Anna was putting her belongings in the office, her new manager, John Walker, also came to greet her.

"Hope you are not too shocked with the outfit and other stuff," Anna said. "In Ukraine, we love all of these traditional things. It seems a little overboard for Polaris, but I couldn't have it any other way. This is part of my culture—it's very important for me and my family."

"Hey, I think your outfit looks absolutely lovely," Bernard said. "And all of the decorations for your office are splendid as well. I am now thinking of bringing more things from Uganda to decorate my office. I have a couple of small statues, but I could definitely have more."

John agreed with Bernard. "In my opinion, staff

would only look better if from time to time they wore what is traditional in their home country. Preserving your cultural identity is important. I'm so glad that I caught a glimpse of Ukrainian culture today. Thanks for that, Anna. Please go ahead and get settled. If you have any problems—do let me know."

The next day, Anna—this time conservatively dressed in a dark-gray jacket with a pencil skirt—ventured out of her office to explore her surroundings. With her stiletto heels brushing against the soft carpets, she quietly wandered around the corridors to get familiar with her floor and study the name plates on the various offices. That eventually brought her to an office which had an "Emily Roberts" plate on its door.

Anna's face instantly lit up. *Aha, this is where her office is! I'm so lucky—we ended up working in the same department. Now I'll be able to stop by at any time, especially if I get in some trouble, or have a burning question.*

She could see Emily's charming profile and soft blond curls easily through the glass door. Emily's makeup was flawless, like usual, and her eyelashes were so long that they looked like butterfly wings, softly fluttering from time to time. She was wearing a chic navy-colored belted dress with bracelet-length sleeves.

The office appeared very well-organized. Emily had quite a few colorful economic books in her possession, as evidenced by three packed bookcases, and multiple awards hanging on the walls. On her desk stood several photos. One of them featured the cute orange muzzle of the faithful Fofo. Another was of a portrait of a man, but Anna could not discern the face from her angle.

Anna waved and opened the door triumphantly.

"Emily, I am here, at Polaris! In the same department as you of all places! Who could guess, right? Let's go out for coffee! I have a million things to ask you."

Emily smoothed out her curls and stood up leisurely, then gave Anna a brief hug. "Anna. Wow… You are really here… How wonderful to see you. But—I have a deadline for an important project. Really sorry. I'm kind of swamped."

"An important project? Sounds so exciting!" Anna smiled, so proud and happy for her friend, and sat down at the roundtable which stood in the corner of the office. "What kind of project is it? Tell me!"

"It's a large lending operation in Burkina Faso," Emily said reluctantly, stretching out her every word and at the same time anxiously eyeing Anna as she was getting comfortable in her chair, stretching out her legs and leaning back. "I'm a deputy team leader. The project is going for Board approval in two months."

"Way to go!" Anna clapped her hands. "You're a big shot here, I can tell right away! You'll get promoted very quickly, I'm sure."

"I sure hope so." Emily smiled subtly.

"Just look at all these awards and diplomas you have on the wall!" Anna said enthusiastically. "And you have so many lovely, framed group photos… Where was this one taken?" She pointed at a large and colorful photo featuring thirty people or so, some spectacular skyscrapers in the background, which was standing on one of the bookshelves.

"Singapore," Emily squeezed out, starting to fidget in her seat. "I organized a learning visit for our African counterparts last winter…"

"And what about that one?" Anna pointed at a photo

of Emily with another large group, taken in some tropical setting.

"Oh, this is from the team retreat in South Africa a few months ago. Our whole department went there, it was a nice trip."

"So cool! I hope I can go one day as well. And I see you have a photo of Fofo, of course. Did I tell you I got two dogs, Lapa and Zirka? They are coming to live with me in a month or so. And who is—"

"Listen, Anna, I'd love to chat with you some more, but I really need to finish an important project document now. We are on such a tight deadline. I'll stop by your office tomorrow afternoon?" Emily raised her hands in a mock outrage. "I should have more time then. You'll tell me about your dogs, whatever their names are, and anything else you'd like."

"Oh, of course, not a problem. Coffee tomorrow is perfectly fine with me." Anna slowly rose from her chair, although she would have much preferred sitting in this spacious and cozy office for another hour, chatting with Emily and getting a glimpse into what a job at Polaris was like. Her college friend had sure come a far way, with her important projects, conferences, the travel, and all. Hopefully, Anna's future would be similarly exciting.

"Great." Emily got up and started walking Anna out of her office. "I'll see you tomorrow. Take care till then!"

"Yes, of course." Anna stopped in the doorway for a brief second. "My office is on the other end of the hall, next to Bernard's. You can easily find me. I don't have much to do yet. Just learning about everything. My first day was just yesterday. I can show you the Ukrainian flag and various pieces I brought from home. And I also have a nice group photo on display, the one with all the Global Associates at the orientation in Tunis."

"I simply can't wait to see it." Emily smiled with her widest and sweetest smile before firmly closing her office door behind Anna.

Chapter 11. The First Project

Washington, D.C.

Anna looked at her watch. It was already past seven in the evening of the following day. Most of the staff had already left for the day. She walked by Emily's office to check if she were there. No. The office was dark. Probably went home by now. Or maybe she was in some meeting.

"Very strange," she whispered to herself before brightening, "Well, she probably got tied up. With her project and all other stuff... I'll just stop by tomorrow!"

Anna kept waiting for Emily's visit for a whole week, but the other girl never showed up. Every time Anna passed by Emily's office, her friend was either not in the office, or on the phone, or talking to somebody. At some point, Anna figured it was time to look for somebody else she could direct her questions to.

She timidly popped her head through the open door of Bernard's office. "Hey, Bernard. I have a few questions to ask about Polaris. Do you have time to meet over a coffee?"

"Coffee? Of course!" Bernard smiled warmly. "I'm up for coffee at any time. Let's go!"

Anna quickly realized that Bernard was an excellent resource for her. Not only did the guy know everything about everything, but he also loved sharing his knowledge. He joined Polaris as the Global Associate five years ago and had plenty of recommendations as to how Anna could succeed in the organization.

"First of all, I suggest to play it safe this year," Bernard said, as he was savoring his delicious cappuccino with skim milk at the Polaris coffee shop downstairs. With many Polaris folks being coffee enthusiasts, the café was pretty crowded. Anna and Bernard got the last table.

"I know that ambitious newcomers like you want to make their name known right off the bat and lead some really challenging project, but this is not the best strategy. I can tell you for a fact—nothing really prepares you for a job at Polaris, even if you were an important official before. You need to learn a lot. Also, keep in mind: your job is in a bit of a jeopardy this year."

Anna went pale and even dropped her spoon on the floor. What was he talking about? Did Bernard somehow guess that she didn't belong here? That she had lied on the application?

"What jeopardy?" she asked quietly, trying not to look at Bernard.

"Well, you do know that as a Global Associate, you hold only a one-year employment contract, right?"

"One year contract?" Anna perked up her ears. Bernard was talking about something else. Not about her lie on the application. Okay. Deep breath in, deep breath out. No need to panic just yet.

"Yes, you signed a one-year employment contract when Polaris sent you the papers. This is the approach they use with all their Global Associates. After one year, most of the people in your class will graduate to become a regular employee of Polaris and sign a new contract.

But not everyone. Some will be let go. Polaris is a competitive organization. It would be too easy if you got into a program and got a job for life, wouldn't it?"

"Well, the program itself is already so hard to get in that I kind of expected it to offer a long-term job," Anna offered nervously.

"This is not the way our inventive management thinks!" Bernard laughed. "Usually sometime mid-year they will hold a big meeting and discuss all the Global Associates one by one—all their achievements and failures, their strengths and weaknesses. They will then make a decision who will continue with Polaris and who will not. If somebody failed their project during the year, or behaved inappropriately—do you think they would want to keep these people? Absolutely not."

Anna's face darkened. When she accepted this offer, she had been sure this would be her job for the next thirty years. That was if nobody found out about her lie, of course.

"In your case, I think there will be no issues," Bernard assured Anna. "You were an adviser to the Minister of Finance before, you know how things work."

"Right. Of course I do," Anna said weakly and felt her face gradually turn red from chin to forehead, while her neck suddenly became sticky.

"Just make sure you do not take on some challenging project, that's all. Go for some study, if you can, it's much easier to pull off than an investment project. And try to get along with everyone, which shouldn't be hard for a person like you."

"Yes, of course." Anna nodded. "I wanted to ask you about our manager, John. Any advice on working with him? Anything to worry about?"

"Oh, John? You struck gold," Bernard announced proudly. "He is the best one at the whole company—fair, honest, and highly intelligent. Just work hard, and he will be on your side at all times."

"Nice! How about the projects I will work on? When will I know that?" Anna smoothed out her skirt and straightened in her seat.

"Hold your horses. Everyone just got back from summer vacation. A big staff meeting is planned for next week. That's when you will be assigned your first project. For now, make sure you do your online learning to continue familiarizing herself. Polaris has a whole online academy and all the staff can pick from thousands of training courses in both soft and technical skills."

This time Anna was not going to mess it up. She'd already signed up for ten courses which were recommended for new staff and had completed them ahead of schedule.

****

For her first big staff meeting, Anna arrived on Monday at nine. Well, actually a few minutes before, just in case there was some delicious snacks up for grabs.

The food selection didn't disappoint. Anna glanced through all the delicacies—muffins of all kinds, flaky croissants, pastries, yogurt parfaits, scrambled eggs with chicken sausages, pancakes, smoothies, and several varieties of juices, tea, and coffee. They also had a huge dish of fruit of all kinds, full of delicious raspberries and strawberries, ripe mangoes, golden pineapple, and sweet apricots.

This is a feast! But there are no large plates... That's not going to work.

Anna quickly went to her office, grabbed a large

fruit platter she'd brought from home and loaded it with all the delicious items which caught her eye. She then leaned back against her chair, admiring like an artist the beauty which she just assembled on her plate.

Should I take a picture and post on social media? Anna held the phone in her hand, contemplating. It was so tempting! But other staff in the room might find it too "touristy." Plus, she'd already startled everyone with her Ukrainian outfit... Maybe it was better to stay under the radar for a bit. Anna reluctantly put her phone away and started observing the staff arriving at the meeting.

About twenty people walked in, their heads held high, all impeccably dressed. John showed up with a large brown folder under his arm. He started shaking everyone's hands vigorously while smiling widely. John was short and scrawny, but his incredible enthusiasm made him look like an indisputable leader in the room.

Emily was the last one to arrive, strolling in slowly and gracefully, like she was gliding on ice. She only said hello to John, carefully adjusted the ruffles on her skirt, and took a seat next to him. Emily poured a small cup of coffee for herself and ignored all the other delicacies. She took very small sips, making sure that her lip-gloss stayed on perfectly.

Finally, the meeting began.

"Tanzania is now one of the most important countries for Polaris," John announced proudly to the staff assembled around the large round table. "Our senior management is very supportive of projects there. Just recently, Polaris Director General travelled to Tanzania and met with the President and her team to discuss various areas of cooperation. The most important and urgent project on the agenda is to support several microfinance institutions with implementing digital tools. Whoever leads this project would be in the spotlight from top management."

There were several other tasks up for grabs—projects to rehabilitate several rural roads connecting various villages, install irrigation systems to help farmers, develop curriculum for various rural schools, undertake several surveys and prepare a new analytical study about prospects of economic development in the archipelago of Zanzibar—an autonomous territory of Tanzania.

"Finally, we have a project which I find especially interesting, albeit challenging—the rehabilitation of the Tourism Institute of Zanzibar, or TIZ for short, and an adjacent training hotel, called Grand Peacock Hotel. The President hopes to fix up their buildings and significantly expand the school to serve students from the whole of Tanzania and potentially other neighboring countries as well."

John passed around copies of the projects list for all the meeting's participants and opened the floor for everyone in the room to discuss the projects they would like to take on.

Anna carefully glanced through the list. She figured she'd better play it safe and just stay quiet for the time being and see what happened. Most of the projects were quickly delegated to other attendees. In particular, Emily was assigned the flagship microfinance project and she looked quite proud of herself.

"Anna, and what do you think?" John finally asked. "I see you have been quite busy with your breakfast. Glad that at least somebody is enjoying the food. So, has anything on the list caught your eye?"

"I should probably work on the study about Zanzibar. That seems very interesting." It was also one of the assignments still up for grabs, and it didn't seem too complicated. Anna was quite good at research back at business school and had co-authored a couple of research papers together with her professors.

"Yes, I think it would be a good fit for you. I have a few ideas about the content of the study." John nodded. "I will send you a couple of earlier research papers we have done. And then you can collect the information before you travel to Zanzibar."

Anna took out her notepad and wrote a reminder for herself to get the documents from John. Bernard gave a glance of approval to Anna. Good choice of project. Not difficult, yet interesting. Need to start your career on the right foot.

Right at that moment, a familiar voice chimed in. "I really apologize, John, but may I suggest something?"

It was Emily, who'd clearly been listening the whole time.

"Yes, of course, Emily. If you have any additional ideas, we are all ears," John said.

"Well, I was just thinking that Anna was an adviser to the Minister of Finance of Ukraine before, not some small job. So, we need to give her an opportunity to shine as much as possible. The Zanzibar study is undoubtedly a fantastic project, as you correctly pointed out, but to me, the tourism institute is the flagship task which you should assign to a bright star like Anna. From what I understand, it's not been assigned to anyone yet." Emily looked shyly under the table.

John tapped her on the shoulder and broke into a big smile. "Emily, I did not think about that at all. Thank you so much for bringing this up. I am always amazed about how deeply you care about all the staff in our department. Of course, Anna should get the project fit for a star."

Then John turned to Anna. She could feel her face grow red and, after choking on her muffin, she started coughing violently.

"Anna, everything okay? Did you hear Emily's suggestion? How about the tourism institute? As I said, this is my favorite project of all that are on the table, but it is not an easy one compared to the study. It is one of those high risk-high reward projects which do not always work out. I'll leave the decision to you."

Anna finished coughing and looked at John hesitantly. Her gut reaction was not to accept the tourism project and come up with some excuse why she could not take it on. She was a finance major in business school. What did she know about tourism institutes and training hotels? Nothing, obviously. What if she completely failed the project and then got kicked out from Polaris? With the study, there would likely be no hiccups and Anna would keep her job. She had plenty of experience with research.

But… I could probably become famous at Polaris if I chose the tourism institute project and managed to pull it off!

During the orientation in Tunis Anna had heard that at the end of every year, Polaris management gave out awards to several best performing teams. The profiles of the winners were featured on the company intranet. A big ceremony was organized to celebrate their achievements. The tourism institute was exactly the type of impactful project which would win an award. Her winning energy from her tennis days fueled visions of success.

Bernard noticed Anna's hesitation and then passed her a note.

—*Don't take it. It's a trap.*—

Anna glanced at the note briefly, smiled, and gently pushed it away. "Absolutely," she responded to John. "I am ready to try the TIZ project."

"Great," John said, sounding very pleased. "You and Emily will be leading two really important projects for our division."

After John ended the meeting, Bernard dragged Anna to his office.

"Anna, I do not know what you were thinking!" Bernard exclaimed as soon as they shut the door. "Don't you see—Emily was trying to play you and force you to accept the project which was already doomed!"

"Why would she do that?" Anna said stubbornly. "She is my friend. I think she was trying to help. She wanted both of us to lead important projects."

Bernard looked at Anna skeptically and didn't say anything.

"I could definitely do some good things with the tourism institute," Anna continued, her competitive nature taking over. "How hard can it be? And the reward, being famous in Polaris, would be worth it."

"Anna, you have never even been to Sub-Saharan Africa yet! This is your first project at Polaris ever, and it's such a complex one… I already see several potential challenges. First, it might be extremely hard and expensive to renovate and expand this school. We don't know what the current state of their facilities is and what needs to be done. Our management only approves projects with an adequate internal rate of return, so keep that in mind. Second, you could face significant resistance from various stakeholders who benefit from the status quo in some way. It happened to me several times in my projects—luckily, I have a lot of experience and I was able to resolve those problems, but it was not easy, I can tell you! I am really worried that this project will sink you…" He sighed. "Well, we cannot change anything now—you were thrown in the water, now you need to learn how to swim—and really fast."

Anna finally realized the gravity of the situation, with the adrenaline of the moment, and the attention, fading from her body. Cool clarity flowed over her. Emily wasn't her friend anymore. She had been looking for a way to torpedo Anna's career and brilliantly orchestrated this whole situation, pushing all the right buttons. Naturally, Emily didn't want to meet and talk to Anna earlier. She had never been happy for Anna for having gotten into a prestigious program like the Global Associates.

"What… what should I do now?" she asked weakly. "How do I begin?"

"Well, first you need to write the concept paper and submit it for John's approval. I will send you some examples. It is just a short note on what you know now about the project and what types of activities you are expected to fund and approximate estimate of funding required. You will also need to put together a team to work with you. You get a preparation budget for the project. This should be enough both to cover your time and support of several experts."

That sounded reassuring. Anna felt the color returning to her face.

"How do I get a team?" she asked. "What about

you? Can you be on the team? You already have so much experience, which would be super helpful."

"I can certainly advise you, but I cannot be on the team. I already have five projects of my own. You will have to contact some specialists at other departments of Polaris. I presume you will need an engineer, a tourism specialist, and an education specialist. I can give you some names of people I have worked with in the past."

****

That evening, Anna sat in her office motionless for several hours, thoughtlessly staring at Pennsylvania Avenue and car lights. Nothing was going as easy as she had hoped it would. Anna now needed to prove that she belonged at Polaris, when she herself still did not fully believe she should be here.

But Anna could not go back home to Ukraine. It would be too humiliating. She did not have a choice. She had a good head on her shoulders—somehow it got her through the interview—now she needed to put it to good use.

In the days that followed, she started reviewing documentation about the tourism institute and putting together a team to work with her. She carefully reviewed the list of names Bernard sent her way, calling each as she went down the list.

First, she hired Fiona Murray, a tourism expert. She was an older lady, very experienced and highly energetic. With her two daughters all grown up and off to college, Fiona was up for trips at any time. The earlier the better.

"Can we leave for Tanzania tomorrow?" Fiona asked as soon as Anna clued her in on the details of the project over lunch. "I can pack very quickly. Let's fly tomorrow morning. Some seats might still be available—I can check."

"Tomorrow might be a bit early," Anna said carefully. She needed to curb Fiona's enthusiasm. Anna still had to find some more team members and also get things organized for the first visit. "I'll let you know once everything is sorted out. Hopefully, we can travel very soon."

"O-o-kay," Fiona said slowly, ending on a sigh. "I'll have my suitcase packed and ready to go, just in case. I really have nothing to do at home, so let's try to get on the plane as soon as possible. Sitting in the empty apartment is the worst for me."

Karen Kalpanian, an experienced education expert, was the second member to join the team. Karen would be helping with the development of the educational curriculum for the school. He was a great family man, with a lovely wife and two young kids at home. Unlike Fiona, he was in no rush to travel.

The last member to join the team was Marcelo Roca, an engineer expected to make an estimate of the funding required to renovate the facilities. Marcelo recently moved from Bolivia to Washington. Apparently, he applied for a mid-career position through the Polaris website and eventually was selected for the job.

"How do you like living in the States now?" Anna asked, as they were sitting down at the Polaris coffee shop.

"Being away from my family and friends has been quite hard." Marcelo sighed. "It was quite a shock in the beginning. I went from hundreds of friends and relatives in La Paz to knowing nobody at all in Washington D.C. I'm now slowly getting to know people here, but it takes time. Hopefully, I'll find a girlfriend to share my life with as soon as possible."

"This sounds familiar." Anna nodded. She felt a slight pinch in her heart as she thought about her own loving family back in Ukraine. Naturally, she talked to her parents and Grandma regularly, but seeing them through a cold screen was so different from sitting in the same room, feeling their warmth and kindness. "Luckily, I had met a great guy some time ago, when I flew in to the Polaris interviews. He's been out of town, but we'll be going out once he is back. I can't wait."

Chapter 12. The Black Pearl Restaurant

Washington, D.C.

A couple light raindrops landed on Anna's nose. "Karen, are you sure you want to walk back to our building? We could take a shuttle. What if it starts pouring down rain, and we get soaked?"

Polaris occupied five large buildings in the downtown D.C. and they were located on several different streets. Polaris staff could either take a shuttle bus which circulated between the buildings every hour, or just take a short walk.

"We'll be fine. It's not going to rain." Karen held out his phone and showed the weather app to Anna with the confidence of an expert. "Besides, I want to buy a Polish sausage and a pretzel at that stand next to the Farragut Square."

"It's only ten thirty in the morning, and you're already hungry?" Anna shook her head and smiled. "All right, fine with me. Let's walk."

To kill the time, Anna and Karen started trading jokes along the way.

"Here is the joke about my native city of Kyiv," Anna said, as they crossed the busy Connecticut Avenue. "You must know about Kyiv cakes, right? When you go to Kyiv, you buy a Kyiv cake. It's delicious. It has two layers of meringue and hazelnuts, chocolate glaze, and a buttercream-like filling."

"I have not tried the cake, but heard they are very good," Karen confided, before asking, "What's the joke?"

"Okay. Imagine: Tokyo, Japan. The Japanese just bought the recipe of the famous Kyiv cake and decided to make these cakes themselves. For some reason, no matter how hard they tried, the cake does not come out as good. In fact, it is completely inedible! The Japanese are in complete despair. What's going on? What are they doing wrong? All the quantities of ingredients are correct, and still it does not work. They call the head of the cake factory in Kyiv.

"Hello, we are calling from Japan. We are trying to use the recipe of the Kyiv cake we just bought from you and it does not work.

"I see, says the head of the Kyiv cake factory. And do you have an Aunt Mania working at your factory?

"Aunt Mania? ask the Japanese. No, we don't have an Aunt Mania! Who is Aunt Mania?

"Well, Aunt Mania is the one who steals nuts and other important ingredients from the cake!"

Karen laughed really hard. He was cheerful and relaxed. They had just stopped at his favorite stand, and he was now holding a Polish sausage in one hand and the glossy pretzel in another, taking bites from each one in rotation, while squeezing his folder with documents under his arm. "Good thing you like jokes. I think we make a good team. I must also say funny situations just follow me. Sometimes I do not believe myself."

"Did anything funny happen on your recent trips?" Anna checked, giggling.

"Oh, something funny happens all the time! Just last

month, I went to Tajikistan. You know, most people speak Russian there, right? Anyway, I am the only team member who speaks Russian, everyone else has no clue. So, the team leader hires a translator for sequential translation from Russian into English, a very standard practice.

"Now imagine the situation. The whole team goes to an important meeting with the Minister of Economy. I am half an hour late because my plane got in late and, when I arrive, I immediately try to figure out what's going on. I glance at the translator. She looks a bit odd from the start. Mini-skirt, too much makeup, super high-heeled boots, definitely not the way to dress for an important meeting. Then I start listening to what she is saying and cannot understand anything. At first, I think that maybe I am just too tired from the trip and the jetlag has hit me too hard.

"Then I realize that no, the problem is not with me. This girl is not translating but just saying whatever gets into her head! She's only had some basic English in school and is just translating some familiar words and adding the rest from her own imagination. And the worst of all, she kept doing it with a very serious face, as if she knew what she was doing! Of course, I told her to go back to where she came from and then went back inside and did all the translation myself!"

"Wonderful story," Anna said, wiping her tears from the laughter. "I am so much looking forward to the adventures on our upcoming trip."

Karen and Anna stood before the Polaris building. After ascending the stairs, Anna reached into her handbag to find her badge. She always had a ton of stuff which made the search complicated—lipstick, hairbrush, sunglasses, headphones, a bag of gummy bears, a pink golf ball—how *did that* get there?—and various other items.

As Anna was digging in her bag like a squirrel for nuts, she glanced around for a second and saw a shiny scarlet red motorcycle zipping along Pennsylvania Avenue. The driver parked the bike right in front of Polaris and took off his helmet. Anna stuck her neck out to see who he was.

Of my goodness. It's Jean!

And he looked as great as before—or maybe even better than Anna remembered. The wind was ruffling his blond hair and his shiny sky-blue eyes were piercing deep down into her soul, setting everything on fire.

It's him, it's him! I knew it. Of course, he got accepted into the program!

Jean looked up, passing over Anna and Karen, before coming back to Anna. His eyes widened and his face lit up with astonishment.

"Is that you, Anna? Thought I'd never see you again… How have you been?"

Oh, the soft French accent which drove Anna crazy the first time around… She was now standing on the stairs as if her legs were glued to them, unable to move or say anything. She should have prepared, rehearsed for their first meeting. Finally, Anna found some words, but they came out as gibberish.

"Yes, it is me! And I am doing great! So much work to do. I have a very nice office. Oh, and this is my colleague, Karen. Have you met Karen? We're working together." Anna pointed at her friend.

"Nice to meet you, Karen," Jean said calmly.

"Good to meet you too. You've got quite a

motorcycle over there!" Karen exclaimed. He had been peaking at Jean's motorcycle from the start.

"Yes, this is the electric bike of the year. I like it. For urban environmentalists like me, it is completely perfect."

"Electric, hah? Very nice bike! So shiny! So red!" Anna kept mumbling, while also constantly straightening her clothes, fixing her hair, clearing her throat.

"Which country are you working on, Anna?" Jean asked softly.

"Tanzania," she murmured, while looking down at her shoes and fiddling with her handbag.

"Congratulations. I lived in Tanzania for a few years. I had a regular NGO job, but I was also actively involved with the Africa Today photoblog. We focused on capturing the daily lives of people living in Africa and then the images were posted on social media."

"Did you get a lot of followers?" Karen asked.

"Hundreds of thousands. I think it hit 280,000 at some point. I haven't checked lately. There is so much interest in Africa these days, and several Africans— bloggers, photographers—instantly became social media sensations."

"We should look this photoblog up on social media sometime," Karen said to Anna. "Right, Anna?"

"Sure." Anna nodded, and continued fidgeting.

"We actually have a meeting in ten minutes," Karen said while meaningfully looking at Anna. "It's at a coffee shop across the street. We'd better get going."

"Meeting? Oh yes! Then we definitely should get flowing. Oh, going that is."

"Of course," Jean said and nodded. "I also have to

run. It is my first day in the office after my Sierra Leone trip. I just arrived this morning. Thousand things to do. Nice to meet you, Karen. And Anna, I think there is going to be a networking event for our Global Associates class next week. I hope you are coming?"

"Yes, I received an invitation. Black Pearl Restaurant, right?"

"Yes, that's the one. I will see you there."

"See you soon."

As Jean disappeared into the Polaris building, Karen dragged Anna across the street to a small coffee shop. "Are you okay? I have never seen you like this. What happened?"

Anna innocently blinked her eyes. The best course of action was to play dumb.

"Sorry, I think I just suddenly started feeling sick… Got dizzy when going down the stairs. It's probably because I did not have anything to eat this morning. I am better now."

"Oh, that explains it." Karen sighed. "You should never leave home without having breakfast. Make sure you at least have some cereal or a muffin. Sometimes, I feel that I eat a bit too much, but it's better than fainting from hunger! Here, have some cookies. They should make you feel better in a flash."

When Anna returned to her office, she was finally able to breathe. What a disaster the meeting with Jean was! She had been embarrassed before, but never to this extent. Somehow, she managed to make herself look like a complete fool in front of the one and only guy she really liked. Good thing Karen came to rescue.

Anna shut the door, sat down in her chair, stretched out her legs, and closed her eyes. Naturally, meditation would not make the memory go away, but at least she would calm her down a little and help her take a more positive view of things.

Today was not my best. But there is still hope to impress Jean. He is coming to the Black Pearl restaurant. This is a perfect chance for a re-match.

****

When Anna reached the Black Pearl restaurant, a lot of Polaris folks had already gathered. Some tables were set up on the patio, while the dinner would be served inside. White-gloved waiters circulated around the patio and offered appetizers and drinks to the guests.

Anna was wearing the outfit she bought the day before—a floral mini dress, with a round neck and three-quarter sleeves, and metallic strappy sandals with an open toe and high stiletto heels. She felt like a tropical bird: flittering about happily in a spray of color. Hopefully, Jean would notice her!

She recognized a number of her fellow Global Associates and representatives of Polaris senior management who were also invited in order to give advice to the newcomers. A couple of Global Associates brought their wives and husbands. Mia, the only baby at the party, was resting happily in the arms of her mother, Wendy Stevens, and serving as a magnet for all the ladies at the event.

One day it would be nice to get a little Mia of my own, Anna thought to herself. She could not help touching Mia's little hands, soft and warm, patting her on the little red dress, and looking into her deep blue eyes. *It's mind-blowing that some people in the class are already married with kids, while others can't even get a decent boyfriend.*

Thinking about boyfriends, the object of Anna's attention was missing. Hopefully, he would show up like he promised. For now, it was time to put her worries to rest and try to network.

Anna ended up standing in a small group with Alex, Wendy, and the Polaris Vice President, Eduardo Martinez, while she drank a glass of white wine. Among the five Polaris Vice Presidents, Eduardo was the youngest one. He was probably in his late thirties. Anna remembered seeing him on TV several times.

Eduardo had a lot of advice to give to the newcomers. He recommended everyone to try new things in the first years at Polaris in order to find their best fit.

"How about your own career path, Eduardo?" Wendy asked. "Could you share some highlights with us?"

"Of course." Eduardo proudly looked at Wendy. "I started at Polaris twelve years ago, then went to grad school to get my MBA, then came back. My first assignment was in the Nigeria satellite office. It was quite a challenge, as I didn't know much about the Africa region at that time. But I learned fast. It's a fascinating continent. Then I worked in several other countries—India, China, and Bangladesh. Later I was promoted to director and then a Vice President."

As he spoke, Jean joined their group and stood right next to Anna, holding a bottle of beer in his hand.

"*Bonjour*, Anna." he gave Anna a look which seemed to last a week. His gaze ran down her beautiful tropical outfit, his mouth smiling sweetly. No doubt, Jean was enjoying what he saw.

She had to restrain herself from jumping up and

down in delight. *I knew it—he wanted to see me as much as I wanted to see him!*

Eduardo welcomed Jean with a grin and casually asked, "You are back from Sierra Leone already?" They must have met before.

"Yes, I am back for a little bit, but I'm definitely traveling back again at the end of the month." Jean's voice sounded calm and smooth. "In just a month's time, the kids will have a great new school. Cannot wait to see those happy faces. This is what our work is all about."

Eduardo was visibly pleased. "I knew you were the right person for the job. I took a bet when I gave the project to Jean to manage. But he delivered beyond everyone's expectations."

Anna surreptitiously glanced at Jean.

Eduardo then noticed an incoming call on his phone. "I have to take this, but I will see you all later."

With Eduardo gone, Alex gave Jean a high-five. "Nicely done! Wendy, Anna, please meet my office buddy. Jean's office is right next to mine."

Wendy gracefully extended her hand. "Good to meet you, Jean. I'm Wendy, and this is Mia," she said while pointing at her daughter.

"Nice to meet you both. Mia is adorable, congratulations," Jean said. "And I already know Anna. We had met on the interview day."

Alex was astonished. "Really? Nobody else from my day made it, just me. I thought only one person from a particular day of interviews gets into the program, but probably there are exceptions. Is anyone else from your interviews in the program now?"

"Yes, we also have Rosie," Anna said, lightly running her fingers through her hair. She had bought a special hair mask to make sure her locks looked irresistible tonight.

Right at that moment, the waiter brought some appetizers of juicy shrimp and scallops and small sandwiches with red caviar. Anna was starving, so she grabbed several.

"Speaking about Rosie," Alex perked up, "is she here today? I have not seen her lately." He started looking around anxiously.

"No, Alex, I knew you'd be asking." Anna laughed, confirming to herself that Alex had a crush on Rosie. Every time they talked, he wanted to find out something about Rosie. "She is not here. She finally found a placement. Last time we spoke, Rosie mentioned several new projects she was taking on. She's no longer worried about her career prospects here at Polaris."

"This is great to hear! Yet, I wish Rosie could have been here tonight... Now everyone is starting new projects and beginning to travel. It will be hard for all of us to stay in touch," Alex said wistfully. "We definitely need to go out to dinner together very soon—you, me, Jean, Rosie, Wendy—we need to hang out more before the work whirlpool sucks us all in."

"Great idea!" Anna said eagerly and briefly looked at Jean. What did he think about that? A lot, it seemed. He smiled right at her and even moved an inch closer. Their shoulders were now almost touching. Anna's whole body started trembling. *It is getting really hot.*

Suddenly, she heard a familiar melodic voice.

"Don't forget me, please! I'm not in your fancy class, but can I come along to your dinner, too?"

Anna turned around and froze. Emily approached their table. What was *she* doing here? The event was supposedly open only for Global Associates and their families, significant others, and senior management. Maybe she imagined that she was now part of senior management? Quite unlikely. Emily had a big ego, but she wouldn't make a mistake like that.

Nevertheless, Emily was definitely at the Black Pearl for a reason, given that she was all dressed up for the occasion. She looked glamorous in a lovely blue knit dress layering magnificently around her body and silver tone pumps with rhinestones reflecting the evening sun. Emily's blond hair was gathered into a stunning updo with a shiny crystal comb in the back. She must have spent the afternoon at the hair salon.

Who could she be possibly trying to impress here? Eduardo or some other Vice President?

The answer was found in no time.

"Of course, beautiful, I didn't mean to exclude you," Alex apologized. "You can come with us anywhere. Jean, your girlfriend never ceases to amaze me. Every day she looks more and more gorgeous."

Anna's lips started trembling for a different reason this time. She felt a rush of blood to her head. No, no, no. Jean could not be dating Emily! This was a mistake. A joke. They hadn't even met—Jean went to Sierra Leone right after joining Polaris!

But within a split second, Emily took her place next to Jean, subtly pushing Anna to the side. The blond beauty put her arm under Jean's and nestled her head on his shoulder. For a brief moment, she even softly ran her fingers against his starched white shirt. No doubt, they were dating.

"So wonderful to see my dear friend Anna here," Emily sang, her voice as sweet as honey. "Darling, you probably do not know this, but Anna and I have been great friends since college. Imagine, she even came to me to consult before the interview. I gave her all the tips! She practically owes this job to me. I was so delighted to hear the news when she called me to say she got in. How is everything going at work, sweetie?"

Anna measured Emily with a cold look. *Sweetie? What the heck? She didn't even want to have coffee with me since I've started my job.*

"Everything is going really well, thank you, Emily," Anna tried to respond in a calm and relaxed voice, but her teeth started clacking inadvertently. She no longer felt comfortable in her light tropical dress and now wished she had brought a warm jacket. The sun disappeared behind the clouds and a strong breeze rose up. Anna's whole body started shivering.

"I'm so happy for you." Emily gently patted Anna on the shoulder with a spare hand. "If you need anything, please feel free to reach out."

Then she turned to Jean and looked at him slyly. "I have something to tell you, *mon amour*. Today at a management meeting I heard that the Polaris General Manager himself, Mr. Anthony Clark, mentioned your name and what a fantastic job you are doing with the Sierra Leone school."

"Thanks Emily," Jean said.

"You'll never guess what happened next!" Emily's excitement had no limits. "You might know that Mr. Clark is now looking for his Special Assistant, right? This is the type of job which propels you to the top of Polaris... Well, Mr. Clark mentioned that he would give the job to you, if you're interested."

"I think I would have to pass on that, Emily." Jean

looked displeased.

"What? This is an opportunity of a lifetime, Jean!" Alex yelled. "I heard all current Vice Presidents have been Special Assistants to the Director General before. I put in my application. Why would you pass if Emily says you could have the job?"

"Well, I happen to disagree with some of Mr. Clark's policies, that's all," Jean explained. "I feel that sometimes he refuses to take a firm stand and instead tries to sit on two chairs at once. For example, I know for a fact that Polaris financed a couple new coal plants under his leadership. It was never publicized, while news about the green investments are all over the media. It's unacceptable from my point of view. Polaris should completely divest from fossil fuels."

"Maybe the coal plants were financed in some very poor nations where it might have made sense?" Wendy asked. "I am not an energy expert, but it's possible that no cheaper alternative existed."

"Well, I firmly believe that coal is not the way to go under any circumstances."

"Okay, guys, let's just change the subject away from Mr. Clark before we get in some trouble." Alex looked around. Several managers were standing relatively close to them, chatting with other Global Associates. "Since I am still hoping to get the Special Assistant job, I need to maintain neutrality. Anna and Wendy, you probably don't know much about Jean's Sierra Leone project. Would you like to hear the details?"

"Of course!" Wendy quickly jumped at the idea, lifting little Mia high in her arms, then tossing her up lightly and catching her. Both the mother and the daughter laughed heartily as they were looking at each other with tremendous love and affection.

Time dragged on, the conversation sounding unclear, as if it were articulated in a foreign language. Anna gave a weak nod. That's all she could manage. Her whole body was hurting and her head was cracking apart. She held herself still, eyes on the ground, so nobody could see the disappointment and sorrow filling her up with every word spoken since Emily was introduced to the group.

She should have found some excuse and gone to another group as soon as Emily showed up. Why did she stick around? She should have at least found a place to sit down... A few chairs had been placed on the edges of the patio. Now she was stuck, forced to observe Jean and Emily together. She couldn't leave now, when Jean was just about to tell about his trip to Sierra Leone. Even though they couldn't be together, she still wanted to listen.

"Okay." Jean put down his bottle and wiped off his lips. Emily immediately wrapped her arms around him and flashed her biggest, most charming Hollywood-style smile. Anna felt a dagger going deeper and deeper into her heart.

"Back in May, I received a call about being accepted to the Global Associates Program. Soon after, Eduardo contacted me about an urgent school project in this remote village of Sierra Leone. I got on the plane to Freetown the very next day. I then traveled by bus to reach the village called Gbahama in the south of the country."

"I cannot even imagine," gasped Wendy. "I'd never be able to do it. In a new country and all."

"It wasn't that hard, really. I've lived in Africa

before, so I am familiar with the way things are done. Anyway, I later tried to find a hotel to stay in or near Gbahama. The city didn't have any hotels, just small guesthouses with a couple of tiny rooms. Of course, they had no air conditioning, which would have been quite useful in the ninety-degree heat, and meals were pretty basic. But I got used to all of that. Afterall, people live like that every day."

Wendy sighed. "It breaks my heart to know that. Look at Mia. She'll have a wonderful life here in the United States. We are so lucky."

"Yes, life in parts of Africa is difficult for many people," Jean agreed. "They have some ultra-wealthy families but many people live in poverty all of their life. That makes education even more important. I was proud to be selected to lead the Polaris project in Gbahama, so I headed to the school construction site as soon as I arrived. Well, I quickly discovered that the contractor who was recruited by the previous team leaders essentially siphoned the money and never built anything. I recruited a new team who were considered reputable and who were able to start immediately, saving funds and the project."

"Wow," said Wendy. "Great way to start your career at Polaris."

"Thanks," Jean said with a smile. "I really didn't think that what happened was impressive when I was doing it. I was just living in the moment and trying to do the right thing. The kids in the village need this school. It's my obligation to fulfil their dreams."

The conversation was cut off as everyone was finally called to dinner. What a relief! Anna made sure to move slowly and separate herself from Emily and

Jean. She found a seat at a table far away from them and occupied herself by reading the menu. A few minutes later, Alex sat down right next to her. He could not decide what to order for his entrée and then ordered a meat dish which turned out gigantic—as big as his head!

As the dinner progressed, Anna briefly glanced in the direction of Emily and Jean, and regretted it immediately. They were visibly engaged in an animated conversation with one another. Emily was completely in her element at the Black Pearl restaurant. Like a giant octopus, she was holding Jean firmly with her eight long arms covered with suckers, and not letting anyone else approach him. Jean could never get out of her tight grip.

It's time to stop fantasizing about Jean.

He was taken. In love with someone else. He had no romantic interest in Anna whatsoever. All they had was one lunch eight months ago! It was stupid to think that Jean could have possibly developed feelings for her over something so small.

It sure seemed that he looked at her with admiration back then, and even today—he appeared happy to see her. But it must have been because he was a nice guy.

It was time to be real. Emily was beautiful, smart, confident, witty. Capable of making people laugh. Heiress to a large family fortune. She had this formidable glow about her—the aura of privilege and wealth—which separated her from the crowd, and especially "commoners" like Anna. It was no surprise that Jean was smitten with her.

And what did Anna have to offer to Jean? A kind and loving heart, not much more. The scale was clearly tipped in Emily's direction.

"Bye Alex, I'll see you around! Thanks for keeping

me company today." Anna picked up her handbag and slowly walked through the restaurant to the exit, passing by the tables of laughing and smiling Polaris folks, digging in to their plates and clinking their glasses. Some people were still not done with their dinners, probably because of chatting too much and enjoying themselves.

Anna stepped outside. It was dark now, and nobody would notice that her eyes were full of tears. She could finally cry as much as her broken heart desired.

PART II

If I have ever seen magic, it has been in Africa
John Hemingway

Chapter 13. Karibu Zanzibar!

Dar es Salaam and Zanzibar, the United Republic of Tanzania

Anna's flight to Tanzania was through Addis Ababa. To play it safe, she got to the Dulles Airport three hours before her flight. But life was easy for business class passengers—getting through check-in and security took thirty minutes at most.

She settled in the airline lounge, full of people similar to her—in business clothes and with lightweight carry-on spinners. Some were eating, others reading newspapers, and many were working non-stop on their laptops.

At one point, Anna's phone started ringing. It was Grandma, who video-called her a few times a week.

"Anna, is this really happening? You are off to Africa?" Grandma's eyes were shining, full of joy and excitement. "Up till now, I had a hard time believing...You'll be the first one in our family to visit the incredible Africa! Your Grandpa would be so proud of you. If only he could see you—all grown up, so brilliant and confident. Working for a top company.

Ready to conquer the world."

Anna drew in a shaky breath, and the flood of emotions started overwhelming her. This voyage was so much more than a work trip. It was going to connect her family's past with the present. It was going to open the door into the colorful world which her poor Grandma never had a chance to explore fifty years ago. She had started packing her suitcase, but the terrible tragedy cut her preparations short. Instead, it was Anna, her granddaughter, who would set foot on the African continent and explore its wonders.

"Yes, Grandma, I'm about to board my plane," Anna said proudly. "I'll make sure to take lots of pictures and videos for you."

The flight turned out very long and Anna did not sleep much. By the time she arrived in Addis Ababa, she was starting to fall asleep, but was forced to get off the plane and wait for her connection.

Stepping out of the jetway, she could already tell she was in a different world. The people, the shops, the food—everything looked so different in Sub-Saharan Africa. Anna got situated in the airport lounge waiting for the flight to Dar es Salaam, which was expected to be in a couple of hours. She was a little bit sleepy at first but pretty soon she perked up listening to the announcements of flights to various African destinations. Ouagadougou, Dakar, Kampala, Kigali—all these unfamiliar names which sounded so thrilling, promising of great adventures.

"Ladies and gentlemen, the Dar es Salaam flight is ready for boarding," announced the pleasant female voice on the radio.

****

"Guys, it's great to see you here in Tanzania!" Anna gave hugs to everyone on her team as they arrived in Dar es Salaam the same afternoon and started checking in at their hotel. At first glance, the team looked a bit disoriented and jet-lagged, squinting in the bright light.

Anna smiled as she remembered herself traveling to various tournaments on the junior tennis tour. Many of the events were in Europe, so she didn't need to endure the jet leg, but going to the United States and Australia was no walk in the park. Luckily, Anna usually recovered in a day or two, but her mother suffered much worse than her, barely dragging herself out of bed in the morning and stumbling around the room in the middle of the night, unable to get any sleep.

"The important part is not to fall asleep right now, so we can all quickly adjust to the new time zone and sleep well through the night," Anna said cheerfully, glancing with a lot of sympathy at poor Marcelo who could barely keep his eyes open.

"Yeah." Marcelo yawned, as he was sinking deep into the lobby armchair. "I'm very tempted to go to bed right now, but I see your point. When are we meeting with TIZ, by the way? Today or tomorrow?"

"We'll be sailing to the island of Zanzibar early in the morning on a large and luxurious boat," Anna announced. "I personally cannot wait to get to this charming island and see what it looks like."

"Me too!" Karen yelled excitedly. "It will also be my first time in Zanzibar. I started reading a short travel guide which I bought at the airport. Turns out, Zanzibar is a very ancient place—people lived there 20,000 years ago! They even had sultans in Zanzibar, did you know that? Back in the eighteenth century the Omani Sultan moved the capital from Muscat, Oman to Stone Town in Zanzibar. At that time, many spice plantations were established, growing cloves, turmeric, cinnamon, cardamon, you name it. Some of these plantations are still thriving and we could even visit them. It's no wonder that the archipelago is often called the 'Spice Islands.'"

"Spice Islands… How romantic." Anna immediately remembered all the Jules Vernes "voyage extraordinaire" books she read in her childhood. Similar to her favorite characters, she'd now be traveling to a faraway island.

"Let's stop by the Polaris satellite office for a couple of hours?" Anna suggested to her team. "We can check in with the local staff and print some documents."

The Dar es Salaam office was small, but growing, as the Polaris program recently started expanding in the country. Irene Asiimwe was assigned to work with Anna's team.

"Irene, do you know anything about the TIZ?" Anna asked hopefully. "We have to visit them tomorrow. They don't have much of a website, and only very limited information is available on the web."

Irene shook her head. "I've heard of the Institute, but I've never visited it. I called them last week and secured the meeting for you tomorrow morning."

"Who are we going to meet?" Fiona asked.

"The president, Albert Kimaro, and his deputy, Rosemary Matanda." Irene looked down into her notebook. "They will probably bring some other staff as well to participate."

"Sounds good to me." Karen nodded. "The key is to make sure we have enough time to inspect the facilities.

175

It's not a big deal for me, as I am mostly concerned with the curriculum. But it's definitely important for Marcelo, as he needs to see what it will cost to fix up the school."

"True. I'll need a couple of hours to look at everything carefully to make sure we account for all the potential expenses," Marcelo said with a big yawn. "For now, I think I need to head back to the hotel and get some sleep. Otherwise, there is a good chance you might be traveling to Zanzibar without me."

****

After a rough crossing on the boat the next morning, the stunning sign stating "Karibu Zanzibar" welcomed Anna and her teammates at the ferry station.

As the liner was docking at the port, Anna stood for a few minutes on the upper deck, admiring the sign and the view of the turquoise Indian Ocean with lovely white sailboats scattered near the shore. *Unbelievable! We are finally here.*

With the hundreds of tourists arriving at Zanzibar at the same time, going through immigration took Anna and her colleagues a bit of time. There were several lines, and Anna ended up standing in the slowest one. A large family did not have the right documents, and the line was not moving.

Ugh, how do I always pick the wrong line? The back of her neck was getting covered with sweat. She wanted to go to TIZ as soon as possible. Important people were waiting for them!

Finally, all the formalities were finished, and the team got into one of the taxi cabs, which were quite abundant at the ferry station.

"Good morning. Please, take us to the TIZ. Do you know where that is?" Karen asked the driver.

The cab driver nodded. "Yes, the institute is not far from here. I know it very well. My niece used to go there."

Pretty soon, the Polaris folks reached the destination, got out of the taxi, and looked around. Surely, a distinguished building would be in close proximity. Most likely, something big and tall.

But nothing of that kind was anywhere to be found. All that the team spotted were three small brown structures scattered around a green lawn with a huge swamp and a thick tropical forest in the back. The buildings were tiny, looked to be in poor physical shape, and unpretentious, with large cracks going through the walls. They were definitely in a great need of a paint job.

Could this possibly be the TIZ? thought Anna, horrified. *No way!*

All the universities she'd known in Ukraine were tall and massive, sometimes looking like museums. The Taras Shevchenko University, for instance, was a true work of art! The magnificent university, named after the famous Ukrainian poet and writer Taras Shevchenko, was painted bright red, with high columns in the front. When walking through its hallways, one felt like a little grain of sand in the enormous universe.

The building Anna saw now was the complete opposite of the Taras Shevchenko University. But this indeed was TIZ. Given the signs, there could be no mistake. One building even had a crooked sign "Grand Peacock Hotel" but it was not grand by any stretch of the imagination. It looked neglected and was falling apart.

"Yes, folks, this is the place." Karen shook his head sadly. "I guess it is not quite what we expected."

"The land behind the institute does not seem well-maintained at all," observed Fiona. "That looks like a large mosquito-infested swamp in the back… It will need to be drained if we ever want any tourists staying here."

Anna stayed quiet, unsure what to say or do. Was this mission impossible? Could she actually pull off the TIZ project? It sure seemed that the universe was telling her yet again: *you lied on the application. Any project you start will be a failure—no matter what you do. Just go back to Uncle Stepan's shop. That is the right place for you. The tea kettles are waiting!*

Finally, Anna gained her composure and gestured to her team. "Guys, let's go inside for a chat with the management of TIZ. I know this looks very disappointing, but we can work together with them to improve the school."

The project team timidly walked into the first building, trying not to trip on anything. The floor was dusty and some tools were laying on the floor.

"Good morning. Where can we find Albert Kimaro and Rosemary Matanda?" Anna boldly walked up to the receptionist. He looked very young, maybe a student himself. "We are from Washington. We have a meeting scheduled with them."

"Yes, I'm aware, come with me." The receptionist looked like a deer caught in the headlights. He immediately ushered Anna and her team to an old and dusty staircase and opened an empty room on the second floor. "Please wait for a few minutes. I'll inform them."

Anna cautiously glanced around the run-down room, only equipped with a table, some wooden chairs, and an old-fashioned phone which she had seen in old movies. The imitation velvet curtains on the windows were long, spotty, and moth-eaten. The air was heavy and hot.

"Achoo! Achoo!" Marcelo sneezed loudly as soon as he entered the room. He looked around for a tissue box, which was nowhere to be found, then fished a tissue out of his bag.

Fiona walked up to the window and tried to pull apart the heavy curtains to look outside. Suddenly, she recoiled and jogged to the other side of the room where everyone else was standing.

"What's up?" Karen asked cheerfully, as he was trying to chase a couple of sassy mosquitos circling around his face. Quite a few were flying around, happy to see new juicy victims.

"There was some type of animal on the floor under the curtains." Fiona's eyes bulged. "I hope it was just a rat or a mouse, but I'm not sure, could be something worse—we're in Africa after all. It disappeared through the cracks in the wall…"

"Well, as long as it wasn't a black mamba, we'll be fine. No need to panic." Karen laughed.

"Black mamba?" Anna asked with interest. "Sounds pretty cool. What's that?"

"Just Africa's longest venomous snake," Karen explained. "It's one of the fastest snakes in the world. I saw a documentary about it on the plane. The black mamba can move up to twelve miles per hour. With my belly, I could never get away from a snake like that."

"Oh come on, Karen, they can't have a snake living here," Marcelo objected, while at the same time moving further away from the window and nervously looking around. "Where are our counterparts?"

Finally, two ladies—one in her early fifties, tall and heavy, and the other one a young girl, very pretty and petite—appeared. They looked the visitors over and came in.

"Please sit down," the older lady said in a loud and unpleasant voice. "My name is Rosemary Matanda. Thank you for coming."

"The pleasure is all ours," Anna said respectfully and looked around anxiously. The chairs were so old, covered with dust, standing on thin, shaky legs. It seemed like they were about to break. Just in case, Anna sat down on the very edge of the chair. All the Polaris folks took out their notebooks and got ready to start taking notes from the meeting. Karen, who was sitting next to Anna, wrote a header "Meeting with TIZ" in a bold handwriting and paused like an artist, holding his pen in hand.

"Will anybody else be joining from TIZ?" Anna asked hopefully and plastered a weak smile on her face. "We would really welcome any staff of the Institute who you think might be useful for the discussion. I presume Albert Kimaro is coming as well?"

"No, it will be just two of us—myself and Jennifer," Rosemary stated abruptly and shot Anna a look. "Mr. Kimaro is currently not available. He just had an operation at the hospital on the mainland."

Jennifer quickly turned her head to Rosemary, the large red hoop earrings jiggling in her ears, opening her mouth as if she wanted to say something, but Rosemary motioned for her not to interrupt.

"Oh, I am sorry to hear that Mr. Kimaro is sick," Anna said. She felt a lump in her throat. This woman did not look friendly. Hopefully she would warm up to them.

"Well, we can start the meeting now. I am not quite sure about the purpose of your visit." Rosemary stretched her legs. "I did receive a call from your office in Dar es Salaam to schedule this meeting and I agreed, but I do not know what exactly this is about. I hope you can explain."

"Yes, of course," Anna said, blushing and her voice trembling. This was her first time ever introducing herself and her team. Luckily, Rosemary wasn't aware of that, or she would probably growl. "We are from Polaris International Corporation. We have come to work with you on the renovation of the institute. My name is Anna Levenko and these are my colleagues— Karen Kalpanian, Fiona Murray, and Marcelo Roca."

With the trembling hands, Anna took out her business card case out of her briefcase and respectfully handed the card to Rosemary. The others followed Anna's lead. They waited for Rosemary's business card, but it never came.

"Polaris? Never heard of it." Rosemary looked the cards over for a quick second and then negligently stuck them all in the pocket of her mustard yellow jacket, like in a black hole. Anna swallowed as she witnessed the sad fate of the first business card she ever handed out in her career. The next step for it was probably a trash can.

"I cannot keep track of all these international organizations, there are hundreds of them, and they keep growing like mushrooms," Rosemary said dismissively. "Every once in a while, we do get visitors from various NGOs. Everyone wants to help with something—at least so they say—but does not really understand our problems or the country we live in. Sometimes I feel they just want to visit Zanzibar and get a day at the beach. Nobody has suggested anything worthwhile. It's just a waste of our time."

Anna bit her lip from disappointment. Where was that beautiful and romantic "Karibu Zanzibar"? The authorities were supposed to be rolling out the red carpet for them… Maybe even greeting them with flowers, as she had seen in movies!

Okay. A red carpet was a bit much. But at the very least, Rosemary and everyone else at the TIZ should have been looking forward to meeting their team and working with them. Instead, they had never even heard of Polaris. How was that even possible?

"Rosemary, if you would allow, let me explain why we are here," Anna finally said. "We want to help you make the TIZ into a very strong and reputable educational institution, one of the best in East Africa. I see that things are not going very well now, but we can work together to—"

"What makes you think that there is something wrong with our institute?" Rosemary interrupted. Her face, which reflected indifference before, had turned angry.

"TIZ is doing great. We have a lot of students who are excited about studying here. Yes, we do face some challenges but who doesn't? There is nothing we cannot overcome."

Anna went completely pale. Rosemary was misinterpreting things. The rest of the team members exchanged looks as if saying "what are we doing here?" Karen started fiddling with his pen, while Marcelo and Fiona subtly began checking messages on their phones.

"I'm sorry, Rosemary. That's not what I was trying to say," Anna tried to correct herself. "All I meant was that you have a great school and, if you want to work with us, we can do much more together. Our organization could potentially provide a grant to your school for redevelopment, if you are interested."

Rosemary measured Anna with a look of contempt. "Do you know how many of these 'experts' I have seen over the years? Dozens. And we are still where we are. If you really want to help, fine, why do you not buy me and Jennifer laptops? That could be a good start. Some new furniture for our office would not hurt either. Then we could talk."

Anna figured out where this was going. Rosemary was not really interested in making their school into a better institution. However, she was hoping to get a few nice things for herself and her colleagues, if Polaris had some money to give out.

"I apologize, Rosemary, but this is not really something we at Polaris can do," Anna said. "If we develop a whole project to support the Institute, then, of course, we'd include funds to equip the teachers and administration with the necessary equipment after we've done a thorough assessment. It would all be a part of the package—new vision and strategy for the institute, renovated hotel, new curriculum, new equipment… But we cannot just buy a few ad-hoc things, it does not work like this. Nobody at Polaris would approve that."

"Then we really have nothing to discuss." Rosemary snorted. She got up and gestured to Jennifer for her to do the same.

Anna made one final attempt to turn things around. "Rosemary, how about we just do a brief assessment of the institute now that we already flew all this way and brought several experts with us?"

Rosemary paused for a minute. "Well, I do not care, to be honest. If you would like to have a look at the school, go ahead. We have nothing to hide here. Jennifer can show you around."

Karen closed his notebook. Clearly, there were no notes to take in this meeting. "How about the curriculum?" he asked weakly. "Perhaps you could send it to us to have a look?"

"Yes, Jennifer will provide it," Rosemary reluctantly agreed.

"We'll collect all the information and then prepare a report to share with you after we return home. We could discuss it when we visit again," Anna said. The idea of seeing Rosemary one more time made her sick to her stomach, but hopefully the second visit would be more satisfactory. It couldn't get any worse than this, that's for sure.

"Maybe. You know where to find me. Now I have to go. Nice meeting you." Rosemary left the room, not shaking anyone's hands, with her lips curved in a dissatisfied grimace. She quickly headed downstairs, walking very fast for her size.

Jennifer reluctantly stayed and looked at Anna and her team anxiously, like a mouse would look over a group of cats surrounding her. "Let me walk you around the school," she said softly. "I will send the curriculum document to you when I get back to the desk."

The group started walking around the campus. Every time the sun peaked through the thick clouds, it became unbearably hot. Even the breeze from the ocean didn't seem to help. January was one of the hottest and driest months in Tanzania—great for laying on the beach, but not so much for outside work meetings.

Nevertheless, magnificent surroundings helped Anna to forget about the heat. The luscious green grass brightened the view and felt soft under the shoes. *The greenery of Zanzibar is amazing*, she thought, glancing at various trees growing on the TIZ territory—graceful acacias, coconut palms, mango trees and glossy ferns. With some effort, the campus could be transformed into a charming garden.

Jennifer was very quiet at first but slowly warmed up. Apparently, she'd been a student and, upon graduation, landed a position in admissions and was also helping the school's leadership. She was just a couple of years older than Anna.

Maybe we can find out from Jennifer why Rosemary gave us such a bad reception? Anna kept walking close to Jennifer, in the hope she would confide some details. But no luck. Jennifer didn't say a word about Rosemary. She focused only on neutral subjects.

Jennifer had a lot to tell. Turned out, three hundred students were attending the Institute this year. Given that tourism was such an important industry in Zanzibar, there had never been a shortage of applicants, but the capacity of teaching staff and the quality of training facilities were a significant constraint. The students received various diplomas but gained very limited knowledge in the field they chose, leading to limited opportunities for employment.

"Our students might be able to secure jobs in some small hotels, but large hotels prefer better trained staff from the neighboring Kenya," Jennifer explained. "It's a lost opportunity, since we have so many hotels here on the island."

"The ideal thing would be to enable TIZ graduates to obtain jobs with the big hotel chains," Marcelo suggested, taking a long look at Jennifer's tall and slim figure, so attractive in her fitted African dress, the combination of bright yellow and orange colors. He had been shooting glances at her the whole time. "The hotel industry is expanding so much in Zanzibar and the whole of Africa, and there will be plenty of opportunities for the students."

"What kind of instructors do you have here at the TIZ?" Karen cleared his throat. He was breathing heavily from the heat and carrying his jacket on his shoulder. His white shirt was sticking to his back. "Do they have the right skills and knowledge to teach the students?"

"Not at all." Jennifer sighed. "Many instructors at the school have very weak knowledge of their subject areas. They would definitely benefit from training courses. The facilities also need a serious upgrade. Just look at what we have to deal with over here."

She led the Polaris folks into the classroom where cooking classes were being delivered. Anna glanced inside and immediately spotted an ancient stove which she had seen only in old movies. There were a couple more pieces of equipment in the classroom—a microwave and a toaster, both rusty and falling apart. The classroom was also extremely small. No more than five or six students could watch what was being demonstrated.

Jennifer kept moving on, revealing other facilities to the visitors. The laundry room, where students were supposed to learn how to do laundry, was also in terrible shape. It featured one old washing machine, several plastic water basins, and a lot of ropes on which various clothes were hanging. Anna shook her head. Nobody could learn anything useful with this type of equipment.

"Let's go into the Grand Peacock Hotel," Jennifer

proposed. "The original plan was to use it as a training facility for hospitality students, but it has never had any visitors, as you can probably guess."

The lobby was mostly empty with the exception of two large ugly statues of deer and antelope and some sort of a strange-looking straw alcove hanging over the front desk. Anna and her colleagues examined a double room at the hotel. It was so small that only one person could be in the room at a given time. Even a suitcase would not fit! The walls were shabby looking, and there was no furniture other than an old bed and a mirror. Of course, no air-conditioning, no wi-fi, no lamp, and other important amenities in the modern world of hospitality.

"Thank you, Jennifer, for the tour," Anna said as they returned to the main building. "This was very helpful."

"It's my pleasure. I'll send the curriculum and other documents to your email addresses."

"You have mine, right?" Marcelo asked anxiously. "If you have any questions, feel free to email me at any time. And if you are ever in Washington, I'd—*we'd* be happy to give you a tour."

"This is very nice," Jennifer said with a small smile and looked away shyly. "Yes, I have everyone's contact information. Safe travels."

With nothing else to do there at the moment, the team left the hotel.

"Well," said Marcelo, as they were walking out of the complex to the main road, "I'm looking forward to preparing some designs for the TIZ when I'm back in D.C. This was not the most successful first meeting, but for some reason, I still feel pretty good about it. I can't wait to start!"

Naturally, Anna smiled subtly. After Jennifer's lovely tour, Marcelo seemed to have already forgotten that the spiteful Rosemary even existed. It was good to have at least one motivated team member.

"What improvements are you thinking about so far?" Anna asked.

"The easiest thing to do would be to tear all these buildings down and build a new complex from scratch," Marcelo said confidently. "We have a lot of land to work with, and we can build a fantastic school and a new three-star hotel. The Grand Peacock Hotel will finally live up to its name. This is a beautiful area, and I am sure the hotel could eventually attract a lot of visitors. I will quickly prepare some designs and a detailed cost estimate."

At the sight of four potential customers standing in the road, one of the cabs driving by quickly stopped. Anna took one last look at the Grand Peacock Hotel. She could not wait for the day when this hotel would finally welcome tourists.

Chapter 14. The Grand Party

Washington, D.C.

During the month of December, Polaris management hosted a number of holiday parties. Obviously, parties for each department were held in each office. These smaller events included good food and music, but were not the parties everyone coveted. What one really wished for was to be invited to the exquisite, private parties at the residence of one of the top executives. These were by invitation only, and it was not easy to get invited to them.

Anna did not know too many people yet, so she was invited to only one private party this holiday season. But it was a big one! The Vice President for Finance organized a holiday party at his house and invitations were scarce, but Anna managed to get one. John had put in a good word for her.

A lot of people approached such parties strategically—to put themselves on the radar of the influential executives at Polaris, pitch new ideas, even potentially secure new jobs. Anna did not have a particular agenda this time, but she had a feeling that something important was going to happen.

She arrived at the residence of Mr. Roberto Nieve, Vice President of Finance on a Saturday evening. As Anna appeared at the door, she was immediately greeted by Mr. and Mrs. Nieve, very cordial hosts, and ushered to a spacious living room, decorated in a tasteful shade of pastel blue with silver accents.

Inside the living room, she instantly spotted some of the people she already knew—her manager John, Rosie, as well as Teresa. Of course, being a Chief Economist, Teresa was invited to all the top parties at Polaris.

What an impressive lady she is, Anna thought to herself.

Teresa had an air of a queen at all times—whether at a country club or at a fancy party. She had an aristocratic look, but in the best sense of it—radiant, sophisticated, elegant.

Tonight, Teresa clearly stood out among all the guests. She breezed into the room in her scene-stealing black evening gown, with a high up-do and a small flower in her hair. Stunning jewels were glittering on her wrists and neck.

"Anna, how delightful to see you here!" Teresa was ecstatic as she saw Anna approach. "How have you been? You know that ever since you started playing tennis with Erica, she talks only about you now? You are her greatest hero."

"Thank you, Teresa, it's nice to hear about Erica's feelings. They are completely mutual. She is such an adorable girl," Anna said with a big smile, as she was observing other guests trickling in.

She hadn't been to a fancy party like this since that New Year's Eve gathering at Emily's house several years ago. *I'm moving on up*, she thought proudly. This time, she didn't need a friend to invite her to her parents' party, she warranted the invitation herself.

"Wonderful!" Teresa gracefully took a sip of golden

champagne she was holding in her hand. "Anna, I want you to finally meet my husband. He's here at the party, so it's a good opportunity. He is usually very busy, traveling all the time. Let me go grab him."

"Of course." On many occasions, Anna heard Erica talk of her wonderful father. *The best Dad ever*, Erica always said. "I'll wait here."

When Teresa returned with her husband, Anna turned around to meet him with her most charming smile. She already knew what she was going to say—

Then her jaw dropped. In front of her was none other than… Lenny Jameson.

He was wearing a tux, seemed to have lost some weight, and looked surprisingly attractive, but all Anna could see when looking at him were the orange trunks on the Tunis beach. She was not quite sure how to start the conversation, but Lenny spoke first.

"Nice to see you, Anna. So, you are the wonder woman who Erica talks about all the time! That explains so much. I'm not surprised." Then he turned to Teresa. "Believe it or not, sweetheart, turns out I actually know Anna from the Global Associate orientation in Tunis. She was in the class, and I could already tell she was brilliant then. Of course, I had no idea she was a former junior tennis player in addition to all her other merits."

"This is fantastic," exclaimed Teresa. "I'm so happy you already know Lenny. If you need anything at all, please turn to him. He's always been a great mentor to younger staff, and I am sure he could teach you a lot. He could be a valuable resource for you."

"Of course!" Lenny said. "Anything at all. Both Teresa and I are here for you."

Anna glanced at Teresa and Lenny, standing side by

side. They were a striking couple and appeared very much in love. Maybe her earlier suspicions were completely wrong?

"Thanks a million for the offer," she finally said, nervously shifting from foot to foot. "And, of course, I will stay in touch with Erica. In fact, we were planning to do something this coming weekend. Maybe skating— you know how much Erica enjoys going to the skating rink. I'm trying to learn as well."

"Terrific!" Lenny said, his face beaming with delight and kindness. "Now please excuse us. Teresa and I have to talk to Roberto about something very important." Then in a lower voice he added, "It's related to the two-billion-dollar infrastructure project in Brazil." He looked at Anna meaningfully. She dutifully nodded in response, as if she knew something about this project.

"We're not saying goodbye, and we'll keep an eye on you." Teresa smiled.

The couple walked away, with Lenny's arm around Teresa's bare back. Anna followed them with a gaze full of longing. *Only I could have thought something inappropriate about Lenny*, Anna thought as she shook her head. Lenny and Teresa were the two nicest people, two love birds, unable to get enough of each other. Her face was burning with shame.

In an effort to distract herself from the debacle, Anna looked around for some familiar faces. She quickly spotted Rosie who was standing by herself and intently checking messages on her phone.

"Hey Rosie, how have you been?" Anna approached her friend with a big smile.

From the first glance, Rosie looked stunning but was dressed somewhat inappropriately for the occasion. She wore a very small leather dress barely covering her butt, super high stilettos and had her hair in a high ponytail, with large golden earrings hanging down. Clearly this was an expensive designer dress and a nice outfit for a night club if she wanted to pick up some guys, but a bit out of place here, at a holiday party, in the Vice President's mansion.

Nevertheless, Rosie smiled as she put her phone away and spoke to Anna excitedly. "You won't believe what happened, Anna. A couple of weeks ago, I went to Paris for a high-profile energy conference. My presentation on new approaches to generating renewable energy turned out to be a big hit. Everyone was talking about it. Our department's flagship project will now be managed by me!"

In the space of three short months, Rosie had gone from being a newbie to being the project manager of the most important project with twenty people under her control.

"Great job, Rosie." Anna hugged her friend. "I am so proud of you!"

"And what's new with you?" Rosie looked at Anna intently, as if trying to read what was happening in her soul. "How are you holding up… given the Jean-Emily situation? Anyone new on the horizon?"

"Meee… Nobody new. Not that I've been looking really hard, you know. It's a bit difficult to stop thinking of Jean. He had been on my mind far too long—ever since we had that lunch together during the interviews. Silly me. Hopefully, I'll get him out of my head someday."

Anna had confided her heartbreak to Rosie after the dinner at the Black Pearl restaurant several months ago.

Jean and Emily's relationship did not show any signs of slowing down. Just a few minutes ago, Anna had spotted them standing at the far end of the living room, holding hands.

"What about you, Rosie?" asked Anna. "I think you hit it off with Alex, am I right? All he talks about is you."

"Oh yes, Alex…" Rosie replied without too much enthusiasm. "Yes, he's been calling me over the past few months. A nice guy. But not sure he's my type."

"That's too bad," Anna said with some sadness in her voice. Alex was such a fantastic match for Rosie. "I'll go check out the buffet and be right back. Need anything?"

"No, it's fine. Trying to watch my weight. Too much good food on my trips. I'll wait for you."

When Anna returned with her plate of food, Rosie was gone.

Where did she disappear to? Oh well, maybe it was for the better. The whole point of going to such a party was to network and meet new people.

The first person Anna talked to was Dalcy Tozaka, a young girl from the Solomon Islands. Apparently, Dalcy worked at the Ministry of Tourism at Solomon Islands and was at Polaris at the invitation of the Director for Pacific Islands as a secondee. She would spend one year at Polaris working on various tourism projects and later return to her home country with a lot of new experience to deploy.

"At some point, you should come and visit my country, Anna!" suggested Dalcy. "You will never regret coming. We have pristine beaches, reef lagoons, crystal-clear waters, and amazing animals."

Anna assured Dalcy that she would definitely visit

her homeland sometime in the future. This seemed an especially attractive proposition once Anna found out that Dalcy's family owned ten islands and Dalcy herself had her own island.

Continuing through the room, she started talking to a lady from her part of the world—a Belarusian named Larisa Golubeva Berg. She was a former model in Belarus who had gotten a business degree and somehow landed a job at Polaris as a strategy officer, first in the Minsk satellite office and later in Washington. Her biggest achievement in life, it turned out, was getting married to one of the Polaris directors, a German national about fifteen years her senior, as soon as she got to Washington.

At that point, Anna got a little bit tired of her networking and decided to take a walk around the house, and maybe give a quick call to Katie who was very curious about the Polaris party. Katie's small auditing firm didn't have anything of this sort. All they offered to their loyal employees was a pitiful buffet with spaghetti and meatballs.

Anna kept walking down the corridor with a champagne glass in her hand until she made it to the back of the house. She slipped into the library, sighing as she stepped out of sight from the rest of the party.

Nice and quiet, Anna thought. *Now all I need is a cozy sofa to sit on, and then I can sip my champagne and gossip with Katie.*

Anna quietly pulled the door of the library which closed behind her, and was about to walk in when she suddenly froze at the entrance. Yes, they did have a cozy and soft sofa in that library, but it was not empty. It was actually getting a good workout.

What the heck is this? Anna's eyes widened.

Rosie was sitting on top of Lenny Jameson, kissing him passionately, while his hands were right inside her unzipped leather dress. The whole thing looked like a scene from a cheap porno movie. The only thing missing was some nasty guy with a camera yelling "action!"

Lenny was turned away from the entrance, so he could not see Anna, and he was so consumed with Rosie that he had no idea that somebody had entered the library. Rosie, on the other hand, immediately spotted Anna at the entrance.

A couple of seconds later, Anna shook off her stupor and ran out of the room as fast as she could. She returned to the living room and caught her breath. Everything looked the same, but her world now seemed upside down.

Poor Teresa. Poor Erica. This was so unfair, so terrible. They didn't deserve it. Why on Earth would they have such a horrible husband and father?

Hope I don't see Teresa again tonight, or I will freak out. Anna looked around anxiously. She didn't see any familiar faces around her. Good. Hopefully, Anna could sneak out of the party unnoticed and get as far away as possible. But, as if she heard Anna's thoughts, Teresa appeared.

"How's the party going for you?" she asked breezily, a warm and kind smile curving her lips. "I bet you met a lot of new people. I always enjoy Roberto's parties. He invites the cream of the crop."

Anna mumbled something incomprehensible and went completely pale.

"Anna, what's the matter? Maybe you need some fresh air. Please, lean on me!" Teresa looked at Anna anxiously and tried to support her.

"I-I need to take a walk," Anna muttered, looking down at her feet, refusing to meet Teresa's gaze. "Thanks so much, Teresa. I should feel better soon."

She hurried out of the mansion, away from the horror she witnessed. As she was walking towards her car, somebody called her name. She turned around and saw Rosie running to catch up to her.

"Anna, please wait, let me explain!"

Anna stopped and looked at Rosie furiously. Just a couple of hours ago, she thought that her friend was an incredible star, and now she regretted knowing her at all.

"Rosie, are you completely out of your mind?" Anna finally yelled. They'd walked far enough from the mansion so as not to be overheard by anyone. "Can you imagine what would happen if somebody else saw you? Luckily it was me, but it could have been somebody from our management. You could lose your job, and everyone would be looking at you as a cheap prostitute. This is so incredibly disgusting that I cannot even talk about it."

"Sorry, things really got out of hand!" Rosie looked at Anna pleadingly.

"This is what happens when somebody shows up in an inappropriate leather dress to an office party," Anna said bitterly, casting a disappointed gaze over Rosie's outfit. "I cannot believe you were making out with a guy you literally just met, and in the Vice President's mansion of all places!"

"Well, I didn't *just* meet him."

"Okay, that was a figure of speech. Obviously, we all first met Lenny in Tunis during the orientation a couple of months ago. He did that presentation on commodity exchanges."

"That is true, but there was more than that… A LOT more actually…" whispered Rosie who proceeded to tell Anna the whole story. Turned out, that same day when Anna saw Lenny at the beach, he also met Rosie there. She was walking around the beach collecting shells when he approached her and started chatting casually about the weather, the sea, and other general stuff.

"I thought that maybe by talking to Lenny, I would advance my chances to get a placement," Rosie explained. "You remember, at that time it was a sore subject… He invited me out to dinner and drinks and I said yes.

"Believe me, Anna, I did not plan on having an affair with him! Far from that. To make sure he did not get any wrong ideas, I even underdressed for the evening. No makeup even.

"I was so impressed with Lenny. He clearly seemed a very sensitive and kind guy, who took my problems to heart. He was there to mentor me, not for any other reason.

"Then the conversation somehow drifted to the dialogue about relationships. Again, Lenny seemed very sincere, talking about how he was separated from his wife, who never understood him and how that supposedly left a big wound in his heart. He told me that he was ready to get out there again and potentially find a new relationship."

What a liar, Anna thought. *And also an idiot. He has a beauty queen right there at home and the most talented daughter on Earth. The greatest family one could imagine.*

"We kissed as we were getting into the elevator, and somehow it felt right to head not to my own room but to

Lenny's. None of this was planned, Anna, I promise! Then at some point we met at a random seminar at Polaris and an invitation to drinks followed. Somehow Lenny ended up in my apartment. Then he started calling, inviting me out more and that's how we got to this point. Well, to be completely honest, I did choose this dress to turn him on a little bit. But we are falling in love. Why is that so wrong?"

It was now absolutely obvious that Rosie had no idea what she'd gotten herself into.

"Rosie, let me quickly clue you in," Anna said sharply. "First of all, I know Lenny's wife. She also works here at Polaris. Remarkable and classy lady. I can assure you that they *never* got separated, or anything he might have told you. It appears that Lenny likes playing on the side. He tried to pick me up in Tunis as well, *but I ran away from him.*"

Rosie listened carefully, sniffling her nose a little bit.

Anna continued. "You have to stop this whole relationship. Now. Before anyone gets hurt. I will try to forget about what I saw today and support you as much as you need. But if you decide to continue, do not count on me. This will ruin your life. Your career. Remember that we are on probation this year. Management can easily not offer you a position after the end of the program if they detect inappropriate behavior. Lenny's job is not on the line, but yours is. You cannot hide an awl in the sack. Eventually it will come out. You will be returning to the Philippines in no time."

Rosie nodded, tears streaming down her cheeks. She looked completely crushed.

"I'll end it right away, Anna," Rosie finally said

fiercely. "I'm truly sorry. Thanks for being such a good friend."

Anna gave Rosie a hug, trying to console her. Good thing the other woman had finally come to her senses. No guy was worth a career at Polaris. Especially not Lenny Jameson.

Chapter 15. The Unexpected Guest

Washington, D.C. and Jekyll Island, GA

The second half of December was a very slow season at Polaris as most of the staff began taking time off to see their friends and family. Anna's floor, usually bustling, became emptier with each passing day. It was time to think of a vacation of her own.

John stopped by her office for a chat, a coffee cup in his hand. "You going anywhere for Christmas, Anna?" he asked. He often walked around the floor to check how everyone in his team was doing and if they had any questions.

"Yes, as a matter of fact I am," Anna announced proudly. "I'll be visiting Professor Thompson and his wife at their home on Jekyll Island. When my parents and I lived in the States, we used to drive to Jekyll Island together every summer."

Professor James Thompson was a chairman of the finance department from her alma mater and Anna's own professor of finance. In addition, he was a personal friend of her parents.

"Lovely." John nodded his head in approval. "Isn't that the place where a bunch of millionaires used to spend their vacations?"

"Exactly. Back in the late 1800s James Hill, George Baker, William Rockefeller, William Vanderbilt, and some of their contemporaries were looking for a good place to spend their winters. In the end, they selected Jekyll Island. The exquisite Jekyll Island Club was constructed there. Its clientele controlled an enormous one-sixth of the world's worth!" Being a finance major, Anna was always fascinated by the stories about the powerful American financiers spending their winters on this legendary island.

"Must be a nice place to visit. Enjoy. Maybe you'll find yourself a millionaire husband there." John gave Anna a wink and kept on walking.

****

"Anna, dear, thank you so much for coming! We missed you!" Mrs. Thompson exclaimed as Anna walked into their house on Captain Wylly Drive, dragging the small suitcase behind her. It was almost ten in the evening. It had taken Anna a good twelve hours to drive to Jekyll Island.

"How are your wonderful parents? I wish they could've come as well. We have not seen them in so long."

"Thank you so much, Alice." Anna carefully put her suitcase in the corner and gave Mrs. Thompson a big hug. "Everyone is fine. My dad is doing his work at the newspaper, and Mom is always busy with her tennis students."

"It's so wonderful that you moved back to the States! We hope your parents will follow."

Anna started taking off her coat and boots when she heard several other people approaching from the living room.

"Anna! Finally! Hope the drive was not too exhausting." A tall and good-looking man appeared at the door. James Thompson was around sixty years old but looked much younger. Like always, he was dressed in polo shirt and slacks. He was together with his daughter Jenny, who was about Anna's age, and some other guy—probably Jenny's boyfriend. Anna had heard that he was supposedly a doctor. They all welcomed Anna warmly.

On the other side of the living room stood another man who Anna didn't recognize at first. But when he heard some commotion at the door, he turned around.

David.

What is he doing here, Anna thought in a complete panic. She felt her blood rush to her face and her legs suddenly get shaky. Professor Thompson had specifically mentioned that his son had other plans and would not be coming!

Anna would have definitely thought twice about this trip, had she known David would be visiting his parents for Christmas… This was so incredibly awkward. The last time they spoke, Anna broke up with the guy while he begged her to give him a chance! How was she supposed to stay in the same house with him now?

She couldn't help but stare at David for a minute. She had not seen him for a good five years. *When did he become so smoking hot?*

Now in his early thirties, David was tall, with a bright smile, shining black hair, expressive and large brown eyes, and an athletic build. His soft white linen shirt was open at the collar, exposing his strong neck and chest.

Anna reluctantly took her eyes off her ex-boyfriend. Perhaps she'd been too harsh on him? They had some good times together—she just didn't appreciate them enough back then. She had been too young and idealistic, confident that her prince charming was already on his way, ready to sweep her off her feet and make her head spin with the greatest romance story of all time. But her prince never showed up, while David was still around. Right there, in front of Anna, to be precise.

All of a sudden, colorful memories of their relationship started streaming in Anna's mind, making her pulse race and her body tremble.

David surprising her with a big bunch of red roses after her team won the school case competition.

David putting together a mix of her favorite music.

David buying the books she urgently needed for her research project.

Emily had mentioned he moved back to Washington... Maybe they could start over again, now that they both lived in the same city? It was a crazy idea, but it suddenly made all the sense in the world.

Or... maybe not.

Behind David was standing a striking young lady. She was wearing a champagne-colored evening gown and sky-blue satin pumps with a crystal buckle. A diamond bracelet was glittering on her wrist and a ring with an immense emerald—on her finger.

Anna anxiously looked over her own humble ensemble—sweatpants and a gray sweater. Of course, she wanted to feel comfortable during the long drive. But maybe she should have still worn something a little more sophisticated. Come to think of it, she didn't even bring *any* pretty clothes with her, just a few T-shirts and yoga pants. What a disaster.

"Anna, glad to see you again," David said cheerfully, putting his hand around the waist of the young lady next to him. "Welcome! Mom just told me you moved back to the States from your home country. Was it… Albania? I forget. Please let me introduce my girlfriend, Helmi."

Albania, eh? Anna frowned.

"Nice to meet you," she said quietly and shook Helmi's perfectly manicured and moisturized hand.

As David and Helmi started walking upstairs, holding hands, Anna couldn't help but follow David with a sad gaze. That was *her* David, and now he belonged to somebody else.

****

It was an early morning and everyone in the house was still asleep. But Anna could not wait another second to explore. She quietly walked to the door and snuck outside. Hopefully, she didn't wake anyone up.

A gentle sun was subtly peeking through the clouds, illuminating the pretty garden with several tall palm trees and a large oak covered with Spanish moss in the back. It didn't even remotely look like winter, but much rather like spring.

As Anna kept walking around, she heard a familiar voice.

"Up so early?" David smiled as he approached her.

"I collapsed after I got into the bed. I was so tired after that long drive," Anna said. "But this morning I really could not wait to go out to see these gorgeous surroundings. The sun, the air, the light breeze—it's perfect weather."

Anna sat down on a white wooden chair and showed her face to the tender sun. Unlike in the summer, the sun was so pleasant now that she could probably sit in this chair all day reading a book, and never get bored.

"Yes, it's lovely outside. I should probably start coming here more often," David noted. "My parents spend all their free time at Jekyll Island—Mom managed to write three children's books here—but I always end up stuck in the office. It's my first time here in two years!"

"Where is Helmi on this glorious morning? She is not a big nature enthusiast, hah?"

"Oh no, not at all. Nature is not her thing," David confessed. "She likes to dress up. The outdoor terrain doesn't quite agree with high heels."

"Yes, everyone is different. Where is Helmi from anyway? I couldn't figure that out, and I didn't recognize the name."

"She is Finnish," David explained. "We are both in the same PhD program and started dating a few months ago." David stopped there, glanced at Anna stretched out in the chair, and then continued.

"I want to apologize for being a bit of a jerk last night. Of course, I know you are from *Ukraine*. There is no other country in the world like yours—I would know, since we spent that July there together years ago. I have the images of the St. Volodymyr's Cathedral imprinted in my mind—the bright-yellow towers and sky-blue domes with the golden stars. We stayed so close to it and I loved waking up and looking at it through the window every morning... Anyways, it's been awhile since we last saw each other, and I reacted badly. It won't happen again, Anna. I am *really* happy to see you."

"Oh, don't worry about it." Anna blushed and turned her face away for a second. "I was also in a bit of a shock seeing you. I had no idea you'd be here."

"I wasn't supposed to be. Really. We were going to

spend Christmas with Helmi's family. They were planning a big party, but her father wasn't feeling well and everything got cancelled. I convinced Helmi to come here instead. Her father should be fine, he just needs some rest. What are your plans for today?"

"I have so much to do! I just broke free from the winter cold in Washington, so I am up for anything. I want to go to the beach, walk around the downtown area and check everything out."

Anna did not mention that she wanted to go shopping as soon as possible. They had a big mall in the neighboring Brunswick, as far as she remembered. Of course, it wouldn't have the latest fashion boutiques, but the stores should be good enough to find something suitable.

"Sounds like a plan." David nodded. "Well, let me know if you are also up for a game of golf. The weather is supposed to be perfect all day today. We could play eighteen holes."

Anna arched her eyebrow. "I don't remember you playing golf. Is that a new thing? I recall trying to get you to the golf course back when we were still dating… You did not seem too much into it."

"I was an idiot, what can I say? I started playing when I was at the consulting firm in New York. We had a lot of outings and one needed to know how to play. I'm not a pro, of course, but I picked up some golf in the last couple of years. You'll see."

Anna blinked her eyes in amazement. "Why don't you get us a tee time at one? That should give us enough time to finish before dark, if we play fast. How about Helmi? Do you think she would want to play?"

"She doesn't play golf. High heels, remember? I'll

ask Jenny and my dad. I'm sure they would love to go with us."

****

Later in the morning Anna visited the Brunswick shopping mall which was about thirty minutes away from Jekyll Island.

"This is not a bad selection at all here," Anna murmured, as she was going through the rack with various colorful dresses. "This blue one would be perfect for daytime. And this one with a golden belt is quite sophisticated, I could wear it if we go to some restaurant... Okay, I'll just get these seven dresses. I also need a few cute golf outfits..."

With the shopping completed successfully, Anna impatiently headed for a walk at the beach. She realized that being at the beach on Jekyll Island in winter was a very different experience from summer. She should have worn a sweatshirt, not a T-shirt. Although the sun still shone brightly and the sky was blue, the strong gusts of the freezing wind made the beach experience much less enjoyable.

Just a couple of people were walking along the sand. The wildlife was virtually undisturbed. A few sand crabs were running sideways across the strand and hundreds of seagulls walked near the water line. A flock of six brown pelicans flew above the ocean in search of some fish for lunch. They were quite a ways from the shore, but the pelicans' long beaks made them easy to spot.

Finally, after lunch, Anna headed to the golf course. As soon as she got out of the car, a familiar starter came to help her put the golf bag in the golf cart—a smiling old man with a white beard.

"I remember you," he said. "You used to come here

with your parents, right?"

"Good memory," Anna commented. She and her parents played a round pretty much every day when they were down at Jekyll Island. They always took advantage of the "afternoon" special, which offered a substantial discount, and allowed even people with modest means like Anna's family to enjoy golfing—while feeling like millionaires.

"Which course are we playing?" Anna asked David. Jekyll Island boasted four magnificent golf courses—Indian Mound, Pine Lakes, Oleander, and Great Dunes.

"Indian Mound, of course. You think I forgot your favorite course?" David grinned.

As in the past, Indian Mound was home for all kinds of animals. During the round, Anna spotted at least a dozen deer. Whenever one hit the ball on the fairway, one or two deer would often slowly come up to it to have a look and see if that was something edible.

Alligators, turtles, and even snakes inhabited the course. Although Anna had not heard of any accidents here, she exercised caution, especially around large alligators. Some of them crawled outside the ponds and opened their wide mouths showing off their big teeth. It was definitely not a good idea to hit a ball anywhere near them.

The round itself was a lot of fun. Professor Thompson and David played a really superb game. To Anna's surprise, David had made impressive progress in golf. Those outings at his firm must have done the trick. He hit the ball with precision, hardly missing any fairways.

Jenny was the only Thompson who was having a bad golf day. She managed to hit the ball pretty much in every sand trap on the course and then spent most of the afternoon trying to get out of them. Anna pitied the girl. It was a difficult sport and Jenny had never been athletic.

"Jenny, will you finally stop hooking the ball?" David said cheerfully after the third time it happened. "I think you've lost a dozen balls in the bushes! Maybe I should ask Helmi or Mom to go with us next time. It's almost too painful to watch you."

"Shut up, David," Jenny snapped, breathing heavily as she walked up the hill. "I'm doing just fine. And stop that bullshit about Helmi and Mom, please. Helmi can't even hit the ball. And with Mom, you'd be playing till midnight."

David laughed. "True. Our women's golf team really sucks. Good thing we have Anna to make up for your game, otherwise I would have quit a long time ago."

Anna indeed was hitting some excellent shots during the round and even hit a couple of birdies. Her game further improved when she caught David's gaze on her tight-fitting golf skirt.

The golfers got back home in high spirits. The plan was to have dinner at the Sparkling Waves Restaurant—one of the Thompsons' favorite restaurants on the island. Everyone quickly changed and left together, Helmi and Mrs. Thompson in toe.

The Sparkling Waves Restaurant boasted an extensive menu of various types of seafood and different Southern delicacies. It also featured the artwork of numerous Southern artists—paintings with the Golden Isles landscapes and sculptures of local animals and birds. All the artwork was for sale, and many customers would walk out of the restaurant not only with a full stomach from an excellent meal but also one of the astonishing art pieces which had been on display.

The conversation around the dinner table centered around the game. Mr. Thompson was very proud that he could still golf a round in the low nineties, Jenny was happy that she hit a couple of good shots in the end, and David was talking non-stop about Anna's excellent play.

"Anna, I still can't believe your birdie on number seven, the par five. Your drive was amazing, and then you sunk that long putt in the end."

"Oh, that has always been my favorite hole on the course," said Anna. "For some reason I always hit my drive very straight on that hole, which puts me in a good position for the birdie. The green definitely has a lot of break and today my putt was not straightforward, but sometimes one gets lucky, you know."

"You are like a magician on those greens, Anna," added Jenny. "I couldn't get the speed right at all. All my putts were either too short or rolled way past the hole."

"Yes, one needs to get used to these greens," Anna explained, as she was ready to dig her teeth into the juicy stuffed flounder just brought by the waiter. "Next time, you might want to practice before the round. They have a good driving range and a practice putting green right next to the clubhouse."

"I am so happy to hear that all of you had such a wonderful time," Mrs. Thompson said, smiling whole-heartedly. "Golf is such a delightful game for everyone—both the young and the young at heart." She pointed at her husband and gave him a pat on the shoulder.

As the dinner progressed, Anna observed Helmi from the corner of her eye. David's girlfriend was the only person not interested in the golf conversation, just eating quietly and periodically checking messages on her phone. Helmi didn't seem the kind of person to show much emotion on her face, so it was hard to understand what she was thinking.

But still, David's clear partiality to Anna did not go completely unnoticed. A few times Helmi's face darkened and she bit her lip. Writing her off was way too early. She could still come up with something.

Chapter 16. The Millionaires' Club

Jekyll Island, GA

The following morning, Anna was woken up by the birds cheerfully chirping by her window. She cracked one eye open and tried putting a pillow over her head. However, sleeping peacefully with these fluffy tenors around was no longer a possibility. They did not stop their tunes even for a minute. She slowly rolled out of bed, giving up on sleep.

Anna spent some extra time at the mirror styling her curls and put on one of the dresses she had bought yesterday—a glacier white one with some pretty ruffles. She also brought a book—to make her plans to see David in the garden again less obvious—and gracefully descended into the garden. David wasn't there yet, but hopefully he would be coming soon. For the time being, Anna sat down in the white chair, subtly looking around.

But David never showed up, no matter how many times Anna looked up from her book searching for him. Eventually, she gave up, returning to the house, her feet dragging and her face covered with a thick layer of disappointment.

Mrs. Thompson was in the kitchen busy preparing breakfast, while Jenny was sitting at the table with the Islander newspaper in her hand. Bright yellow eggs were loudly squawking in the pan. "Anna, do you want something to eat?" Mrs. Thompson asked kindly. "We'll be having breakfast shortly."

"Sure, I'm hungry." Anna sat down next to Jenny and looked around in search of David. He was nowhere to be found. "Alice, would you like me to help you cook? There are really a lot of people in the house. I can make a few Ukrainian dishes for everyone to share." David would probably appreciate the cottage cheese pancakes which melted in the mouth, or the heavenly big and thin pancakes. They would bring back all the happy memories.

"Of course! Ukrainian dishes are so delicious," Mrs. Thompson said. "But we don't need much, since only the three of us are here for breakfast. James went fishing with his friend. David and Helmi are gone, too—they left very early this morning. They decided to bike around the island. I think it's a wonderful idea."

"Yes, that's just wonderful." Anna leaned back against her chair. Now she could not relive the memories with David while making breakfast. She probably wouldn't be able to talk to him all day.

"We also need to think of something to do after breakfast," Mrs. Thompson suggested. "How about a walk together along the beach today? You, me, and Jenny?"

Anna nodded weakly. All her enthusiasm about Jekyll Island had suddenly gone out the door. A walk with Mrs. Thompson and Jenny along the beach would have sounded awesome a couple of days ago, but today she would have much preferred hanging out with David... A few years ago he had been head over heels in love with her; nobody else existed for him. *She* had been the one to end it with *him*. But one cannot step in the same river twice.

David and Helmi continued biking the whole week. Christmas went by, and the New Year was quickly approaching.

"I just don't understand men," Anna gloomily announced to Katie one evening. "I can't even talk to the guy anymore, he is always out. We have barely exchanged a few words. I thought we are starting something again, there was a spark between us, but Helmi quickly distracted him. I just… I want to know if we still have something, like we did back in university."

"Sorry to hear that." Katie sadly waved from the screen. "Well, who knows, something might still change. You have a couple more days. I'm sure you'll find time to chat with him."

"I doubt anything will change now." Anna sighed. "If only I could get David alone for a few hours, just to talk. But Helmi is always around him, like she's glued to him. There is no way she would leave us alone."

"Hey, just keep your hopes up. If you wish for something really hard, it might actually happen. Look at me—I didn't have any boyfriend for like ever, and then out of nowhere appeared Nick. We are going to the Kennedy Center tonight. Have a look at the presents he got me for Christmas." Katie twirled around in her blue-green evening gown in front of the screen so that Anna could get a good look. She also proudly showed her new emerald colored cork purse. "These are both handcrafted, vegan and sustainable."

"Incredible. At least one of us has a great boyfriend. That makes me feel much better… All right, enjoy your evening. I'm going on a 'date' with Jenny. We decided to order some takeout tonight—burgers and milkshakes—and hang out and gossip in the garden."

"My mouth is already watering. Say hi to Jenny for me!"

The food arrived promptly, and Anna and Jenny got comfortable in their white wooden chairs outside the Thompsons' house. They had a perfect view of colorful Christmas lights which Mr. Thompson had draped all over their palm-trees and the oak tree.

The night was warm and breezy. The nocturnal wildlife, always so rich at Jekyll Island, did not disappoint, and the parade of animals began as the sky turned to dusk. First, an owl started hooting somewhere close by, alerting everyone that the night was approaching. Then several graceful deer slowly passed by the house with their heads held high, sort of saluting the ladies, and a couple of rabbits hopped on the lawn as well.

A few moments later, a big fat cat with a long and fluffy tail and shining eyes appeared on the grass. But only when she looked more closely at it could Anna tell this was actually not a cat but a chubby racoon. She watched as he almost proudly proceeded to the trash can which was standing on the side of the road.

"These racoons are such bandits," Anna commented while sipping on her milkshake. "When we used to stay at the hotel here in Jekyll, we always saw them going through the trash cans outside the hotel late at night or early in the morning, having a big feast, stuffing their faces with leftover bananas, muffins, eggs, and everything else... Then they would leave a terrible mess on the ground and bail. The racoons look kind of cute, but they are not really nice guys!"

"Definitely," Jenny said.

Anna and Jenny thought they could continue with a quiet evening until they heard a commotion at the house. David appeared outside rolling a bright purple suitcase and headed to the garage without saying a word.

"Weird," Jenny said stretching out the word as she turned her neck sharply in the direction of the garage. "He wasn't going anywhere today, and what's the deal with the suitcase? It's clearly Helmi's. I remember seeing her arrive with it."

"Let's go inside and find out." Anna quickly got up from her chair. "Something must have happened while we were sitting here."

When Anna and Jenny got into the living room, warning lights immediately started flashing in their heads. The air was full of anxiety. Helmi was standing in the middle of the room, her face pale and eyes teary. She was intently talking to somebody on the phone.

"Poor Helmi," Mrs. Thompson said, her voice low as she approached Anna and Jenny. "She just got a call that her dad was hospitalized. He's been having some heart problems for years. She's been on the phone with her mom trying to coordinate."

"I'm so sorry!" exclaimed Jenny as she patted Helmi sympathetically on the shoulder. "Please let us know if we can be of any help."

"Is her dad in D.C.?" Anna asked Mrs. Thompson.

"Her family lives in Richmond. She got herself a last-minute ticket to fly home tonight, so she can be with her parents. David is taking her to the airport." Mr. Thompson said. "Helmi is such a wonderful girl, so close with her family. I'm glad David met her."

****

There he is, working on his laptop yet again. Should

I maybe jump up and down a couple of times?

Anna watched David plugging away on his laptop in the far corner of the living room, oblivious to everyone and everything around him. He didn't even notice that she'd put on some risky shorts this morning! And they looked so hot with the new stilettos she had bought...

This was really a bad sign. Helmi was no longer in the house, yet David didn't attempt to reconnect with Anna at all, as if she didn't exist. He was plunged in his own world, far away from here.

After Helmi's departure, David was either in his room, or downstairs and not talking to anyone. As he had explained to Mrs. Thompson, he had several deadlines to meet on his dissertation, and there were also a few things he needed to finish for his work. How true this was, nobody knew, but given the situation with Helmi, not a single person in the house dared to bother him with conversation. Anna included.

Finally, New Year's Eve came. Whenever the Thompsons were down in Georgia for winter holidays, they and their guests always spent New Year's Eve at the Jekyll Island Club restaurant. This year would be no different.

When everyone in the Thompsons' house started getting ready for the party, Anna also went to her room to start getting dressed. But first, she checked her messages on social media and made a few calls as the New Year wishes started pouring in.

New Year's Eve was one of the biggest holidays of the year for Ukrainians. The saying was that you will spend your new year as well as you celebrate New Year's Eve, so people tried to find the best parties and go to the most interesting destinations to meet the new year.

Anna of course talked to her family—her parents, Grandma Maria, Uncle Stepan and his family, as well as Uncle Tolik—who were celebrating all together in Kyiv, where the clock had already struck midnight. They were at the Emerald Hotels & Resorts, the best venue to celebrate New Year's Eve. When Anna called, her family was in a festive mood, clinking champagne glasses and holding sparklers.

"Anna, anything new with David?" Olena asked anxiously as soon as she answered Anna's call.

"Happy New Year to you too, Mom." Anna laughed. Her mom was always so predictable. She wore her emotions on her sleeve. These days, the David situation was at the top of her mind. Likely because Anna had mentioned she was spending the holidays with the Thompsons.

"Right! Happy New Year, dear! Well, I hope you manage to win David over. You could never find a better guy, believe me. He is my dream son-in-law."

"I know that. You told me many times," Anna assured her mom. Olena clearly had a bit of a crush on David herself... Why else would she be his strongest advocate over the years? Back when Anna was weighing the pros and cons of a long-distance relationship with him, Olena drove her insane trying to persuade her to give him a chance. Of course, Anna had followed her heart at that time. But now it looked like Mom was right all along. "Tonight we are going to New Year's Eve party all together. Let's hope something good will come out of it."

Anna then talked to Dima, who was in Vietnam for the New Year's together with his family. They always picked some exotic far away destination which offered big fireworks, bigger parties, and nice weather for their celebration. Dima would have plenty of content for his blog.

Finally, she called Katie, who was celebrating the winter holidays with her moms, like usual, and was just about to sit down to a quiet family dinner. Quite an opposite celebration from Dima.

To her great surprise, when Anna was checking her inbox, she came across an email from Jean Rolland which contained a beautiful wintery postcard for New Year's Eve and kind wishes for the new year. It even included a nice little poem. It was very thoughtful, but rather odd, she thought, as they had not spoken since that fateful dinner at the Black Pearl Restaurant.

What does this mean? Could it be more than just a card—like he is trying to tell me he is thinking of me? Or is it just a polite greeting and nothing more?

Anna kept reading the message over and over, trying to find any hidden meaning. But it was impossible to tell. Maybe Jean was just sending greetings to everyone he knew. Some folks did that to be friendly. Quite possibly he was one of those.

In the end, Anna decided that it was best to just put Jean out of her mind. She had already mistakenly imagined that he was interested in her—or potentially *in love* with her—after a simple lunch together. Right now he was probably getting ready to go out with Emily to her parents' grand celebration. Or maybe they were in Paris, heading for some romantic dinner…

Anna could not possibly continue chasing some elusive love. There were some limits. And she had a great guy here—if she could just get him alone and talking. He was somebody who used to love her and could potentially love her again.

With a lot of excitement, she pulled her dress out of the closet. It was a gold sequin column gown which fit her like a glove. The dress was very simple yet splendid—sleeveless, with an open back, two thin straps, and a long skirt which shimmered beautifully. She chose her exquisite sultanate set—necklace, earrings, and ring—which she had bought during her vacation in Turkey some years back. The jewel changed color depending on the light, and its sparkles were totally irresistible.

Finally, Anna decided to leave her hair flowing down over her shoulders as opposed to any complicated up-dos. With a light evening satin shawl and gold stilettos, her outfit was now complete. She was ready to ring in the New Year.

When she came to the living room, everyone was already there except for Jenny who was taking a bit longer. All the men looked extremely handsome in stylish tuxedos, while Mrs. Thompson was very attractive in a lovely navy blue, lace gown with long sleeves.

"Anna, what a gorgeous dress, and it fits you so perfectly!" Mrs. Thompson said loudly.

David, who was sitting on the sofa busy sending some emails on his phone, looked up to see what his mother was talking about and froze. Anna could read delight, affection, even desire on his face in that instant, even though he didn't say a word. There was no need for a compliment—David's lingering gaze was a compliment enough.

Finally, Jenny came down in her black mock-neck halter dress and everyone was ready to go. They took two cars—Michael drove Anna and Jenny, while David drove Mr. and Mrs. Thompson.

The weather was beautiful for New Year's Eve—in the seventies and with a light breeze. The forecast included a chance of heavy rainstorms later in the evening, which were quite common, but for now there was no sign of them. The moon was shining brightly in the clear skies.

"I am feeling quite melancholy that the Christmas holidays are starting to come to an end," Mrs. Thompson complained as everyone was sitting down at the large roundtable and looking at their special menus for the evening. "A few more days—and everybody will start leaving. I wish we could be here together forever!"

"I fully agree with you, Alice," Anna said. "I feel the same. These are my first winter holidays here, but I can now fully understand why all those millionaires spent their winters here. Superb weather, gorgeous nature, fresh air, great company. I think we have flawlessly replicated their experience here. I cannot even imagine how to go back to all the noise, cold, snow, and work in D.C. I will truly miss this paradise!"

"Mom, you and Anna would have fit in perfectly here during the Gilded Age." Jenny laughed. "You could be part of the women's social circle, having all those elaborate picnics on the lawn in front of the clubhouse, eating five course meals, gossiping all day, and driving all the servants crazy. Our beautiful Anna would have met a millionaire. You know, history shows that some young ladies did find their matches at Jekyll Island."

"I don't think Anna needs to go back in time to meet a man," David suddenly said, staring straight at Anna as he was sipping his margarita. "She could easily find a great match now and get married, if she weren't so stubborn."

Everyone looked at David. But David chose just to let his words hang in the air before changing the subject.

The dinner was served promptly. Everything was delicious, like always, and service was impeccable. A piano concert accompanied the dinner, and everyone listened to the performance by an award-winning pianist.

At midnight people in the dining room started clinking their champagne glasses to wish each other happy new year. As the Thompson party came out of the restaurant and looked around, they were mesmerized by the Christmas lights tangled around all the grand oaks surrounding the clubhouse and its lawn. It was such a gorgeous view: a picture from an illuminated enchanted forest.

"Does anyone want to walk around and look at the Christmas lights before we go?" asked Anna. "I also want to take a few pictures for my parents. They would be so curious to see what the club looks like during the winter holidays."

"Sure, I'd love to come with you," David volunteered. "They also have a stunning Christmas tree on the lawn, I'll show you."

"I'd love to come as well!" Jenny yelled as she was walking woozily. "Let's walk all night! Let's go dancing somewhere too! I think I see J.P. Morgan walking down the lane… Let's catch up to him and get some autographs!"

"I would recommend that you, Jenny, head straight home," said Mrs. Thompson firmly. "You are a bit, I dare say, tipsy."

"Who? Me?" Jenny protested. "I am totally fine. I

am staying here."

"Out of the question," said Mr. Thompson and turned to David and Anna. "We will take Jenny home, with Michael's car. Why don't the two of you take your time and just come back in David's car? Mind the forecast, they are calling for thunderstorms later this morning."

Anna and David started walking down the lane, while the rest of their party dragged Jenny to the car, stuck her inside, and took off.

"Like always, Jenny can't hold her liquor," David observed. "We need to keep the champagne away from her next time."

"Yeah, I thought she was getting a little too talkative during the dinner but I did not notice she was drinking so much," said Anna. She sighed as she took in the colorful lights, shivering in the cool night air, thankful for her shawl.

"Thanks for staying with me, it would not be too interesting for me to walk around the grounds by myself. Do they have these lights here every year?" Anna asked as she and David reached the Moss Cottage, which had a large colorful wreath in the middle of its façade.

"Yes, I believe so. I don't come down every year, but every time I've been here, they've had these lights. It's pretty amazing, look at the Christmas tree over there!"

"Oh yes, it is lovely!" Anna said as she looked at the large tree in the middle of the lawn shining with all different colors, a golden star sparkling on top. "Let's get closer and take a picture for my parents. I am sure they would love to see."

"Of course. Let me hold your hand, I don't want you

getting stuck in the lawn with those stilettos."

As a true gentleman, David supported Anna while they walked through the lawn. The picture taken, they headed back to the car. David suddenly let go of Anna's hand and took a few steps, but then turned around sharply.

"You know, I can't do this. I don't want to let go of your hand. I don't want to let you go even for a minute. The second I saw you in that dress this evening, it reminded me so much about how we used to be together." He shook his head, then continued. "Remember that one time we went out? All the guys were just staring at you, ignoring their girlfriends or wives. When we were leaving, one guy who was passing by us just said, 'Wow!' At that moment, I felt like I was the luckiest man in the world."

"Of course, I remember," whispered Anna.

"Throughout this whole vacation, I have not been able to think about anything but you," David added. "It was really hard with Helmi around... I didn't want to hurt her. But from the first moment I saw you, I knew it was over with her. I want to give us a try again. And if it doesn't work out, we won't have any regrets."

"I have also been thinking about you a lot since I got here... It was possibly a big mistake that I let you go back then. But we are both in D.C. now, and we could give it another shot."

They kissed in the middle of the colorful lights and trees, the wind blowing through Anna's hair—one of those romantic kisses which every woman dreamed about. Then small raindrops started falling, lightning illuminated the sky right after.

"I think we better get going," David suggested,

anxiously looking at the sky. "Put my jacket on."

They ran the rest of the way to David's car and got in before the big rain started.

"You've got a... Bentley?" Anna asked when they got into David's shiny silver car. "I did not quite look at your car before as it was in the garage. This is a beauty! Last time we dated you had a rather simple car."

"Thanks," David said proudly. "You probably remember my grandma Adelaide, on my mom's side? Well, she passed away a couple of years ago and left Jenny and me ten million apiece. So, you have officially met your 'millionaire' here on the island. Not quite a J.P. Morgan, but I can still give you anything you want."

Handsome, intelligent, rich, and still completely in love with her. Unbelievable. Why did she ever look for anyone else?

David drove to the Thompsons' house as the rain started falling in sheets. The thunderstorms in Georgia, and Jekyll Island in particular, were usually very powerful, and it was hard to see anything while driving. Luckily, David and Anna were on a small road with no cars on it and just ten minutes away from the house.

Finally, they reached their destination and Anna ran into the house while David was putting the car into the garage. She grabbed a towel once inside and dried her outfit. Thankfully, the dress was okay. David's jacket was a lifesaver.

She stood by the window, looking out at the raging forces of nature. She adored watching the rain. Obviously, the view was much better from inside a warm and dry house. The sky was covered with dark gray clouds and the rain kept coming strong and drumming loudly on the roof. All the trees were swaying from the fierce wind, and the lawn in front of the house was already flooded.

Anna heard David enter the room and close the door behind him. He probably wanted to check on her and get his jacket back. She continued watching the rain, shivering for another reason.

"Look," she exclaimed. "The rain is getting worse and worse. I am so glad we escaped! I definitely would not want to be outside now."

"Yeah," said David, standing right behind her in his perfectly starched white shirt, so tall and broad-shouldered. "It's going to rain all night, I bet. We were really lucky it didn't start before we could see the lights around the club house."

They stood in silence for a moment, when Anna felt a tender touch of David's soft hand slowly moving up and down her neck. David then gently and slowly pulled off the light straps of her dress and started kissing her shoulders. It felt really good, so Anna did not resist. She kept standing by the window as the rain continued pouring down with an incredible force and the lightning was illuminating the sky. A minute later, Anna turned around and David's hot lips met hers. He lifted her up, and carried her to the bed, like he used to so many times before.

"Finally," he whispered. "You are mine again. I can't wait any longer."

Chapter 17. The Love, the Jealousy, and the Crying Baby

Washington, D.C.

"Anna, you've been looking absolutely radiant these last couple of weeks," her neighbor Pablo said one morning. "It's so cold and gloomy outside, yet your face just glows with sunshine. I need to start putting on sunglasses when I'm next to you. I bet you have either a new boyfriend, or won the lottery. Am I right?"

"Ha-ha, Pablo, you are really observant," laughed Anna. "I think it is actually both."

Since that magical New Year's Eve, things had really been going well with David. The morning after New Year's Eve, David had immediately and unambiguously announced to his surprised family at breakfast that he and Anna were back together again and asked them to refrain from any questions or concerns on the matter. For a moment, there was total silence—everyone in the house was completely shocked, especially given that Helmi's departure was just a few days earlier.

Anna ducked her head, expecting a hostile reaction from Mr. and Mrs. Thompson. However, a few minutes after the initial shock passed, everyone quickly agreed that they were a much better match. Once that hurdle was overcome, David called Helmi that same morning to break up with her.

The following days, Anna and David were inseparable, playing golf, walking along the beach, and going to all of Anna's favorite restaurants on the island. Finally, the vacation had ended but not the fairy tale. David and Anna met pretty much every day in D.C. He called and texted her a few times a day and quickly became the most important part of her life.

And what a lovely house David had! Anna was in a complete awe. His home was located up on a hill on McArthur Boulevard with a magnificent view of the Potomac River. He'd moved in a year ago and had the place remodeled perfectly.

If Anna had to pick her dream home in D.C., this would be it. The modern and chic two-storied house featured large glass walls, allowing for maximum light flow and breathtaking views of the river and the dazzling sky from every spot in the house. On cold winter afternoons, Anna adored sitting together on the sofa in his spacious living room, enjoying some snacks and watching the spectacular views as the falling snow blanketed all the hills and trees.

She quickly informed her family and friends of the news. Of course, everyone was ecstatic. Except for Dima.

Anna had not seen Dima for quite some time, although she was still up to date on his whereabouts. Thanks to his social media channels, of course. Apparently, Dima had been sucking up to Erica over the winter. His persistence paid off as Erica did a joint video with him for his cooking channel.

A couple of days ago, Dima arrived in Washington "on some business" and texted Anna.

IncredibleDima—*Just landed in D.C. ! Want to meet up tomorrow?*—

Anna—*Tomorrow's no good. Busy at work*—

IncredibleDima—*When?*—

Anna—*Saturday. I'm organizing a party at my apartment*—

IncredibleDima—*SYS*—

The party was scheduled for seven, but Dima showed up right at six.

Great, she thought as she gave Dima a reluctant half embrace. *Why is he here so early? Doesn't he understand I have to prepare food for the party?*

Anna showed Dima to the living room where David and Katie were standing, and went back to the kitchen to continue working on appetizers. From time to time, she stuck her nose out of the kitchen to check on what was happening. Hopefully, Dima was going to be nice and friendly.

****

"Nice to meet you, Dima," David said respectfully as soon as the new guest walked in and extended his hand. "Welcome. You're Anna's friend from Ukraine, right?"

"Oh yes, we have known each other for ages." Dima shook David's hand with all of his force and smiled from ear to ear. "Anna probably told you, she and I were dating sometime back… Now we just hang out together. So to say. You know what I mean. Ha-ha-ha. No strings attached."

A shadow appeared on David's face, but he said nothing.

"Dima runs this super popular travel blog," Katie said quickly in order to slightly defuse the situation. "I read all of the articles, they are just so interesting."

"Yes, I travel all around the world," Dima said proudly. "This New Year's Eve, for example, I went to the lovely coastal city in Vietnam, Nha Trang. The hotel covered all my expenses, like always, in exchange for content on my blog. I wish Anna came with me. I invited her, but she was not ready to travel so far away, with her new job and all. Next year, Anna is definitely coming with me. The readers totally love reading about our adventures together. Anna and I do all kinds of crazy stuff. Maybe we could go sky diving or swim with the white sharks in South Africa. I will come up with something super cool."

David frowned and continued drinking his beer in silence.

Dima, however, seemed intent on continuing his attack. "So, David, what do you do?"

"I own an international consulting firm," David replied reluctantly.

"Your *own* firm? Now, this is something… Quite a shocker actually. You've done quite well for yourself, my friend! Looking at you, I would never guess that you were a brainiac or anything of that sort. And what types of services do you provide at your firm?"

"Various advisory services primarily to corporate clients. M&A, IT consulting, lots of different things. The majority of clients are within the U.S., but we also recently opened several offices overseas."

"Very interesting." Dima scratched his head. "M&A? The market was quite hot this past year."

"It sure was," David replied abruptly and demonstratively turned his back to Dima. "Katie, so Anna told me you're dating a guy who established a very promising new business, is this right?"

"Oh yes!" Katie said proudly, glancing at Dima in her peripheral. "My boyfriend, Nick, started the company *Fresh and Healthy*. It's going to revolutionize the food market. They are producing various food items with healthy natural ingredients and miraculous extracts which have been used for centuries by various tribes in Latin America. Nick's Dad is from Peru, and that's where he got all his ideas."

"Sounds cool."

"You bet! I hope you can meet Nick sometime, I wanted him to come with me tonight, but he had to travel to meet some prospective investors. They need to raise some money very quickly, as demand is growing, there is a huge buzz about their products—"

"Happy to meet Nick whenever he is back. Hope he finds some investors."

****

Sensing the tension building in the room, Anna stepped out of the kitchen and reappeared with a plate of cheeses and cold cuts. Dima was standing alone in the corner, frowning like an owl.

Right then, the rest of the guests arrived—Pablo and Ben together with Sausage, Rosie, Alex, Karen with his wife, Sirvat, Wendy with her husband Phil and daughter Mia, and a bunch of other people from work.

Mia had grown quite a bit since Anna saw her last at the Black Pearl Restaurant and she had gotten even cuter—a chubby little baby smiling widely at everyone. She was wearing a pretty little red ribbon in her blond hair and looked like such an angel. It seemed that nothing could ever upset her.

One more baby was in attendance this time. Another

co-worker, Mary Jones from the accounting department, brought her little son Sammy with her as she could not find a babysitter that evening. He started crying and refused to be put down even for even a second. Sammy also grimaced all the time, which made him look a little bit like a pug.

Anna was starting to wonder how she could possibly motivate Mary to go home. Every time they started a nice, relaxed conversation, Sammy would start screaming from behind, scaring everyone. A couple of times Sammy frightened Sausage so much that he crawled under the sofa and refused to come out.

Eventually, the situation resolved itself. Mary walked out of the door with a stinky Sammy, his diaper full, and everybody was finally able to relax. Sausage even abandoned his refuge under the sofa and was happily prancing around the room.

"When are your dogs supposed to arrive, Anna?" Ben asked, gently lifting Sausage up in his arms. "They were supposed to be here soon after the New Year, no? Sausage has been quite anxious to meet them."

"Oh, I forgot to tell you… There is going to be a bit of a delay," Anna said gloomily and shook her head. Lapa and Zirka again got themselves into a mess. They were unmatched experts in that.

"So, here's the deal. The pooches went to the dog park together with my grandma for a nice leisurely walk and—surprise, surprise—got into a big fight. This time with a rottweiler."

"Oh no!" Ben yelled in shock. "A rottweiler! This story isn't going to end well, is it?"

"No, it won't… The battle was short but fierce, and largely one-sided. Eventually the owners pulled the rottweiler away. Zirka did not get too hurt. She is a strong dog and a good fighter. She just lost some fur and had small bite marks in a few places. But poor Lapa suffered several deep wounds in her leg and side. Grandma had to take both dogs to the neighborhood vet. The prognosis was good, but travel for Lapa is now out of the question."

"So sorry to hear that." Ben patted Anna on the shoulder. "Hope Lapa gets well soon. How is your project, by the way? I remember you had a lot of challenges on your first trip."

"Well, the problems are still there unfortunately, but we'll try to get them resolved. Right, Karen?" Anna asked her team member who was standing close by.

"Of course!" Karen replied—even though his mouth was full of food.

Unlike Karen, Anna was worried. With all the excitement of the last weeks, she knew that she needed to start getting ready for her second trip to Africa. This next visit was necessary to get things moving. In just a month, Polaris management would be evaluating the performance of all this year's Global Associates and making decisions about who would be leaving the organization for good. Anna really needed to get the project on track.

The conversation ebbed and Anna went to catch up with Alex who she had not seen for a while. He was in really good spirits and had a lot of news to share. First, he finally heard about his application as the Special Assistant to Mr. Clark; he got the job! Second, their mutual friend Emily was moving to another department of Polaris and even more, to another country!

"Unbelievable!" exclaimed Anna. "I know how

much you wanted this job. Congratulations! But what is the deal with Emily? Where is she going?"

"Well," said Alex mysteriously. "*Something* happened. You remember that Emily was dating my buddy Jean, the French guy?"

"Yes, sure," Anna replied as calmly as she could manage. Alex was not aware of her crush on Jean from a while back. "So, what happened? Tell me!"

"A big scandal. That's what happened." Alex explained that apparently Jean and Emily were not together anymore. Emily had been caught making out with Jean's brother, Arnaud, by her *sister,* Lauren. Apparently, the thing between the two had been going on for a while.

"Oh, no!" Anna's eyes bulged. "Poor Lauren! I met her before, and she is a really nice girl. She does not deserve it. I believe she just recently got married to Jean's brother."

"Yes, that's right. They've been married for less than a year. I heard that Emily's father made some calls to Polaris management and got her a position in Saudi Arabia, to send her far away from Arnaud and Lauren, and calm the situation down. Lauren is pregnant! And Arnaud works for the Emerald Hotels & Resorts where Emily and Lauren's father is a big exec, so he has some leverage… That's what Jean told me."

"What a drama!" gasped Anna. "How is Jean holding up?"

"Oh, Jean seems fine. He handled it like a real gentleman. Now everything is over between them, of course. But let's talk about you. I understand that you have found your prince charming? You and David look like such a gorgeous couple. I hear he is very successful, too?"

"Oh yes, David is unbelievable. We are so much in love! I'm really lucky." Anna had been saying the same thing proudly over the last few weeks, but this time she did not quite believe her own words. It didn't sound right anymore.

Just a few minutes ago, David looked like the most handsome man she had ever seen. His dazzling smile was capable of illuminating the whole room. His body was so strong and muscular that Anna marveled at his tremendous athleticism and power. But now, when Anna glanced at him again, he appeared quite average, maybe even a little out of shape, his smile was weak, and his nose appeared too big. She must have been out of her mind!

Up to this moment, Anna was sure she had moved past her fascination with Jean. But maybe she still had some feelings for him…

"Hey, Anna, wake up! Are you daydreaming about David?" Alex asked with a smile. "He is right there."

Anna pretended to smile as well. "Oh yes, of course. He is always on my mind. I was just shocked about what happened to Emily…"

What a strange turn of events, Anna thought. Emily had been so happy in Washington and now she was moving away from her family and friends to a faraway country. Saudi Arabia was obviously a very wealthy country, but it had so many customs and traditions which might be hard for Westerners to follow. Especially for Emily who was always used to doing whatever she wanted.

The party began to wind down around ten and everyone started getting ready to depart. It had been snowing earlier and the temperature was in the high teens. The upcoming trip to hot and sunny Africa seemed more and more attractive to Anna in this weather.

In the end, just a couple of guests remained. Katie kept waiting around for Dima to give him a lift, as, being a visitor in town, he did not have a car. But for some strange reason, he kept hanging around and finding excuses why he could not leave yet. First Dima was "helping" Anna with the dishes, when in reality he was making more of a mess by spilling and dropping stuff on the floor. Then he got a big stain on his shirt and needed to get it out, then he received some email on his phone which he urgently needed to answer... Katie finally gave up waiting on him and left.

Dima hung around for at least another thirty minutes, seemingly waiting for his taxi which was very late. At last, Anna ordered a taxi for Dima herself in order to help expedite his departure.

"Thanks for coming, Dima, see you next time you are in Washington!" Anna yelled as Dima finally started dragging himself downstairs, after giving her a long and tender goodbye hug.

"Ugh, finally," Anna said to David, closing the door behind Dima and embracing David. "I thought he'd never leave. He is a super nice guy but, at times, it is really hard to get rid of him. So, how did you like all my friends? Obviously, you knew Katie very well from before, but how about others?"

David looked frustrated. "Yeah sure, everyone was nice. But I don't know about that Dima guy."

"Is anything wrong? I noticed that you did not get along very well. I could not understand what was the matter."

"It is obviously your choice, Anna, but it is really odd for you to hang out like that with your *ex*-boyfriend. He is clearly still into you."

"Oh, David, please!" Anna exclaimed. "Dima has been just a friend for many years. I have no idea why he was behaving like this today. Calling him an 'ex-boyfriend' is a real stretch. We went out a couple of times in high school, but those were not even dates in a true sense. We just went to the movies, that was all. I never had any romantic feelings for Dima and never will."

"Okay. Fine," David agreed reluctantly. "In this case, it's not a big deal. Just—be careful, please, on how you conduct yourself now that we are together. You are a very attractive woman, and a lot of guys would love to go out with you."

"Of course, David. I understand," Anna assured him. "I am so sorry if Dima made some strange comments tonight... You have absolutely nothing to worry about."

"Okay. So, tell me, how are the preparations coming for your trip to Africa?" David tried to change the subject.

"Well, everything seems ready," said Anna, happy that the hurricane had seemingly passed. "I am flying on the same flight with Karen and Fiona through Addis. We are leaving next Saturday morning, arriving in Dar on Sunday. I am staying at the Silver Moon Hotel this time. We plan to take a boat to Zanzibar on Monday morning to hopefully nail down the project. I'll get on video chat on Monday evening my time when I get back from Zanzibar and give you a full report. Then I have my tickets to go back to Washington for Friday night, so I will be home Saturday."

"Great, glad to hear that all the travel arrangements have been made. Please be careful. Don't get on any small boats, I hear they can sink in Africa. And definitely no small propeller planes."

"Oh, don't worry about that. The boat we take to Zanzibar is super luxurious and big. We will not take any small planes."

"Okay, good. We'll see each other next week and can talk more then. Let's go to some special restaurant of your choice, and I will take you to the airport on Saturday morning."

"I like the idea of the restaurant, but you do not need to take me to the airport," Anna said in protest. "I have to leave really early in the morning. You could sleep in. You have been working till midnight for so many days. You deserve some sleep."

"Don't worry about me," David said, starting to kiss Anna's neck and ears. "I could not let the love of my life get on a plane without getting one last good-bye from me. I'll be here at seven on Saturday and take you to the airport in style."

"Fine with me. I will miss you a lot. But I will be back in your arms quickly, and everything will be the same, just like today."

Chapter 18. When All Hope's Lost

Dar es Salaam, the United Republic of Tanzania

"So, how did it go?" David asked as soon as his face popped up on the screen.

"Disaster!" Anna yelled, almost about to bang her laptop against the wall. "This visit was even worse than the first one. Imagine: this morning, we went to Zanzibar to present the results of the assessment, and again, we did not encounter Albert. Rosemary showed up, of course, and told us that he was still sick. Last time, she had at least brought another colleague with her, Jennifer, who was quite nice and helpful. But this time, Rosemary just met us alone. It was such a useless meeting. Ten minutes, and she almost chased us out with a broom."

"Well, did Rosemary at least listen to the assessment you guys prepared?" David asked hopefully.

"No! She just sat in front of us with a blank stare and did not want to have anything to do with our project!" Anna rubbed her face in frustration. "I took the report out of my folder and suggested at least to present it to her—since we spent so much time on it, and came all the way from Washington—but she didn't feel like listening."

"I'm really sorry to hear that, baby," David said sadly. "I know you worked so hard. Can anything else be done?"

"Well, if we could find Albert and talk to him, there

would be some hope, but I do not think we are able to do that. At this point, I don't know if Albert even exists. Every time we called the Institute from Washington, we got Rosemary or her assistant who refused to put us through to Albert. I was hoping we would meet him if we came to Zanzibar again, but you see the result. I think it is all over for this project and my career at Polaris."

"I wish I could help you somehow."

"Nothing can be done now." Anna sat back in her chair and put away the folder she had been fiddling with. When she was first assigned the TIZ project, she had bought a scarlet-red folder and started filling it up with various relevant documents for her project: latest news articles about Tanzania and Zanzibar, overview of the economy and the largest companies, travel highlights, reports about different successful training schools. Anna proudly carried her fancy Tanzania folder all over the Polaris building as she was preparing the project. At one point, Teresa even commented how well-organized Anna was.

And now all of her research could be thrown right into the black trash can in the corner of her hotel room. That was exactly where it belonged. Next to the banana peel and the wrapper from the energy bar she had earlier.

"All in all, it was a fatal mistake to take on this project. Bernard had warned me, but I didn't listen," she bemoaned. "I will definitely not get confirmed in my position at Polaris. I should have never lied on the application… This job was never meant to be mine!"

"Wait. You—You *lied* on the job application?" David asked in a low voice.

"You got it-it… I-I had put on the application that I was the adviser to the Minister of Finance of Ukraine, and that is why they invited me to the interviews. Had they known I worked at the Chervona Ruta store, I would never have gotten a chance."

"One hundred percent agree with that," David said. "I had always wondered how you managed to get an interview with a top company like Polaris. It didn't make any sense. They don't hire anyone unless they have some extraordinary achievements in their career."

"Well, that's how… Believe me, I fully repented for what I did. I'll never do anything like this again. I worked really hard and I thought I deserved a second chance. But repentance is apparently not enough. I have to keep paying for my mistakes. And now, you see, I am about to lose this job anyway!"

"Anna, calm down," David begged.

"No, I do not want to calm down!" Anna continued yelling. "Pretty soon I will need to pack my things and leave Polaris. What am I going to do now? Go back to Ukraine, to my Uncle's Chervona Ruta store selling matches and tea kettles? It will be so humiliating!"

Anna imagined the mocking smiles of Baba Kateryna, Uncle Opanas, and everyone else in the market. *"Back already?"* Baba Kateryna would say in her nasty nasal voice, with a poisonous smile. *"I knew it was just a matter of time. These international companies just chew you up and spit you out. Typical Western mentality."* Anna's eyes burned with tears. She would never be able to wash the shame off. Everyone at the market would be perpetually reminding her about her unsuccessful attempt to build a career in the distant land of opportunity.

David gave Anna a look full of determination.

"Baby, I didn't want to talk about this on video chat,

but you leave me no choice. I wanted this to be done somewhere romantic, but… fine. I assure you, you'll never be forced back to Ukraine to work at your uncle's store. We'll get married and I'll take care of you no matter what. You can work with me at my firm or do anything you want. We have this luxury. We are rich, can't you see that?"

Little by little, Anna's face relaxed and her mouth curled into a smile. Of course, she had David now. She didn't have anything to worry about. "Thank you, my love. You are the only person who cares. I think I am feeling a bit better now. Losing this job is not the end of the world."

"Not at all," David said boldly. "It's just not a good fit. Being a project manager is really hard, so don't worry about it. In any event, would you actually want to spend your career working in Africa? It can't be a long-term thing, especially when we decide to start a family. There are too many risks… I'd ask you to leave Polaris myself in a year or two. At my company, we can put you in charge of public relations or something else like that, nothing too difficult. By the way, you planning to come home earlier now? Or still stay till the end of the week, as planned?"

"Well, I was thinking about leaving early… But Rosemary did mention that she would think about the project and contact me by the end of the week in case she changes her mind. I told her I was staying till Friday. Pretty sure she will not call but it might be worth taking this last chance. I could work on my final report on the project while I am here and maybe I could use the pool a little. It's a really scenic hotel and the weather here is in the nineties."

"Fantastic!" David nodded. "Finally, the glass is half full, not half empty. Just enjoy the things you can and don't worry about the rest. I'll be here waiting for you. Promise you, we'll do something epic when you get back. Anyways, it's getting late, we'll talk again tomorrow, okay?"

"Okay, David. Thank you. You always manage to calm me down. I love you."

"I love you too. Tomorrow will be a much better day. Good night."

The next morning, Anna woke up much more hopeful than she had been the night before. Maybe she rushed too quickly to those conclusions? It seemed too premature to think about leaving Polaris. There was still a good chance that Rosemary would change her mind, or that Albert would be found, or something else would happen, and the project would somehow be saved. Hopefully, all the other team members felt the same.

Anna met with her colleagues for breakfast at the hotel. They sat at the cozy table in the shade under the palm trees, drinking their coffee and enjoying the warm morning breeze.

A few minutes into the conversation, Anna realized that nobody else shared her optimism about the project.

"Okay, boss," Fiona said. "Let me be honest with you. I would love to stay here in this lovely green hotel waiting for Rosemary to change her mind, but I have a lot of other projects to attend to. In particular, the team working on the Ethiopia project needs me right now."

"Yes," Marcelo chimed in, as he was carefully spreading delicious cream cheese on his whole-wheat bagel. "I received an email from the team leader on the project in Ethiopia, too. They are in Addis right now, and they need my help urgently. Their project is on track to be approved next month, way ahead of schedule! I've heard that the project manager, Pietro, is one of the best at Polaris. I know that both Fiona and I committed to your project first and we will stay if needed, but our time could be used much better in Addis. I would love to be part of an award-winning team."

"I understand," Anna said sadly. Her project wasn't going to win any award. Quite the opposite. And the lovely assistant Jennifer was no longer around to motivate Marcelo. "I certainly cannot hold you hostage. Please go to Addis. How about you, Karen? Would you like to stay? Rosemary might still call us."

"Well, I don't have a particular project to go to, but… I don't think anything will happen here." Karen was hiding his eyes. "Sorry, Anna, I wish I could be more positive, but things sure look bleak. You know, my boys in Washington would really appreciate if their dad came back a bit early. They have an important hockey game with a rival team coming up."

"I see. Family is equally important. Then why don't all of you call the travel agency and change your tickets? I'll stay here by myself, just in case the project can be rescued by some miracle."

****

After a short flight, Jean landed in Nairobi and immediately proceeded to the airport lounge. He'd been there many times. Jean first wandered around the lounge, which had several rooms and hallways, just in case somebody from Polaris happened to be sitting there. It was kind of boring on his own. Nairobi was a big hub for Polaris, and many of his colleagues flew in and out of this city on any given day.

Not spotting any familiar faces, Jean picked a table by the window and got himself a soda.

Time to start working on my back-to-office report. Jean pulled out his laptop. It was always good to get a head-start on the report, while the memories of the trip were still fresh.

"Hello." A short and stocky man approached him and stood right by his table. "It seems like you are from Polaris as well? We have met before I believe... I am Karen Kalpanian from the education department. Sorry, I forgot your name."

Jean looked up and smiled widely. "Bonjour! Indeed, we have met, not sure where though. My name is Jean Rolland, I work in the West Africa department. How nice of you to stop by Karen! I would love some company. Feel free to join me."

Karen pulled in a chair. Jean was in luck. Now he had a companion and did not have to sit alone for four hours.

"So, Jean, where are you heading now?"

"Flying back to Washington, but I'm planning to stop in Paris for a week to see my mom and sister. Just finished a very interesting economic conference in Kigali, Rwanda on Monday. You might have heard about it. It's on the future of Africa."

"Oh yes, it's an annual one, right? I think a lot of the heads of African states come to that one."

"Correct. Rwanda has made this conference into 'the event' of the year in Africa. All the big shots are there. I was on the panel for early childhood education presenting our experience in Sierra Leone."

"Oh right, you are the team leader for the Sierra Leone project," Karen said excitedly. "I heard so much about it! Great work."

"Thanks so much. How about you? Where are you coming from?"

"Dar es Salaam, Tanzania. I was just there for a project which regrettably did not work out. We were supposed to stay for a week in order to discuss the details, but it looks like it's all over now. So, I left early and am hoping to give my twin sons a huge surprise when I show up for their hockey game."

"Tanzania?" Jean asked dreamily. "My favorite country in Africa. I wish I had known about your project earlier. Maybe I could have helped. I lived in Tanzania for several years. Oh well, it seems too late now… Sounds so exciting about your twins. How old are the boys?"

"Eleven. Tigran and Artur. They are my greatest pride. How about you, do you have any kids?"

"Ha-ha, not yet, although I adore kids." Jean laughed. "I do not even have a girlfriend. I have not had good luck with girls, to tell you the truth. About a year ago I invited the girl I really liked on a date, but she just disappeared on me. No good-bye or anything. Then the one I was dating recently cheated on me."

"With your looks, girls should be all over you!" Karen exclaimed, while patting Jean on the shoulder. "You are probably choosing the wrong girls. Look at me—I am no movie star to say the least and I have dated a lot of lovely women before settling down… I am sure the tide will turn soon and you will find a great girl."

"I hope so too." Jean sighed. "For now, it is just me."

"I am going to get myself something sweet to eat," Karen said. "Do you want something from the buffet?"

"No, thanks. I am fine. Still have my soda and a

couple of snacks," Jean replied, pointing at his plate. All this time, he had been trying to place Karen. Where had he seen him? Jean was always so good with faces, and he just could not stand it that he was not able to remember from where he knew Karen. They clearly did not work on the same projects and they did not meet at any parties. Where did they meet then?

Suddenly, an alarm went off. Karen was the guy with Anna when they met at Polaris that first day back to the office! Maybe he had some news about Anna and what she had been up to?

After breaking up with Emily, Jean had made a weak attempt to contact Anna through a happy new year message, as he just could not think of anything better. After Anna walked out on him following the interviews, the last thing he wanted was to put pressure on her and end up receiving a restraining order.

Yet, he couldn't help but feel incredibly drawn to Anna ever since he first laid his eyes on her. He didn't want to give up yet. But he needed to take it slow. Maybe someday she'd become interested in him. He surely wanted to try. The Ukrainian girl was worth all the time in the world.

Karen came back with a big plate of desserts and a cup of coffee.

"They have some good sweets here," he announced. "I got some banana bread, a chocolate cake, chocolate chip cookies, and even some ice cream. I think this is enough for now. Feel free to share."

"Thanks," Jean said, watching Karen carefully arranging all of the food on the table. Now was a good opportunity to sneak in a question about Anna. He needed to sound very casual in order to not look like an idiot in front of Karen. "By the way... I wanted to ask you. You are friends with Anna Levenko, right? How's she doing?"

"Anna? Yes, for sure. We were just in Dar es Salaam together. She is the team leader for this project which failed. She is still there, waiting at the Silver Moon Hotel, poor thing, hoping that the client will call her and agree to another meeting. She is staying till Friday night. But it is completely hopeless, I can assure you. That's why I left."

"I had no idea!" Jean exclaimed. "If she fails the project, she will not receive a full-time contract at Polaris."

"Yes, that's right," Karen said, putting half a slice of the chocolate cake in his mouth and rolling his eyes up in total delight. "I think it is her first and last project at Polaris. Unfortunately, nothing can be done. We tried everything, believe me! The client does not want to work with us, they want to leave the institute as it is now."

Karen continued enjoying his chocolate cake while Jean quietly sat for a few minutes, thinking. Clearly something could be done. Anna's career could not come to an end like this. It wasn't fair. Working at Polaris was her dream, and she was a perfect fit for the company. She just happened to pick the wrong project. She needed a second chance.

Jean left Karen to enjoy his sweets and quickly walked up to the front desk of the lounge where a smiling Kenyan lady in a bright red uniform was standing.

"Good afternoon. I wanted to check at what time the flight to Dar es Salaam is leaving? And are there any seats?"

The receptionist looked the flight up in her

computer.

"In forty-five minutes. Yes, there are plenty of seats. Would you like me to change your reservation, Mr. Rolland?"

"Yes, please. And I will depart from there on Friday evening to go to Paris and after that to Washington? You can just use my miles for the extra ticket."

The lady made a few clicks.

"Done. Here is your new boarding pass. You must hurry, sir, they just announced boarding."

Jean ran back to his table and grabbed his carry-on bag and his backpack. Luckily, he never checked any luggage. One never knew what could happen, like in this particular case.

"I just had a change of plans," Jean quickly explained to Karen. "I have a different flight to catch. I won't be going to Paris right now. Hope we'll see each other when we are in Washington. *Au revoir*!"

Jean reached the Silver Moon Hotel at around six thirty pm and checked in easily—the hotel had plenty of vacant rooms. After dropping off his luggage, Jean went in search of Anna. He had visited this hotel in the past, so he was pretty familiar with its facilities. The Silver Moon was a small and cozy two-storied hotel immersed in the greenery of bougainvillea, sugar cane, and palm trees. They did not have much of a lobby, so patrons usually stayed either in the garden, by the pool, or in their rooms. Nothing had changed since he was here last.

As soon as Jean walked into the garden, he saw a lonely figure sitting at one of the tables under a big sugar cane bush, working at a laptop. *It was really easy to find her*, Jean thought to himself, as he approached Anna. She looked cute in her casual T-shirt, shorts and flip-flops, her hair up in a high ponytail.

"*Bonsoir*," Jean said, as he slowly walked up to Anna's table.

****

Anna heard the familiar French accent and looked up in disbelief. She was definitely not expecting to see anyone from work at the Silver Moon Hotel, much less Jean. What was he doing here?

"Jean! Are you staying here as well? I did not see you earlier," Anna said warmly, trying to hide her frustration. Had her project been successful, it would have been so nice to tell Jean about it and try to impress him with it! But all she accomplished was wasting her and her team's time and Polaris funds. She was by far the worst in their Global Associate class.

"Yes, I just arrived today," Jean replied. "Had some business in the area, but now it is all finished... How have you been? I ran into Karen and he told me your project had some problems. Anything I can help with?"

"Oh, I don't think so." Anna shook her head. The last thing she needed was to drag Jean into her failed project. She needed to figure it out herself. "All my team left. I decided to stay. You know, when I used to play junior tennis, I was told to fight until the last ball. So that's what I am doing right now. But so far, I have no new ideas and no miracle has happened."

"Well, why do you not just tell me everything about your project?" Jean suggested, sitting down at the chair next to Anna. "I have some time. Maybe we can come up with something and create our own miracle."

Anna looked at Jean skeptically. What could he possibly do in this situation? Anna would have declined the offer of help from anyone else, but for some reason she was not able to do it with Jean. His gentle look, his sweet smile, his soft voice mesmerized her all over again… She just could not say no.

"Okay, let me tell you how it all started and where we are," Anna finally said. "Back in September we had a staff meeting and John, my manager, suggested that I take on the project to renovate a tourism institute in Zanzibar—"

Chapter 19. The Perfect Getaway

Dar es Salaam, the United Republic of Tanzania

"Okay. I understand the problem we are facing." Jean picked up Anna's Tanzania folder and started browsing through it, carefully studying every page. "Now let's think who we can possibly know from Zanzibar, who would be able to help us? Rosemary clearly has her own agenda. For some reason, she does not want Polaris to partner with TIZ. We need to find somebody in the position of influence who can lead us to her superiors."

Anna nodded in agreement. "That's exactly what I was thinking about as well. We have to get around Rosemary and speak directly to Albert. But I don't know anybody in Tanzania yet. I've met a few people here and there, but nobody who could help.—"

"Aha," Jean suddenly exclaimed, as he spotted the article in Anna's folder about the Dogani Group establishing a new state of the art milling plant. "Anna, you're a genius!"

"Me? Why?" Anna shrugged.

"And you're asking why! Of course, *Said Dogani* is from Zanzibar."

Anna leaned in. "Dogani Group? Yes, I found a lot of articles about them all over the Internet. They are a huge conglomerate here in Tanzania. I'm sure they're very influential, but so what? We don't know anyone there."

Jean was beaming. "Believe it or not, I happen to know Mr. Dogani, their founder and chairman! As you might imagine, a lot of these top industrialists are very cognizant about their corporate social responsibility and have implemented various initiatives to improve the lives of the people. In Mr. Dogani's case, he is on a crusade to fight against malaria. It is a huge issue here. Our NGO worked with him to help implement a robust malaria prevention program for all the employees of the conglomerate and best practices. I was the team leader of that project. They are also now using a much better drug to treat malaria, so if people do get it, they recover quicker. Let me try to call him and see if he has some suggestions. Obviously, he will not deal with the issue himself, but he will tell me who to contact."

Jean dialed the number; the call was picked up immediately. Anna listened as Jean first explained the situation and then watched him nodding and taking some notes. After Jean hung up, he immediately dialed another number. Once the calls were over, Jean looked at Anna with a huge smile.

"Okay, this is going to be easier than I thought. You just need to know the right people, and everything becomes clear as day. Mr. Dogani apparently was aware about the situation at the Institute as he has been involved in various tourism initiatives in the country. That guy, Albert, the head of TIZ you have been trying to locate, is not sick and has never been sick. I just talked to him. Mr. Dogani gave me his number. Albert never even knew that the Polaris team requested a meeting with him. Apparently, Rosemary was playing some games with you and not telling him about your visits. Anyway, Albert is away at a tourism conference in Arusha, but he will be back to Zanzibar on Thursday and I set up a time to meet him. He is excited about the opportunity to partner with Polaris and hear our suggestions about the improvements at the Institute."

Instantly, a wave of happiness enveloped Anna's heart. Her project now had a chance! She might be able to keep her job after all! But... her team was gone. All her team members were so experienced in their field of work. She was a complete novice compared to them.

"You have nothing to worry about," Jean comforted her, as if he could read her thoughts. "You might be new to Polaris, but I know you're very smart and perfectly capable of handling an important meeting like this on your own. You have the assessment of the institute, that's all you need. I'll go to the meeting with you and help out if needed."

"Fantastic. Thank you so much!" Anna clapped her hands.

"Okay, now that we have a free day tomorrow, waiting for Albert to return, I'll take you around Dar es Salaam, if you don't mind."

Anna looked at Jean hesitantly. It was better not to accept. Being alone with Jean would be really awkward and could cause her more heartbreak. For Jean, who was just looking to kill some time, this would be a simple sightseeing trip, but not for her... She'd be reminded of all the what-ifs and could-have-beens between them.

"I think it's better to just go to our satellite office and work from there tomorrow," she said finally, covering her face so that Jean would not discern the blush burning across her cheeks.

"Oh, don't worry! In the several months that I have by now spent at Polaris, I have learned that all they care about are results. Believe me, you will work plenty of late nights and weekends. But if there is a chance like this, while we are waiting for the client, you need to take it to learn more about the country. This will help you prepare a better project in the end."

"Okay… I guess we can go tomorrow," Anna finally conceded, having run out of excuses. She would just need to be careful and control her feelings in order to not make a fool out of herself. This would be just a short day trip between two Polaris co-workers. A team-building trip, so to say. Nothing more.

****

Jean rented a car and drove them to Slipway—a prominent shopping, leisure, and dining destination in Dar es Salaam. It boasted a supermarket, a big market with various local crafts, several cafes, a travel agency, a children's playground, as well as the boat station from which one could take various trips to neighboring islands.

Anna and Jean headed for Bongoyo—an uninhabited island just forty-five minutes away, supposedly one of the best day trips in Dar es Salaam area. The first departure for the island was at nine thirty am each day, and Jean said it was essential to get on the first boat.

"There are not that many umbrellas on the island and, since they are all free, they all get taken by the people from the first boat. Everyone stays till the evening, so those who arrive later do not get much sun protection and I'm warning you, it gets super-hot there this time of the year. I don't care much about the heat, but you definitely need a big umbrella, or you will roast."

Tickets purchased, Anna and Jean approached the pier and checked out their boat. Anna had imagined that they would be going on a magnificent top-notch liner like the one she had taken to Zanzibar. But that sure wasn't the case. The boat they were taking looked very small and quite ancient, and in a great need of a paint job.

Anna hesitantly walked up onto the vessel, holding Jean's hand, and found a spot on the bench in the shade. To Anna, this definitely did not look like a safe boat, but the island was probably not that far. Maybe even a boat like this could make it.

In the worst-case scenario, Anna was a good swimmer and there were even some life jackets laying around. Hopefully, it would not come down to swimming in the middle of the ocean.

As Anna was contemplating her chances to stay alive, Jean did not seem to share her worries. He was in a great mood. As soon as he got on the boat, he gave a big hug to the captain and warmly greeted him in Swahili. "*Jambo*! Good to see you again, George!"

"Jean! You are back… and with a pretty girlfriend," the captain said with a smile. He was a tall guy in his mid-forties. "Hey, Deo, look who is here!" he yelled at one of the sailors. The guys gathered around Jean, really happy to see him. Anna heard him tell them about his great time in Sierra Leone.

After greeting everyone, Jean turned to Anna. "I have taken this boat with George many times when I lived in Dar a while back. He will take great care of us here."

It was now about ten minutes before departure, and other tourists started getting onto the boat. In the end, there were about fifteen passengers—a few couples, some single travelers and one family with two kids. That was reassuring. At least other people were willing to try this boat and some even brought their kids.

Finally, the trip began, and Anna got a bit distracted by the spectacular landscape. The Indian Ocean was gorgeous, with its bright and clear turquoise waters, and they were passing a lot of different, interesting vessels. Some of them were ordinary boats and yachts which Anna was used to seeing in the States, but others had triangular lateen sails and sharp bows. These boats were both big and small, and some were tiny with just one fisherman sitting in them.

"These are called *dhow* boats," Jean said, pointing at a few of the traditional vessels sailing by. "It is a typical East African boat. In the past, merchants were traveling in such boats all the way to and from India carrying all kinds of heavy items—fruit, water, different merchandise—"

"I love these," she interrupted with excitement. "They are so beautiful and romantic. They look like the vessels from fairy tales."

By now, Anna was no longer scared; she even got up and walked around the boat, enjoying the scenery around her. The boat was moving at a good speed and would be reaching the destination in no time.

Anna tried not to look at Jean but eventually she could not help taking a peek at him sitting on the bench, totally in his element, relaxed with his blond hair flowing in the wind. He took his T-shirt off, and Anna was able to see he had a deep tan and was muscular—maybe a couple of inches shorter than David and also thinner.

How would David carry himself in Tanzania? Anna

laughed at the mere thought of having David on this boat. Of course, he would never set his foot on it and never in a million years allow Anna to take it. David would also never be saying "jambo" and embracing the captain. It was hilarious even to imagine that.

In fact, Anna could not even tell David she went on this day trip. David belonged in his glass house in D.C. and at holiday destinations like Jekyll Island, Miami, Nice, Venice, and the like. *Well, David does not need to know anything about today. No point in worrying him unnecessarily. It is just one trip.*

The boat finally got to Bongoyo island and everyone was safely transported to the shore. Anna and Jean settled in the shade under a nice umbrella. It was now time to go explore the island.

"I bought two snorkeling masks at the hotel shop last night," said Jean, handing one of them to Anna. "I figured these will be very handy. You can spot a lot of coral and many colorful fish in the water. Let's go!" And with that, Jean dove right in with a big splash.

Anna smiled and followed Jean with a lingering gaze. She spent a minute standing in the warm water, listening to the subtle sound of waves gently touching the shore, just savoring the moment. Up till today, she had only been to the Black Sea, which was quite lovely, but certainly not nearly as striking as the Indian Ocean in front of her. Hands down, this was the most impressive body of water she had ever seen.

So this is what paradise looks like—golden sand, robin's egg blue sky, and shiny turquoise water? Anna put on her snorkeling mask and submerged into the crystal-clear ocean which quickly enveloped her like a soft warm blanket. She immediately spotted a school of colorful fish passing by, as well as coral of all shapes and sizes. A bunch of starfish also quickly caught her eye. They looked like lovely red flowers growing on the bottom of the ocean.

"Can the starfish move, or do they just stay in the same place?" Anna asked Jean, who was snorkeling nearby.

"Oh, these guys move quite fast, when they want to," Jean explained. "They have tiny little feet on each of their arms… Once I saw a starfish laying next to one of these beach umbrellas. I was wondering if I should take it into the water, but it crawled there by itself in no time."

Jean later took Anna on a walk around the island, which had quite a few interesting birds and lizards. Then they had a seafood lunch in the island's café.

The fresh seafood was simply exquisite—huge shrimp, juicy lobsters, and kingfish, grilled to perfection and nicely arranged all together on a big platter. Jean took a few selfies of them sitting at the wooden benches, smiling widely, and chomping at the delicious food.

"Give me your phone number," said Jean. "I will send you these pictures and also a few others I took at the beach and around the island. This way, you can have them too."

"Thanks so much, this is a great idea!" Anna quickly received and downloaded all the photos. Such wonderful memories of this fun day.

Still smiling, she said, "This café is simply outstanding. Who'd think that one would get such a treat on a small island like this?"

"The food here varies from day to day. As you can probably tell, they just bring the locals by boat every day for cooking food at the café. The locals don't stay overnight. Depending on what the catch of the day is, they come up with the menu. I think we are really lucky today!"

"This place is a total paradise for me," Anna said. "I wish they had a hotel on this island, I would stay here and never want to leave."

"I feel the same. I think they like keeping this place uninhabited because otherwise all of this peace and tranquility would be ruined. People would take away all these shells and probably scare the fish and the animals away. For now nobody stays here overnight. Whenever people come, it is only for a few hours and sort of 'supervised' by the locals. When I used to live in Dar es Salaam, I would come here almost every weekend. I would just lay here on the beach with some adventure book and not worry about a thing."

Anna looked at Jean and thought to herself how similar they were and how easy it was to talk to him. David would have gotten tired of this place pretty quickly, even if he managed to make it here in some upscale boat. Generally, David did not like the heat too much and rarely was out in the sun.

"How long did you live in Dar es Salaam?" asked Anna.

"Three years, with my previous NGO. I joined right out of grad school and my position was based here in Dar. It was my first time living in Africa. Later they moved me to work in North Africa. That was great as well, although I must say no country compares with Tanzania for me. It is such a gem. My heart is here."

"You are so lucky," Anna said with envy. "I wish I were able to live in Africa as well. I would travel all over the place and see everything. It is a totally amazing continent."

"Well, you never know, maybe you will get stationed in Africa at some point in your career. A lot of international staff take assignments here, and Tanzania is definitely one of the best places."

Anna shook her head. If she were to continue dating David, it would definitely not be a possibility. Moving here would be completely out of the question. She doubted he would ever even go with her for a week, much less for a year or more. He was just a completely different person. Not that it was bad, they did not have to be the same, but it limited her options to explore and experience new things.

"Tonight I am going to have dinner with one of my old buddies here, Jack Carter. He was my neighbor when I lived here. He works for the U.S. Embassy. He and his wife, Barbara, invited me over. Do you want to come with me and see how expats live here?" asked Jean.

"Oh, I don't know. Do you think they wouldn't mind?"

"Of course not. They love to have guests. I had mentioned that I might bring somebody. So they are for sure expecting both of us. We will go there after we get back."

****

The dinner at Jack Carter's house was set for eight o'clock. He lived to the north from the city center, in an area romantically called Oyster Bay—one of the areas where most expats resided in Dar es Salaam. Compared to the rest of the city, it was quieter, with many bungalows available. In order to cater to the taste of the foreign residents, the area also had upscale hairdresser salons, stores, restaurants, pharmacies, and hotels.

Jack Carter and his family lived in a three-storied, snow-white villa covered with pink and purple bougainvillea vines. Their house was five minutes away from Coco Beach, one of the most popular beaches in Dar es Salaam. The house had a large luxurious garden around it with several flame trees covered by dashing red flowers, as well as a diamond-shaped outdoor pool with clear blue water. Even from the first brief look, it was clear that this was a true paradise for its residents.

Anna met Jack and Barbara as well as their two children—Bianca and Noah who were ten and eight years old respectively. The family had been in Oyster Bay for four years already and were content to stay.

"Jean, your girlfriend is really pretty," said Bianca.

"Yes, with such beautiful wavy hair!" Noah said.

"Thank you. You two are such angels."

"Not at all," said Barbara. "You will not believe what trouble these kids almost got us into about six months ago. Want to hear more?"

"Yes, absolutely," Anna and Jean said simultaneously.

"So, Jack was turning forty and we decided to organize a birthday party for him, invite people from the embassy and various other friends we have here. We had not hosted a party like that before. The kids were a little overwhelmed, but we figured, what can possibly happen?"

Anna and Jean shared a look, both thinking the same thing.

"Anyway, the day of the party comes and we find out that at least fifty people will be at our party, even the Ambassador is attending. He shows up with his wife, a very attractive lady named Stella. Her blond hair is in a stunning up-do. She wears this ultra-expensive, bright blue silk dress from some big-name designer which she just bought at a Paris fashion show, lots of big diamonds everywhere, and she is the life of the party as she chats with everyone."

Bianca screeched as she ran past the party before disappearing into a room. Barbara shook her head before continuing, "As Stella walks around the house, I kind of notice that the kids are following and staring at her a bit too much, but I do not pay attention to it. Maybe they like the shiny diamonds, who knows, we have never had such stylish ladies in the house."

She leaned in, her eyes expressive. "Then time comes to sit down at the table and Stella ends up sitting next to Bianca. Stella is very nice and turns to Bianca and starts talking to her. Bianca keeps listening to everything Stella says with an open mouth, without paying much attention to other stuff, and eventually gets so distracted that she spills her glass of cranberry juice all over Stella's dress. A good brother, Noah rushes over to help while holding a huge tuna salad sandwich in his hand, but then trips and the sandwich also ends up on Stella's dress.

Both Anna and Jean burst out laughing. This must have been a hilarious scene.

"So, what happened next?"

"Well, Stella froze with her mouth open. Jack thought he was going to lose his job and pay his annual salary to cover the damage to Stella's dress. I wanted to sink into the ground so that nobody would ever find me. Then, luckily, Stella laughed it off, and so did everyone else at the table. We brushed her off and gave her a shawl to cover up. I think Stella was just a very nice lady who liked kids, and she ended up not making a big deal out of it. We were really lucky. But every time we have some guests over, I always get nervous as I remember the incident. You never know what these wonderful kids will come up with."

The hosts then took Anna on the tour of the house and the garden.

"This is such a fantastic house!" exclaimed Anna. "Jean, did you live in a similar one as well?"

"Yes, almost identical, it was a few houses down the street. A Norwegian family rented it after I left. The real estate in Oyster Bay is in high demand with all the expats coming to Tanzania."

"Absolutely," Jack said, chiming in. "If you work in Africa, Tanzania is definitely one of the best places to be. It is safe, has nice friendly people, great beaches, and various animal reserves, like the Serengeti. Have you been yet, Anna?"

"Oh, not yet," said Anna. "It is just my second time in Tanzania, and I have not had much time to travel around yet. I have been working on this challenging project… But I have already been to Bongoyo island— Jean took me earlier today—and Zanzibar. So, I am slowly learning."

"Yes, getting projects done here in Tanzania is not always easy. Requires a lot of patience and perseverance. But I am sure eventually you will get it right," said Jack. "Luckily, you have Jean to help you. He has worked here enough and knows how to approach different people."

The dinner was served on the rooftop, which had a nice area with a table and chairs. It was pleasant sitting there on a nice warm evening.

"The food is excellent," Anna said as she ate all the

grilled seafood and various local delicacies. "Barbara, you are an amazing cook!"

"Ha-ha," laughed Barbara. "I wish this were true. I am actually one of the worst cooks you can find. All of this feast was prepared by our lovely Farida," she said, pointing at a young lady serving the food. "This is one of the reasons we do not ever want to leave Dar es Salaam. What would we do without Farida?"

As Anna and Jean were heading to the hotel, Anna couldn't help but imagine a life in Tanzania. She could also have a bungalow like the Carters, and she would go to the beach every weekend. It would be like a dream come true.

Chapter 20. The Brightest Star of Zanzibar

Zanzibar, the United Republic of Tanzania

Jean booked them on a Tanzanian airline the following day. Anna had never flown in a small airplane before.

"Are you sure we are not going to fall down from the sky?" she asked cautiously.

"Definitely not." Jean laughed. "This is a twin-engine turboprop, a very safe airplane. I've flown this airline many times and they have excellent pilots. I promise that someday I'll fly you to some fancy place myself, but this time we will have to take a commercial airline."

"Fly me yourself? You, what, can fly an airplane?" Anna could not believe it—this guy could also fly airplanes, in addition to everything else? Somehow none of her other friends mastered such a skill.

"Yes, I can, it is not a big deal," Jean replied modestly. "It's just a hobby. I got my license when I was twenty-three. Do you know that the Dutch king, for example, is a guest pilot of the Dutch airline? He obviously has plenty of other things to do, but he has a pilot's license and likes to practice from time to time."

"Okay," Anna said. "If you think it is fine, then it definitely is."

The flight was as easy as Jean said, and the female

pilot got her passengers to Zanzibar quickly and efficiently. Now it was time for the visit to the TIZ.

"Third time's the charm," Anna whispered.

As soon as Anna and Jean walked into the building of the TIZ, it was evident that the tide had changed. Albert, a tall Tanzanian man in his early forties who was very soft spoken and highly knowledgeable in the field of education, was standing at the entrance to welcome them.

The meeting was arranged in a spacious and well lit conference room—who knew there was one like that at TIZ?—and about fifteen staff from the Institute joined. Everyone was smiling, except for Rosemary who sat in the corner with her arms crossed over her chest.

If the first two encounters lasted for a mere thirty minutes each, this time the meeting took pretty much the whole day. Albert was very interested in the assessment of the TIZ, which of course had never reached him, and he requested a detailed presentation. He was also curious about the report on other tourism institutes which Anna's team prepared, and listened with a lot of attention to the description of schools in Hong Kong, Kenya, and Switzerland. Albert was particularly fascinated by the world-famous tourism institute in Hong Kong—HTI.

"HTI started out with just a few programs," Anna explained, "but over the years they added more and now have a really wide range of degree and certificate programs. Some of these are pretty cool, I would love to get one of those myself—certificates in sushi preparation, European pastry, Hong Kong savory snacks."

"These are some of the mouth-watering certificates," Albert said with a smile. "By the way, I think it is time for lunch. Our team has ordered a buffet lunch for everyone. It will be here in a moment. We unfortunately will not be able to offer sushi or Hong Kong savory snacks, but plenty of East African delicacies."

"This is perfectly fine with us." Anna laughed. "Cannot wait to try those. Pretty soon you can start offering certificates in East African cuisine, I am sure there will be many takers!"

The lunch arrived in no time and everybody enjoyed all the great Tanzanian dishes—flatbread called *chapati*, *pilau kuku* (rice with chicken), *mshikaki* (marinated beef), some green peas and beans, fried plantains, as well as *samosas*—fried pastries with beef and lentil fillings.

"My absolute favorites are samosas," Anna said, rubbing her belly. "Next time I am here, I will get a TIZ certificate in samosa preparation."

"I will be right there with you," said Jean. "These are so delicious. I'd love to be able to prepare them at home."

After lunch, the discussion shifted to the topic of hotels for training purposes. Albert aspired for the Grand Peacock Hotel to eventually become a three or even four-star hotel which would be able to offer luxurious rooms to the best tourists on the island.

"Yes, this is what we should aim for," agreed Anna. "We should try to build the Grand Peacock into something like the T Hotel in Hong Kong. This is a hotel managed by HTI students, and it has been consistently winning awards."

"Believe it or not, I stayed there a few years back," Jean said. "I was in Hong Kong for a conference and my brother who is an executive at the Emerald Hotels &

Resorts and knows the hospitality industry quite well recommended the T Hotel. It was an unbelievable experience. I am sure that the Grand Peacock can one day reach the same standards. Soon enough, TIZ graduates will be working in all the premier hotels here on Zanzibar, catalyzing the development of the tourism industry here."

Albert smiled and then paused for a second. "The only unknown which remains is the oil and gas exploration. You might have heard, large deposits of oil and gas have been discovered in both mainland Tanzania and Zanzibar archipelago."

Jean nodded. "I'm well aware. Petroleum exploration and tourism don't usually mix well. Let's hope that any energy companies selected to work here will have very high standards, apply the latest technologies to minimize impact on the ecosystem, and also that the local government puts the environment first."

"That would be ideal," Albert said. "But I don't trust our leaders. The other day, I saw a big foreign delegation marching into the Malekano mansion. I thought it was rather odd."

"*Malekano* mansion? What is that?" Anna asked, her ears perked up, after hearing such a familiar name.

"Oh, the Malekano family is one of the wealthiest families here in Zanzibar," Albert explained. "They are famous all over Africa and beyond. They own a big conglomerate and also play an important role in Tanzania's politics. Several family members occupy key government posts. They have a historical family mansion overlooking the Indian Ocean here on the island, in addition to a dozen luxurious homes all over the world. It's a very ancient, elite family."

How strange, Anna thought to herself. Of course, Malekano was the last name of her late grandfather. It probably didn't mean anything—it was just a popular name here in Africa—but it was still worth keeping in mind. They could be very distant relatives.

"Do you think the delegation was here because of the oil and gas?" Jean asked Albert.

Albert nodded. "That's my theory. I can guarantee you they weren't here on vacation. Such a large delegation would only come if they smelled some big money. Will they take good care of our environment? I do not know… Can I make one suggestion?"

"Of course," Anna said.

"Let's make the Grand Peacock Hotel the 'greenest,' most sustainable hotel in the world. Since we will be renovating all the TIZ buildings, it would be a great opportunity to implement green practices. Other hotels in Zanzibar could later follow our example, making the hospitality sector of Zanzibar the greenest in Africa. We will not only help to improve the environment, but also attract more tourists to Zanzibar."

"I think my manager John will be delighted about this idea." Anna shot Albert her brightest smile. "I have no doubt we will have financing for TIZ approved. Polaris and TIZ will be excellent partners."

****

"We did it!" Anna exclaimed as they were walking out of the TIZ. "I cannot believe that after all that happened, we managed to get the project back on track. And all thanks to you, Jean!"

"Well, you did the lion's share of the work," Jean said modestly. "I just helped you to connect the dots, so to speak. It's all your achievement in the end."

"When I get back to Washington, I will definitely stop by and tell Teresa Jameson about the project," Anna said proudly. "You probably know her, she is a Chief Economist of Polaris. She has been my mentor. I am sure she'd be delighted to hear the news. She is aware of the problems I needed to overcome...Oh, Jean! I just thought about it. We missed our flight, right? Is there a later one?! Or maybe we can take a boat back?"

"Unfortunately, the ferry does not operate this late, and there are no more flights either. We'll have to stay on the island tonight. Don't worry, we'll just pick up our luggage in Dar es Salaam tomorrow morning and fly home. I think it's even better that we are staying in Zanzibar tonight. It will be a special treat. We need to celebrate!"

Jean suggested that they stay at a boutique hotel, which was just a short ride away. This turned out to be a lovely hotel decorated in Swahili style, with its interior and exterior spaces reflecting the cultural influences of the sultans of Zanzibar.

"Let's meet for dinner at the terrace restaurant at six," Jean suggested after they'd finished checking in.

"Seems a bit early for dinner?" Anna asked, as she was savoring delicious amber-yellow passion juice in a tall glass which the receptionist handed to her a moment ago. Just one of the many signs of incredible African hospitality.

"Well, I want to make sure you see the gorgeous sunset from the terrace, that's all. You cannot miss it! It gets dark pretty quickly here. We can start with some appetizers and then ease into the main course."

Right at six o'clock, Anna appeared at the rooftop

terrace and leaned against the fence, stunned by the view. The Indian Ocean was right in front of her—limitless, majestic, and everlasting, with turquoise waves crawling gently to the shore. The heat of the day finally started fading and a light cool breeze was caressing her shoulders.

"This is such a gorgeous view," Anna said as Jean approached her.

"It truly is," Jean said with a smile as they walked to their table and sat down. "I think we're so lucky to be working in international development and visiting places which other people will never see."

"Of course. I'm so happy work took me to Africa. I've never told you, but my grandfather was actually African. It's a very rare thing in Ukraine, so our family never spoke of it."

"Really! I'd never be able to tell that you hold African blood in you. I am sure the features of your face hold a little bit of your grandfather in them. That is why it turned out so incredibly gorgeous."

Anna blushed at Jean's compliment. "Yeah, amazing, right? Unfortunately, I never met my grandfather. He passed away when my mom was little. Imagine—we know nothing about his family, not even which country he was from."

"You must look for your grandfather's family," Jean said confidently. "Now that you work in Africa, you can do it more easily. I have a feeling that your life will change forever once you find them! It will be like opening a door to a new and exciting world—first peeking through the opening and then immersing yourself in it."

"I'd love to be a part of this world," Anna said,

looking with admiration at her surroundings. "I belong in Africa. I can feel it now."

"Africa is an enchanted land, you know." Jean gave Anna a long gaze. His glowing eyes pierced her soul. Every word which came out of his mouth was pronounced with so much feeling, so much passion, she could listen to him for days and never get bored.

"Africa is not a continent, it's a planet of its own," Jean continued. "It's the land of miracles. Africa gives youth to the old, courage to the fainthearted, peace to the angry. Every time I come here, I feel like a child on Christmas morning—impatient to find out what incredible gifts have been prepared for me this time. This place fills my heart with tremendous happiness. Once you've set your foot in Africa, you'll come again and again! This land holds so many secrets, but it can also make all your most cherished dreams come true. I know it won't be easy to find your grandfather's family, but don't give up even for a second. It will be so worth it. You'll see."

Right then, the waiter brought their drinks. Anna got a glass of white wine and Jean a Kilimanjaro beer.

"Cheers!" Jean said as they clinked their glasses. "For the success of the Tourism Institute of Zanzibar!"

At that moment, the radiant sun started setting and the sky magically began changing its color from bright blue into a hot orange. The wind subsided and nature was so peaceful and quiet. The sun looked like an enormous fire ball glittering right above the horizon; its long golden beams reflecting in the water. The ocean now looked dark and gray, and several fairy-tale like dhow boats with their sharp sails were slowly rocking up and down the waves.

The boats effortlessly glided from one side of the ocean to another, as if they were playing catch-up with each other. Who were the people sailing in them? What were their lives like?

"Thank you for bringing me here, Jean," Anna said, overcome with emotion. "This is one of the most gorgeous sights I have ever seen."

Jean looked straight into Anna's eyes and took her hand in his. Anna trembled and an electric charge ran up and down her body from Jean's touch. She had dreamed of this moment at one point in time.

"This is the least I could do," he said quietly. "If I could, I would show you every single wonder of the world."

Jean leaned in closer, his lips pressing on hers in a hot and ardent kiss, sweet as honey. A few seconds later, Jean gently pulled Anna on his lap, like a doll. He embraced her, lightly running his hand through her hair, along her neck, and down her shoulders. He pressed kisses on her forehead, cheeks, neck, shoulders—everywhere his lips could find. His kisses and touch were intoxicating, so much more than the wine she just drank.

She felt weightless, flying somewhere high in the universe, right underneath that fiery sun which was glittering in the sky. She never wanted this to end and wished to continue floating in the air forever.

Anna finally came back to reality when the waiter brought the appetizers and respectfully placed them in the middle of the table. "*Bon Appétit*! Your main courses are being prepared right now and should be coming right out," the waiter noted calmly. He was probably used to seeing crazy couples on honeymoons who could not stop embracing in public. "Hope everything tastes good, please let me know if there are any concerns."

Embarrassed, Anna quickly returned to her seat. Luckily, nobody knew her here in Zanzibar… What on Earth was she doing, embracing Jean? The last time she checked, she was still in a relationship with David!

Anna realized, however, that since Jean arrived, she hardly even communicated with David, although he was sending texts all the time, checking in on her. Anna did mention that the project might be getting on track, and she would be heading back to Zanzibar again. Of course, she never announced the presence of a handsome Frenchman named Jean, whom she'd had a huge crush on before David! If he knew, he would have been on the first plane over, no doubt.

"Jean, I'm really sorry," Anna finally spoke, while weakly poking the octopus salad with her fork. "I got completely carried away with the beautiful sunset, the wine, the project, you… In reality, I am now in a relationship. My ex and I, we just got back together over the Christmas holidays."

"I didn't know," Jean whispered, then continued with feeling. "I understand. I cannot hide my feelings from you anymore though. I must tell you that I've been smitten by you from the first day. I remember every single moment we shared. When we finally saw each other at the Black Pearl, how I wished I were free from Emily!"

He shook his head. "When you did not wait for me after the interviews, I looked for you everywhere, asked everyone if they had seen the Ukrainian girl from the interviews! I begged the organizers to give me your contact information, but they said it was confidential… I was positive you were not interested in me and we would never meet again. Eventually, I started dating Emily because I thought I had lost you forever. Emily looked like a kind and sincere girl, but it was all just a big mistake."

"Yes, it was so unfortunate that I did not wait for you after the interviews. That was *my* mistake. You won't believe it, but my friend's frog got sick and I had to rush to the rescue. By the time I ran back to Polaris, you had already left. I was so heartbroken when I saw you with Emily at the Black Pearl Restaurant. But then I met David and thought that maybe I would be happy with him... Right now, I need some time to think and understand what is going on in my heart."

"That means I still have a chance," Jean said. "That is all I want. Just know that I am here for you, I want you to be happy. I will cherish the memory of this kiss we shared. It was such a stroke of luck that I met Karen in the Nairobi lounge and found out about the problems with your project—at least that seems on track now."

"In Nairobi?" Anna's eyes bulged. "I thought you met him in Dar es Salaam?"

"Well, in full disclosure, I did meet him in Nairobi. I just hopped on the next flight to Dar es Salaam to help you out. No big deal. Nairobi is right next door anyway."

Just like that, he just hopped on a flight to Tanzania. Who else in this world would have done that for her? Nobody. Neither David, nor Dima. This guy was truly extraordinary. Anna felt strong emotions for him—that kiss they shared was so electric. But was that real, or was it just the romance of Zanzibar? Would this feeling evaporate tomorrow, or would it stay in her heart forever? It was impossible to tell now. Anna needed to go back to reality, to Washington, to find out.

"Okay, let's just enjoy the dinner now, I will shut up. No more revelations," Jean said. The waiter had brought the main courses but they were still sitting on the table untouched. "Your seafood is starting to get cold. I brought you here to have a great dinner and the best time, sorry if I messed everything up."

"Well, I sort of share the guilt," Anna said weakly. She felt a little bit better once she dug into her prawns and lobster tails, cooked to perfection.

As Anna and Jean finished their dinner, Anna took one last look at the ocean from the terrace and paused. It was now dark and there was no trace of that golden sunset which impressed her so much. But the sky was now illuminated by a million stars—big and small, silver and blue green, enigmatic, spectacular, and so unreachable. It looked like the sky was sprinkled with iridescent pixie dust.

"I've never seen a starry sky like this," Anna said in awe.

"Yes, you can see such a breathtaking night sky only in Africa," Jean replied. "Millions of stars are glittering here, but you will always be my brightest star of Zanzibar. The most splendid, yet the most unattainable of all."

They finally left the terrace and walked downstairs. She would be saying goodbye to Zanzibar and going back to Washington. Would she ever share another day in Zanzibar with Jean? Anna didn't know, but she would keep this memory in her heart forever.

Chapter 21. Golden Ticket, Anyone?

Washington, D.C.

"Good morning, sunshine!"

As Anna was getting out of the airport, she immediately spotted David standing in the waiting area. His smile stretched from ear to ear and he was holding a large bouquet of two dozen red roses with a large bow around them. They had not even discussed pickup, and here Anna was, going home in a flashy Bentley, instead of a cab! The last thing she needed—and wanted—at the moment.

As soon as they got to her apartment complex, Anna reached for her keys to open the door. But it wasn't necessary—the door opened on its own. What the heck? Did she forget to lock the door when she left for Africa? Anna's knees started trembling and she looked helplessly at David. What if all her apartment had been burgled while she was gone?

"Surprise!" Olena yelled happily, hugging her shocked daughter.

"Mom? How did *you* get here!" Anna didn't know if she should laugh or cry. She was blinking her eyes, trying to understand how this happened.

Well, it turned out, Olena's visit was David's idea, and he'd paid for her to fly business class to Washington. She had just arrived yesterday and David let her in with his key.

"Thank you, David." Anna smiled softly at her boyfriend as she got over the initial shock. "This is the best present I could ever have."

"Well... I could think of something even better! David has something to show to you outside," Olena said conspiratorially, as she was leading Anna outside the apartment. "I suggest that we go right now, because I personally won't be able to wait any longer."

"Are you sure, Mom?" Anna pointed at her suitcase. "I was actually planning to unpack... But okay."

They walked outside of Anna's apartment and headed across the street.

"Ta-da!" yelled both David and Olena in unison, as they showed a gorgeous Porsche Carrera parked in one of the spaces to Anna. It looked like a shiny toy, not a real car, and resembled a cute bug with big eyes.

"I thought it was a good time for you to upgrade your car!" David said excitedly. "My girlfriend needs to drive in style. I looked at different colors and didn't know which one to get. I thought the sunflower yellow was going to suit you best—it would remind you of the sunflowers back home. I hope you like it."

"Wow, David, this is completely unbelievable!" Anna gasped in surprise. Hands down, this was definitely the most beautiful car she had ever seen.

"Anna, I am so happy for you," Olena said, hugging her daughter, and looking at David like he was a saint. "You have the best boyfriend in the whole wide world. When David showed me the car yesterday, I really had to restrain myself from texting you. I could not spoil the surprise of course, but you know me."

Several neighbors who came to the parking lot to get

their cars noticed the commotion at the yellow Porsche and walked closer to check it out. This was a nice neighborhood but definitely not one where millionaires lived.

"Nice present!" said Nora, a neighborhood dog walker.

After Anna took a short drive around the neighborhood, David suggested that she and Olena take a rest. He needed to go back to the office—he had a lot of important work at his company these days, weekends included.

Anna and Olena returned to the apartment. Anna started unpacking her suitcase, while Olena was giving her a dose of all the news about their friends and relatives. The big news of the family was that Cousin Sveta broke off her engagement with Mr. Banduchenko after he cheated on her with his young secretary, Daryna.

"Now Sveta does not even have a boyfriend and you are closer and closer to an engagement," Olena declared proudly. "Motria is desperate because it looks like you will be married first. She actually pleaded Sveta repeatedly to forgive Mr. Banduchenko, but for once, Sveta held her ground."

Wow, life seemed to go on after Anna's departure, there was no doubt about that.

"So, how was your trip to Africa?" Olena asked cheerfully after she finished with her news. "David was telling me you had some problems, but you resolved them?"

"Yes, things are looking much better now," Anna said confidently, as she took her Tanzania folder out of the suitcase, absent-mindedly browsed through it for a second, and put it on her desk. She felt like warm milk spilled all over her chest, making her cozy and comfortable.

Just a few days ago, she and Jean were going through this folder in Tanzania. Palm fronds were swaying in the breeze and the silver moonlight was bathing their faces in its cool glow. Jean's soft fingers flipped through these same pages. They probably still carried a tiny bit of his warmth. A tiny bit of the affection which filled his heart.

"We are pretty much done preparing the project. I am certain I will receive a full-time contract from my job now."

"Excellent." Olena nodded subtly as she was half-laying on the sofa with a glass of cranberry juice in her hand. "Although I must say I would prefer you to work at David's company. What's the point of working for somebody else and dealing with a myriad of problems, like the one you just had?"

Anna pursed her lips and turned away. Naturally, Olena had already started developing plans involving Anna and David. This was a danger zone, and she needed to get out of it urgently. She had to buy herself more time.

"Mom, I think it is a little bit too soon to start thinking about changing jobs. Let's give it some time."

Olena looked like she was just hit by an electric shock. Her face immediately tensed up and she jumped off the sofa. "What does this mean? Why do you need more time? You are sure that David is the one for you, right?"

Anna gave her mom a hesitant gaze. "Well… Yes, I am pretty sure—"

"Anna, you've been having second thoughts? Are

you out of your mind?" Olena's eyes looked like they were made of stone.

"There's this guy… I had met before Christmas, and-and I kind of like him," Anna said weakly. "I had mentioned him a long while back, Jean. I met him at the interviews. You probably do not remember, which is fine… I am still not sure if it is anything real, I just wanted to see, that's all."

"What kind of guy is he?" Olena asked doubtfully. "Is he somebody who will buy you a car as well? I bet not."

"Oh, he isn't into stuff like that," Anna said. "Jean doesn't even own a car himself. He has an electric bike which is much better for the environment… He showed me a sunset in Zanzibar, it was out of this world. He also thought that I needed to find out where my grandfather was from. I would imagine that if Jean wanted to surprise me, he would take me to watch a sunrise up on Mount Kilimanjaro."

"Okay, Anna, if you want to watch a sunrise, just get your butt out of bed earlier for once and watch it here with David. I am sure he would be happy to go with you. No need to hike up a distant mountain with some random guy."

Anna did not think about it before, but Olena would not easily approve of a relationship with Jean. Why would she? Mom never believed in grand romance but rather a happy union based on common sense and logic. She was a complete opposite to Grandma Maria who enjoyed watching different romantic movies and continued loving her one and only husband, even though she lost him fifty years ago. Up till this day, Olena grumbled at her mother for choosing a man coming to

Ukraine from some African country, instead of a fellow Ukrainian. Growing up, Anna constantly heard from Olena various complaints about her own childhood. It was not easy growing up without a father.

"Please, Anna, it is time to realize that you already have the best guy you could ever find. *David*," Olena finally said, breaking the silence. "We know everything about David. He is a good person and loves you with all of his heart. You know nothing about this Jean. Do not risk your connection with David, I beg you."

"Mom, I know nobody is perfect. But from what I could gather, Jean is an amazing person. He cares deeply about the poor people of the world. He never backs away from danger. He does his best to combat climate change. We share so many values... I have a feeling that Jean might be the one. Can I please try to find out?"

"No, Anna, this is absolutely out of the question!" Olena yelled. "You will mess up your life if you let David go and you'll end up alone. Just think how wonderful it will be for us to be related to the Thompson family, it will be such a win for all our relatives, not just you. The Thompsons are wealthy, highly educated, well connected. It is a whole other level. Do you want to hang out your whole life with losers?"

"Oh, please, Mom! Our friends and relatives aren't losers. They are all great."

Olena snorted. "I also did not tell you yet, but your dad will be getting a job here in the States through the Thompsons. I talked to David and his uncle Phil, you know, the one who owns the business magazine, will be able to hire your dad! Can you imagine? Your dad is so talented—and he has no prospects in Ukraine... We will then be able to live happily all together in the States.

You, me, dad, our dogs. Would that not be wonderful?"

"Yes, but—"

"I also asked David about investing in Uncle Stepan's new ventures on your behalf and he immediately agreed. He already wrote me a check. This is pocket change for him, really. Now you will be a big shot investor and make a ton of money. You know, everything Uncle Stepan touches turns into gold. He just needs capital. If he opens a travel agency, it will be a big hit in no time."

"Mom, I do understand, these are all fantastic opportunities, but *not at this time.* It would be unfair to make David do all these things for us, while I'm not in love with him."

"But what about me? All of us?" Olena exclaimed, with her tears flowing down her cheeks. She pointed at the large photo, which was standing on Anna's table, featuring the whole family gathered near their country house last summer. Everyone in the photo was laughing. Ivan was trying to hold both Lapa and Zirka up in his arms, and they were trying to wiggle their way out.

"You were the glue which kept all of us together. Are you just going to abandon everyone, chasing your dream around the world with some random guy? We want to be part of your life."

"Mom, please don't say that." Anna embraced her mother, as tears appeared in her eyes as well. "We will find a way to all be together. I promise. I will make it happen. We do not need David for that."

Olena smiled weakly. "Is that true?"

"Of course. We create our own destiny. We will be all together. Rich or poor—that I don't know—but we will be together. Dad eating his favorite sandwich, Lapa and Zirka stealing food, you and Aunt Motria bickering about poor marriage prospects for Sveta and me… And you know what, we will even expand our family. I will make sure we find our long-lost African relatives. We will finally learn where Grandpa came from."

Olena's eyes filled up with tears again. Anna brought up the most sore subject of all for her mother.

"There is no way for us to find his family," Olena said stubbornly, as the shadow of grief appeared on her face and she tried to contain her emotion. "He passed away so long ago. His family never tried to meet with us. They didn't care."

"No, Mom, they just did not know where to look. Grandma mentioned to me at her last birthday party that Grandpa's younger sister, Gloria, was looking forward to meeting you. She might still be around… somewhere. There has to be a way to find her. At least we can try. We've never tried!"

"It's useless, Anna. Just forget it. Nobody finds lost family members fifty years later. It was impossible to do it when Grandpa—*Dad*—just passed away. It's even more impossible now." Olena wiped her red eyes with a handkerchief and turned away from Anna.

"Hey, I don't think anything is impossible. We will ask everybody who had known Grandpa. Even Grandma might be able to remember something extra, which she did not tell us before. We will find some leads. Please, don't cry. I promise, we *will* find Grandpa's family."

Olena did not say anything more and quietly left the room. Anna did not stop her and just sadly followed her movements. It was too much for one day. Olena needed some time to recover. Whenever she was quiet, that was when she was in her unhappiest mood, Anna knew that

very well. Hopefully, Mom would come around.
****

How do I tell him? The ideal thing was to talk to David frankly right away, as soon as Anna had made up her mind. The more time that passed, the more difficult it was going to become. The last thing she wanted was to get sucked back into her comfortable routine with David and become complacent.

She could meet with him in some neutral place. Somewhere downtown, maybe a coffee shop next to Polaris? Immediately cut to the chase—that they could no longer be together. Quick and easy, like ripping a bandage off. It would sting for a bit, but both of them would go on with their lives thereafter.

However, finding an opportune moment wasn't as simple as it seemed. Right after Anna's arrival from Africa, David became incredibly busy working on an important new contract for his firm, Thompson Consulting. He worked very late and even needed to travel a lot to iron out the details. They talked several times, but Anna would never break up with David over the phone. No way. She needed to wait till they met.

In order to keep herself going, Anna tried to find some comfort in thinking about Jean and how they would be together, soon, but that also did not help. She had no idea what Jean was up to these days. She had not heard from him since their departure from Africa. He was supposedly in Paris visiting his family, this was all she knew.

Jean had not brought up his feelings to her since that dramatic kiss in Zanzibar. He was quite reserved saying good-bye to her before boarding his plane for Nairobi. Just a light smile, a wave, and a quiet "adieu." They parted as friends, not as two people madly in love who could not live a day without each other. It was a bit worrisome.

She knew Jean wanted to step aside for the time being, given that Anna was in another relationship. That made all the sense in the world. From what Anna had seen so far, Jean had high morals and would not want to pull her into some inappropriate relationship before she made up her mind and separated from David. He wanted to give her some space.

But if Anna's current connection dragged on for too long, Jean could potentially lose hope and possibly even meet somebody else. He would not wait forever, that's for sure. The guy was from Paris, they had some of the most fashionable and stylish women in the world! Models, actresses—all gorgeous and sophisticated… Anna would not be able to compete with them.

Finally, *finally*, David called Anna to announce that he was back in D.C. The contract he had been working on was signed and they needed to celebrate.

Anna sighed with relief. At long last, an opportunity came up to end things with David once and for all. But it was not going to be easy. She still cared deeply for David. Hurting him would hurt her as well. Anna hardly got any sleep the night before meeting with him.

Completely unsuspecting of what was going to come, David picked Anna up that evening in his Bentley. He selected a romantic French restaurant for their dinner and started them off by ordering one of the most expensive wines they had on the menu. Anna sat down quietly at her seat and tried not to look at David. It was too hard.

"We just signed a large long-term contract with

these guys from New York," David announced proudly. "Looks like the word is spreading fast about Thompson Consulting. It's all over Wall Street! The HR team is scrambling to find new hires for us."

This was a tremendous opportunity for Anna, David explained. She needed to join his team as soon as possible and take part in his success. Apparently, he already spoke with the members of the management team that they would hire Anna.

"I think we need to get you out of Polaris as soon as possible," David said excitedly, as he was triumphantly pouring the wine into their glasses. "Even if your current project is going well, there is no need to stay. Our company can easily double your salary now. You will get a large office right next to mine. We will work together and I'll make sure that you don't face any problems, like you did at Polaris."

"Thank you, David," Anna murmured. "I am not looking to change jobs. I-I like my company. I have always wanted to work there. Facing challenges like I did with TIZ is actually part of life… This is the way one learns. By taking an easy road, one can set themself up for failure in the future."

David raised his eyebrow. "You're sure, babe? All right… No worries."

Anna knew that normally he would insist on doing things "his way." But given his success at work, he was probably feeling magnanimous today and did not want to argue about anything.

"It's your choice. You can work at Polaris a bit more… Let's say one year. All I want is for you to be happy. Ever since you came into my life, I have been the happiest man in the world. I love giving you gifts and surprising you. How's your Porsche doing these days? I didn't see you drive it, but I bet heads turn wherever you go."

"Thanks David, it was a generous gift," Anna said carefully. Naturally, she would not be able to keep the car, so she had not even attempted driving it. The Porsche was still standing in the parking lot, where they left it that day when she came home from Africa. A few times she walked up to it just to have a look, but did not open the door or get in.

"I also thought that maybe we should take a trip together soon," David said. "You are much more adventurous than me—I admit it—but I can learn. Here are two tickets to St. Kitt's next month. I bet we can start from there and see if you can turn me into a world traveler."

David was not making this breakup easy. Like a Santa Claus, he was taking out more and more gifts out of his bag. Maybe this was not the right time to break up with him? There might be a better opening on a different evening.

But David did not give her any time to think. To Anna's astonishment, he got down on one knee and opened a light blue box with an engagement ring in it. It had a gorgeous fifteen-carat white diamond—so enormous, pure and dazzling like a star.

"Anna, will you marry me?" he asked with a big smile. "I cannot wait for us to share our lives together."

Anna froze. She had to make her choice right there, right that moment. This evening was not meant to be just a celebratory dinner for David's new contract at work. It was supposed to be the beginning of their forever—either together or apart.

The ball was in Anna's court. And she needed to hit it without delay.

If Anna said yes, her future would be certain. Wealthy life, fancy trips, easy job in which she would be shielded from all the evil by her husband, and even her family by her side from day one.

However, there would be zero chance to find her own path—build her dream career the way she wanted to or find her one and only true love. She would be put in a box. Everything would be pre-programmed to what David considered a happy life together. The benefits they would attend, the places they visit, the friends they socialize with, the number of children they would have… Anna would not be a separate person anymore but an extension of David. Her independent spirit would no longer exist.

What was the right choice?

The answer came much easier than Anna thought.

"I'm sorry, David," she finally said, her eyes shining bright. "I think you are a wonderful guy, and we had a great time together, but I cannot marry you. We are very different people. And-and I met somebody else."

David's triumphant smile vanished from his lips. His face now appeared dark and gray. His eyes slit.

"Met somebody else?" he asked slowly. "What are you talking about?"

"I do not know if it's something real yet. It's just somebody I recently met," Anna said quietly. "David, I am not ready to get married—to you or anyone else. For now, I just need to explore life and hopefully find my true love one day."

"Anna, are you insane? You would throw out everything we had for—for a *chance* to explore some relationship? With a guy you don't even know? That's crazy. Did you think this through? Did I upset you in any way?"

"No, David, there is absolutely nothing you have done wrong." Anna looked straight into his eyes. "Quite the contrary. You are a wonderful guy and I'm sure you will meet the girl who would be perfect for you. She's just not me."

"This is the last thing I thought would happen today," David said absentmindedly, glancing nervously at other patrons in the restaurant. Anna noticed how he kept fiddling with the ring box and did not know what to do with it now that his proposal was rejected so unexpectedly. No doubt, he had carefully thought through every step of the evening, just like he did with everything else. But he did not plan on this scenario. He had been one hundred percent positive Anna would say yes.

"Well, don't expect that I will wait for you and you can rush to me when things go wrong again," David finally said as he put the ring box back in his pocket.

"I guess I will have to take that chance," Anna said firmly. "I can take care of myself. I am lucky enough to have a job with one of the best companies in the world."

"Oh really? The one which you got through your lies?" David laughed. "Don't try to pretend you are such an honest and honorable person who doesn't compromise. I bet your superiors wouldn't be too happy to hear about it."

Anna suddenly felt blood rush to her face. Her heart beat faster and her throat tightened up.

"What do you mean? Would you tell them?"

"Anna, it doesn't matter whether I will or not. They

will find out. With or without me."

David looked straight at her.

"You can't hide the truth forever," he continued. "Your house of cards will fall and you'll end up with nothing. This job wasn't meant for you in the first place. It was meant for somebody who was an *adviser to the Minister of Finance of Ukraine*. That person was the one they selected for the interviews. But instead, you showed up and just happened to answer the questions. Pure luck. So, you got the job, but you will never succeed in it… Anna, it was with *me* that you won your golden ticket! And you can still have it. Just change your mind, and we will forget about this conversation."

Anna got up from the chair. There was nothing else for her to do here.

"David, it's still a no. I never wanted a golden ticket! Just give it to somebody else. I have to leave."

She walked out of the restaurant with pride, straight into the cold, crispy winter air. She was free from David and able to take control of her life—exactly what she wanted. But suddenly she realized that her beloved job and dream boyfriend were now even further away than they were five minutes ago. And the path to them suddenly became thorny.

Chapter 22. The Georgetown Waterfront

Washington, D.C.

Ever since their fight, Olena had only said a handful of words to Anna at best. Yes. No. Thanks. Fine. That was pretty much all. Any invitations to an actual conversation were ignored. Anna tried to come up with a few topics which could possibly interest her mom, but she did not take the bait.

It did not help the situation when Anna came home early from the dinner. Without David.

Anna was well aware of Olena's personality. She was easily capable of not talking to a person for weeks and weeks after a major fight. Anna was the one who would need to start the conversation.

On a cold but sunny morning, without a strong wind, Erica texted Anna that she wanted to meet up at a skating rink in Georgetown, which they frequented on weekends. It would be a good opportunity to get Olena out of the house as well.

"Mom, you cannot keep avoiding me like this," Anna said when Olena came to the kitchen and started cooking her oatmeal in silence. "Let's forget all the disagreements and just do something fun. Erica wants me to go to the skating rink with her. Come as well. The skating rink is right on the waterfront. You will finally meet Erica, the tennis star I told you about."

There was nothing but silence in response. *Will Mom ever speak to me again?* Anna was starting to panic.

"I suppose I could come," Olena said very reluctantly, but with some curiosity in her voice. This was a good sign. Maybe Olena was tired herself of this situation and wanted to make peace.

Anna needed to strike while the iron was hot. "Great! You won't regret it."

"Dima writes about this girl, Erica, all the time on his blog. It will be interesting to see her in real life. She is a good tennis player, I suppose. Is she also good at ice-skating?"

"Very. I had never skated before, as you know, but Erica gave me some inspiration, and now I am actually pretty decent. When we get to the rink, you should rent skates and try, even if you don't know how to skate. You can hold on to the railing. That's what I did for a few times, but now I'm much better."

An hour later, Olena and Anna made it to the Georgetown Ice Rink. Like usual, not too many people were at the rink in the morning. Erica preferred to come at this time so that she had better chances to stay "incognito."

When Olena and Anna arrived, Erica was already on the rink, wearing a white dress with sparkles, a light jacket, and big sunglasses, effortlessly gliding from one side of the rink to the other. Erica always maintained a stunning air position on her jumps and achieved perfect extension on the landing. She also excelled in her spins—Anna especially loved Erica's upright spin which looked so beautiful with her long leg extended up in the air. It seemed that Erica skated with a trail of sparkles behind her.

Teresa was sitting on the terrace of the café next to the skating rink and proudly watching her talented daughter. Luckily, Lenny never came to the skating rink. Anna would hate to see his lying face. As a matter of fact, Anna hadn't seen Lenny since that fateful New Year party. Rosie had told her that she immediately broke up with Lenny after she learned the truth. Since then, he had disappeared and was nowhere to be found. Maybe he crawled into some deep dark hole, like a troll.

Anna and Olena greeted Teresa and waved to Erica. Anna then quickly put on her skates and walked on to the ice, staggering a bit, as usual.

She noticed that Olena was making conversation with Teresa. This was a good sign that mentally she was in a better place now.

Ice skating was definitely not an easy sport to master for a novice. Even though Anna had practiced at least ten times by now, on occasion she still had trouble maintaining her balance. She moved relatively slowly and stayed not too far from the railing. There was definitely no talk about skating fast or any jumps or spins like the ones Erica was doing. For now, Anna just needed to get her basics right. Maybe next season she would try some advanced elements.

At one point, Anna's attention was so consumed by skating that she lost sight of her mom. When Anna glanced at the terrace, Olena wasn't there anymore—she must have gone into the pro shop to rent some skates.

Anna became worried. Olena was very athletic, obviously, but she had never skated before. What if she fell and broke a leg or something?

"Mom, please, be very, very careful!" Anna yelled

anxiously when she saw Olena emerging from the pro shop in the rental skates. "It might seem easy when you watch, but it's pretty hard when you actually try it. You might slip and fall."

Olena stepped onto the ice and started moving along while tightly holding on to the railing. The first time was always hard. So far, so good though. She seemed okay.

But all of a sudden, Olena let go of the railing and skated right into the middle of the rink. She gained pretty good speed and started gliding in all different directions. She then made a couple of spins. Her eyes were shining bright and she had a big smile on her face, like she was doing something she had always wanted to do, but wasn't allowed to.

Anna stopped and stared at Olena in complete shock. Her mom must have done this before—no way she was skating like this for the first time! Her technique was clearly rusty—but she was not a novice. It was incredibly weird.

Olena stopped near the railing to catch her breath and Anna immediately rushed to her.

"Mom, I don't understand! Why did you never mention you skated before?"

"It's not a big deal, really, Anna." Olena dismissively waved her hand and turned away while trying to fix something on her skate.

"It probably isn't, but still?" Anna looked at her mom intently. She was hiding something. It was absolutely clear.

"Well… I learned when I was three or four, I guess. I practiced a lot, pretty much every day. I thought that the skill goes away after not skating for a long time, but seems like it doesn't. Surprisingly, I feel pretty confident on ice, so many years later."

"Where did you learn? Neither you nor Grandma ever mentioned this. Not even once. And we talk about all kinds of sports all the time! What's the deal with skating?"

Olena thought for a second, like she was not sure if they needed to stay on the subject. Then she reluctantly decided to continue.

"I learned skating from Uncle Igor—"

"Uncle who?"

"Uncle Igor. He was our family friend. He helped us a lot after Dad passed away, we did many things together. Uncle Igor took me skating whenever he came to see us. Winters were long, cold, and frosty back then, skating was one of the few activities to do."

"This is the first time I am hearing about somebody named Uncle Igor," Anna said, puzzled. She desperately tried to dig in her memory for a mention of somebody with the name. "I have never seen him in my life. Grandma never mentioned him, either. And she always keeps in touch with all her friends—she is very particular about that."

"True," Olena agreed. "He completely disappeared from our lives. I remember very well that one day, he took me to the ice-skating rink and said he would come again tomorrow. But he never did. I never wanted to skate again. Till today, I guess. When you mentioned ice-skating this morning, I decided I really wanted to do it. The ice looked too inviting. I could not resist."

"This is extremely weird," Anna said. "We will need to ask Grandma about this mysterious Uncle Igor. Especially now that we will be looking for Grandpa's family. He might be able to tell us something useful, give us some clue. Assuming he is still alive, of course."

"I suppose he would be in his seventies now, just like Grandma."

Erica skated up to Anna and Olena to alert them that it was time to leave the rink. Their skating session was over. The rink staff were starting to clean the ice before the beginning of the next session. A lot of new patrons were waiting outside the gates. Olena returned rental skates to the pro shop and Anna put hers in her bag.

"Till next time!" Erica yelled, as she and Teresa were rushing to get into their big black SUV.

"This is one family which seems very happy and does not have any secrets," observed Olena as she was watching Erica's car speed away. "The girl is a total treasure and the mother is so sophisticated. I can't believe she is just a few years younger than me. She looks like a young girl. I bet her life is as easy as it gets and her husband totally adores her."

"Oh, Mom, I would not wish Teresa's life on you." Anna shook her head. "I don't think anyone has it easy in this world, no matter who they are."

As Anna and Olena were walking towards their car, Olena suddenly paused. "How are you holding up after breaking up with David? I didn't ask you before. I'm sorry. I had a lot on my mind. Did you see this other guy you liked—Jean?"

At the mention of his name, she felt like a dagger stabbed her heart. She looked at Olena sadly. At this very moment, she wanted support more than anything. This was her chance to finally reveal the horrible mistake she had made. The lie which had been driving her insane for a whole year. The lie which now could prevent her from being with the guy she thought the world of.

"No, Mom, I have not seen Jean. I wanted to contact him, but I couldn't—" She licked her lips before continuing, "The thing is, I did something really bad, something which I am not proud of. Unless this is resolved, I cannot even show my face to Jean. Also, I am not sure I will stay in Washington D.C. much longer. I might have to return to Ukraine."

"Hah? Is there something wrong with your work again?" Olena asked in astonishment. "I thought everything was going so well with your project."

"Yes, it was. The project is fine, it's actually going great. But there is another big problem which I didn't tell you about yet... Let's sit down, it will take some time."

They found a nice cozy bench overlooking the Potomac River. For a few moments, while trying to gather her thoughts, Anna looked around the promenade. The waterfront was quite busy on the weekend, and a lot of people were walking by, heading to numerous cafes in the area, to the skating rink, or just enjoying a sunny winter day. A few chubby seagulls with long beaks were sitting on the railing, carefully watching all the bystanders.

"So?" Olena asked impatiently. "What is this horrible problem you mentioned? Come on, don't make me wait any longer!"

With a trembling voice, Anna explained to Olena how she had lied on the application and how David threatened her to reveal it to everyone at Polaris. Olena listened, trying to comprehend and make some sense of what she was hearing.

"Anna, dear, how could you have possibly done something like this?" Olena finally exclaimed when Anna finished her story. "Lie on the job application?

Pretend to be someone else? I've always taught you to be an honest person—in sports and in life! You never cheated on the tennis court, even when you were a young child. It never even occurred to you to say that a ball was out when it wasn't, or something else like that… You wanted to win more than anything, but you never attempted to cheat. What happened to that honest girl?"

"I know, Mom, what I did was absolutely terrible." Anna looked at Olena, her eyes full of despair. "When I put in the Polaris application, I was pretty sure that it would be rejected, like all my other applications were. But somehow it worked—and then I was left to deal with the consequences. All by myself."

"Why did you even have to lie?" Olena shook her head. "You worked for a few years at the Energy Institute. They could have given you a good reference. I am positive that Polaris would have appreciated your real experience. Why didn't you believe in yourself?"

"I don't know, Mom." Anna looked at Olena hesitantly. "I thought that the real me was not perfect enough for Polaris… I was a washed up athlete, I worked at Uncle Stepan's shop, all my previous job applications had been rejected. I was sure I didn't have a chance."

"But you did!" Olena objected. "You got all the interview questions right. It was your achievement, nobody else's. And you have now succeeded in preparing such a complex project. Who else would learn about various training institutes in such a short period of time, put together a good team, and charm the socks off their counterparts in Zanzibar? This means that all along, you were the right person for the job!"

"Now I think so too… But back then, I felt that I wasn't good enough."

"I wish I knew about this earlier," Olena said, tightly hugging her daughter. "It must have been so hard for you to keep this inside yourself, day in, day out—You should have told me. You made a mistake, a really bad one, but you should not have been dealing with it alone. Just go ahead and tell the Polaris folks about what you did. Be frank, tell them how sorry you are. They know you well, I'm sure they will understand. It's going to be okay."

"Thank you for understanding, Mom," Anna said, as her tears were fiercely flowing all over her cheeks. She now wished she had told the truth to Olena a long time ago. It was good to finally get some support, as opposed to fighting this battle all alone. Anna felt a warmth suddenly spreading throughout her body and the chills she had gotten so accustomed to were suddenly gone.

"I'll need to find a good time to tell everyone at Polaris. It won't be easy for me to reveal the truth. What if they don't accept my apology?"

"Let's hope they will. But if they don't, then so be it. We'll go back to Ukraine and you'll try building your life and career there. With your brilliance, you'll succeed no matter what. You go down, you get up, and then try again… It's all part of life."

"Oh, Mom, I so much hope my career won't end like this, because of the terrible, stupid mistake I had made. You know how much I have dreamed about this job, how much I tried to do well in it. This would be so unfair."

"I know, Anna, I know. And one thing you can be sure of—I will always be here for you. We will get through this no matter what. If this job had been meant for you, you will be able to keep it. I have no doubt about that whatsoever."

Chapter 23. Fate in Limbo

Washington, D.C.

Anna walked down the corridor and carefully glanced into Emily's office. The other girl was slowly typing something on her computer. She must have been packing earlier. The room was in a total disarray. The table was littered with empty coffee cups and candy wrappers. Several large carboard boxes were standing around with items already inside.

Anna had not seen or spoken to Emily for over a month, and she immediately noticed that the other woman looked very different. Her usual impeccable makeup was gone, and she barely had enough lipstick covering her lips. There was no customary lengthening mascara on Emily's eyelashes. It seemed that her eyes were a little swollen. Could she have been crying? Even her blond hair now showed dark roots.

"Hi Emily," Anna said quietly. "How have you been? If you do not want to talk, I understand. I know we have not been on the best terms these last few months."

Emily looked up and smiled sadly. "No, Anna. It's really nice that you stopped by. These days, I could use a friend. You might be the only one I have. I'm sure you've heard, I am being transferred to Saudi Arabia. I'm also sure you know why."

"Yes, I did hear, Emily, and I am very sorry. Even

though we might have started it on the wrong foot here at Polaris, I have always been your friend and I hope things get better for you very soon." Anna removed the cardboard box from the spare chair in Emily's office and carefully sat down, trying to keep her feet away from the stuff laying on the floor. Never in a million years would she have thought Emily could have such a messy office. Naturally, she no longer cared about anything.

"This last month has not really been a good month for me," Emily said. "My dad even froze all my credit cards. I obviously still have my salary at Polaris, which is enough to live on, but you know, this isn't the lifestyle I'm used to. And this transfer to Saudi Arabia, away from everyone, sucks. My dad told me that I either go there for a year or two till things calm down between Arnaud and Lauren or he will completely disown me. But why Saudi Arabia? It's so far away and I don't know a single person there."

"I'm really sorry." Anna nodded sympathetically and gave Emily a light pat on the shoulder. "Your dad appears very opinionated, I guess he has his own reasons for taking these measures—"

"Well, my parents have always loved Lauren more than me." Emily rubbed at her swollen eyes. "All I heard growing up was Lauren this, Lauren that. I was the pretty one, but I was always crying or complaining. And when Lauren and I liked the same guy, Arnaud, my parents were entirely on her side. Now, they are trying to rescue her marriage for her as well."

"Does Arnaud actually love you, or your sister?" Anna asked.

"I'm not sure," Emily confided, sniffling. "I think-I think Arnaud loves nobody. I think he was taking advantage of both of us. He married Lauren for her inheritance. Then, like an idiot, I continued to flirt with him and he-he decided to keep playing. After we got caught, he had the gall to say he made a mistake, that it was all my fault! Bastard. Of course, he wanted to stay with Lauren."

"I'm really sorry, Emily," Anna said, looking at her watch.

"I hope your love life turns out better than mine." Emily sighed. "I heard from Alex that you started dating David again? I think it's fantastic, he's one of the most eligible bachelors in Washington area. If you don't want to end up like me, exiled to another part of the world, with no family and no money, don't mess it up." She shook her head. "How is it going?"

"Oh Emily, if only you knew," Anna replied quietly. Emily's life was not the only one which had been turned upside down recently. Anna's life was possibly in an even greater disarray.

"It's all over with David. We separated a few days ago. But things are even more complicated than that—" Anna glanced at her watch again. "We have a staff meeting starting in five minutes. I will be making an important announcement which you would not want to miss. Let's head there, so we are not late."

Just two days ago, the decision was finally made on which Global Associates in Anna's class would be given full-time employment contracts to work at Polaris. Several people did not make it, but Anna was on the list. Today was supposed to be the happy day when she would sign her contract and continue her dream career at Polaris.

But could she actually sign her contract?

Anna was debating in her mind whether this was a good time to reveal to her department that she had lied on the application. It was not clear if David would contact Polaris and tell her secret. It was quite possible, although not certain. But even if he never did, would Anna be comfortable working there, with this huge lie hanging over her head day after day? How could she build a successful career at Polaris, knowing that at any moment she could be discovered, and dismissed?

It seemed there was no choice. Anna needed to tell everyone today. At least this way, they would be able to hear her out first, and better understand her background, motivations, and complete repentance. She could still lose her job, but there was a remote chance that people would understand and forgive her.

The conference room was already full of staff when Anna and Emily entered. They found seats at the table and the meeting started promptly.

Like usual, John started out by talking about the various affairs of the department. Several projects were approved, the department received funding for a few more, and overall, things were going quite well.

Anna kept fidgeting in her chair as she was getting ready to tell the truth. After breaking up with David, she no longer had a safety net. If she lost her job, she would be sent back to Ukraine and would never have a chance to work for Polaris again. She would never see Jean again, either. Her dreams would come to an end, if she spoke up.

Finally, John got to the topic of Global Associates. Anna held her breath.

"Colleagues, the next item on the agenda is the Global Associates Program. As you all know, our department has been hosting Anna Levenko, who in the past held an important position in the Ukrainian government—she was an adviser to the Minister of Finance. Anna demonstrated exceptional leadership and technical skills when preparing the project to support the development of the Tourism Institute of Zanzibar. It has been an absolute honor for me to work with Anna and watch her develop professionally. I am positive that Anna will have many more achievements here at Polaris! Anna has a lot of excellent professional qualities which we value at Polaris—team work, perseverance, and integrity. I am pleased to offer a full-time employment contract to her."

Anna got up from her chair to go get her contract. She noticed that many people in the room gave her approving glances and thumbs up. Somebody whispered, "Great job!" Global associates were always the darlings of the organization and everyone wanted to be friends with them.

John was standing there with a bright smile, so proud of his protégée, holding the paperwork in his hands, waiting for Anna to walk up to him. But her legs suddenly felt heavy, as if made of stone. She needed to speak up. Now.

"John, colleagues," she started, "I greatly appreciate all the recognition. But there is something I need to tell you first."

She took a deep breath, looking from Bernard's smiling face, John's kind face, before stopping on Emily's carefully blank face. "It would not be fair for me to accept the employment contract, unless you knew my real background. John just mentioned that I held the position of the Adviser to the Minister of Finance of

Ukraine. Unfortunately, it is not true. I never held this position."

John stepped away, shocked. The kind smile disappeared from his face.

"I don't understand, Anna—What *was* your position then?"

"Well, I did several things after graduation. I worked at my uncle's shop—I had to make some money, as our family is not rich. I also was a research assistant at the Energy Institute of the National Academy of Sciences of Ukraine. This is the job I really liked, and I felt I was making an impact in the fight against climate change, something I am very passionate about. But my dream had always been to work at Polaris. I wanted to work in international development, helping the disadvantaged people of the world and trying to make the world a better place."

"Why on Earth did you say you were an adviser to the Minister of Finance?"

"It's hard to explain." She fidgeted, hiding her eyes from her coworkers. "I figured that none of my jobs were good enough for the Polaris application and, well, I-I decided to somewhat improve my work experience on my CV. I thought it was my only chance to get an interview with Polaris. I now fully understand this was incredibly wrong, and I will never do anything like that again. This lie has been haunting me for months! I hated myself for doing what I did, but I had no way to correct it."

Anna lowered her eyes and just looked at the floor. Her heart was about to jump out of her chest. It was pounding faster and faster. Finally, she glanced up. John stood there, shifting from foot to foot, looking very uncomfortable.

"It is reprehensible to lie on a job application," John noted. "I am glad to hear that you understand it and will never do anything like that again—But this is still a significant issue. Let me think for a minute."

"While you are thinking, maybe I can say something," Margaret suddenly intervened, one of Anna's co-workers. Anna did not get a chance to work with her, but saw her at different meetings. Margaret had a reputation of being a "straight shooter" and her opinion was usually greatly valued by her superiors.

"This is absolutely unacceptable behavior," Margaret said loudly, giving Anna a dissatisfied look. "The Global Associates program is meant to bring the best talent into our organization—staff who are intelligent, professional, and truthful. A person like this has no place here. Somebody who lies once will do so again and again. Anna needs to be dismissed immediately and never have a chance to work at Polaris again."

Anna's heart sank. If John thought the same way, she would be on the next plane to Ukraine, just like she had feared.

"Shush, Margaret," Bernard immediately intervened in Anna's defense. "Nobody was asking for your opinion. You don't even know Anna. She did a fantastic job. And this isn't up to you to decide."

"Thank you for your views, Bernard and Margaret," John finally said. "I have never been in a situation like this before. It is hard to resolve. It is definitely not black or white… I will have to discuss this issue with the ethics committee. I cannot give an answer right now."

Anna swallowed anxiously and squeezed her fists so

tightly that she dug her fingernails deep into her soft palms. She had hoped for a quick resolution. Even if she were going to get dismissed, she wanted to know it right here, right away. Waiting and not knowing how this would end was the worst punishment of all.

"John, what should I do in the meantime?" she asked weakly.

"Until the issue is resolved, you will stay on paid leave at home. My assistant will call you and advise on the next steps," John said calmly, as he was putting Anna's employment contract back in his document folder. It was impossible to tell what he was thinking at that moment.

"One last thing," John said, moving away from the controversial subject with a bit of relief. "As everyone knows, Emily Roberts is now moving to the satellite office in Riyadh, Saudi Arabia. This will be quite a change for her. Emily, do you have everything packed?"

"Yes, for the most part…"

"All right. We will be holding a farewell party for you very soon. I hope everyone can attend. My assistant will be sending out invitations."

"Thank you." Emily broke into a weak smile.

"I hope you enjoy your new assignment," John said.

"I'll try to. This will be a completely new experience for me," Emily noted softly. Anna did not sense too much enthusiasm in her tone, but Emily definitely sounded more positive than when they were chatting earlier. It was clear to Anna that after what just happened, Emily reconsidered her own destiny. Waiting at home until your fate was decided was so much worse.

The meeting then finished and everyone started leaving the conference room. Usually, Polaris folks liked to linger in the conference room for a bit even after the meeting was over. They would grab some more coffee and muffins, laugh and chat non-stop about the main points of the meeting or current projects.

This time, however, there was total silence. Nobody got an extra helping of coffee. Everyone was trying to get out as quickly as possible.

As she was exiting, Anna made a forced smile to her colleagues, but all she got back were a bunch of icy stares—gazes full of judgment and resentment. With the exception of Bernard and Emily, who both glanced at Anna with compassion, Polaris folks demonstratively avoided Anna as if she suddenly caught some terrible disease which could potentially spread to them as well. Just fifteen minutes ago, she was a star of the department. Now she was a nobody. Or worse.

After witnessing this conduct on the part of her colleagues, Anna decided to immediately leave the office and wait at home. She had no idea what the ethics committee was and how it functioned. Probably they would decide her fate quickly.

As she was leaving, she looked at her office with sadness. Hopefully, she would be back soon. But maybe she would never set foot in it again.

Chapter 24. The Icing on The Cake

Washington, D.C.

Two weeks passed and still no word came from John.

Will he ever contact me? What's going on? Anna checked her email and voicemail every ten minutes. Her career prospects looked bleaker and bleaker with every passing day.

"Mom, why can't they just tell me the answer?" Anna moaned as they were carrying groceries. Her cheeks were bright red—partly from the frost outside, but even more so from the painful memories of her lie on the Polaris application.

"I get it, I made a huge mistake. So just fire me, don't make me wait for so long! I'm sure they know perfectly well what they are going to do with me… They are just trying to drive me completely crazy. It's as if they are grilling me on a slow fire, so that my pain is prologued as much as possible."

"Anna, please, try not to worry so much," Olena attempted to console her. "It's out of our hands. They are probably following some process they have in place. They are a big organization. Just be patient. They'll give you an answer. Let's cook something yummy tonight, that might cheer you up! How about the *holubtsi*? We could invite those lovely neighbors, Pablo and Ben, over for dinner."

"Maybe… tomorrow," Anna said without her usual enthusiasm. Holubtsi—the dish of rice and meat rolled into the boiled cabbage leaves—had been one of her absolute favorites since she was a little girl. She could easily eat five or six at a time, and not blink. Olena mentioned once that when she was pregnant, Anna always started happily kicking in her belly when Olena ate a meal of holubtsi. But during the last few weeks, Anna didn't have much appetite. Neither for the holubtsi, nor for life.

At long last, the email came from John's assistant. *Finally!* The message itself was abrupt:

—Dear Anna, Please come to Building 1, Office number 56 tomorrow at two pm for the fact-finding meeting with the Polaris ethics office. In case you cannot make it, please let us know as soon as possible. Sincerely, Teri Melilla—

Yes, obviously, she could make it! Did they think she had anything else to do, other than waiting for this fateful email?

Brimming over with anticipation, she ran into the Polaris offices. Four officials were waiting for her in the meeting room. Without much introduction, they asked Anna to provide all the information she could share with them regarding her case.

"Of course, of course," Anna mumbled, squirming awkwardly in her seat, as strong emotions boiled over in her chest. "Let-Let me start from the very beginning." Her pulse beginning to race, Anna explained how she had seen the ad on social media, how much she wanted to work for Polaris, and how she didn't have the right credentials.

"I regret my decision to lie on the application. I hope I can be reinstated in my job. Please let me know if you have any questions." After her long, emotional speech Anna cast a hopeful look at the people in front of her. They had to believe her and help to get her job back!

"Thank you for the information." Every word pronounced by the ethics officials was clipped and precise. They quickly got up and were getting ready to leave the room, talking calmly with each other.

"What will happen to me now?" Anna asked, slowly rising from the table and smiling tightly. Her eyes were gradually filling up with tears. Her voice was so quiet, as if she'd suddenly shrunk to the size of a tiny mouse. "When can I expect the answer?"

"We cannot give you a particular timeline. Just wait for further communications," the leader of the ethics team answered in a firm, robot-like voice and looked at Anna with a blank stare. Their faces were ice-cold and eyes hard as pebbles, not a single drop of compassion in them. They probably dealt with similar issues all day long and built a strong stamina to handle situations like this.

When Anna got back home from Polaris, Olena suggested, "Why don't you send a message to Bernard? He'll probably be able to tell you what's been happening. These ethics people seem pretty hopeless. They are just collecting information. They are not the decision-makers."

"Of course. Bernard! Why didn't I think about it?" Anna exclaimed and opened her laptop with renewed excitement. Bernard had been such a good friend to her, ever since the first day at Polaris. Now that she was temporarily suspended, he would be her eyes and ears within the company. Even if he didn't know everything, he could give her at least some idea as to what management might be thinking.

Usually Bernard was excellent with emails. He would reply within ten to fifteen minutes. But this time, no reply came—even after an entire day.

Maybe he missed my email by accident?

Normally, he was very thorough, but obviously mistakes could happen to anyone. Even an email machine like Bernard. A follow up was needed. Anna decided to send a text message this time. The message would beep on his phone, and he would respond instantaneously.

Three hours later, Anna was still checking her messages. No response came in. And the app showed that Bernard was active twenty minutes ago.

Crap. He just doesn't want to reply to my texts.

It was pretty clear that Bernard wanted to step away and avoid possible problems for himself. Now Anna had no insider who could help her. Not a single soul wanted to associate with her.

The only way to find out her fate was to endure more and more waiting. Which meant lying awake at night and staring at the ceiling for hours on end. Sitting in front of the TV in the living room, and looking right through it. Talking to Mom and not hearing what she was saying.

When Anna got a call from Teri again to come to another meeting at Polaris, she was no longer excited. She was emotionally spent. Extremely tired. She just wanted all of this horror to be over.

"Thanks for calling, Teri," Anna said, her voice bland and even. "Meet tomorrow? Yes, no problem. I'll be there."

****

Anna got off the red line train and slowly walked into Polaris. The meeting invite indicated the room on the same floor where Anna used to work, so she took a familiar elevator. Just a short time ago, she was entering the Polaris building triumphantly with her Ukrainian arts and crafts, starting an exciting career. How quickly things had changed…

Anna passed by her lovely, cozy office, the "Anna Levenko" sign still on the door. A source of tremendous pride. On her first day, she took at least ten selfies in this office standing in front of the beautiful Ukrainian flag on the wall and sent them to her friends and family. Anna could not resist the temptation of glancing inside, just to relive the happy memories for a brief second.

Oh no!

All the documents, crafts, and family pictures Anna had left in the office were now packed in a neat box which was standing in the corner of the room. The desk and the bookcase were bare. Anna's large world map had been taken off the wall and rolled into a tube, as was the Ukrainian flag.

So that's why she was invited back to Polaris today! To surrender her badge and take any last belongings home. How thoughtful.

There are all my dreams, broken into a million pieces and packed in one box.

For a second, Anna stood in front of her office, remembering her last trip to Africa and the kiss with Jean. It all seemed like a hundred years ago.

"Good bye Polaris, good bye Jean," whispered Anna and continued walking down the hallway. She passed a few colleagues of hers—former colleagues as of today—

who did not say hello and gave her some disapproving glances, like "What are you still doing here? Weren't you dismissed a month ago?"

Heartbroken, Anna dragged her feet to the meeting room. She weakly knocked on the door and quietly entered the room. To her surprise, there was nobody except for John inside.

"Anna, thanks for coming! Please take a seat." John seemed much more relaxed than the last time she saw him. He was probably glad that this situation would finally be resolved and he would not have to deal with Anna and her problems.

"How are you doing?" John asked calmly.

What kind of answer could she give, especially after she saw her office had been packed up? *Devasted? Heart-broken?*

"I'm doing okay," she finally squeezed out. "Not the best."

"I know, this must have been incredibly hard on you," John said, his voice full of compassion. "It took a long time to resolve your case, but now I finally have an answer for you."

And I already know what it is, Anna thought to herself. At least she was prepared for what she was going to hear.

"All right," John said. "Let's get down to business. This was a very difficult decision for all of us. First and foremost, I want to underscore that I cannot abide liars. There is no place for them at Polaris. They would only damage our reputation."

"I understand," Anna said sadly. She hated liars as much as John did. And she hated herself the most for what she had done.

"*But,*" continued John, "I've gotten to know you quite well by now. I feel that the lie on the application was an unfortunate mistake on your part. Such conduct is not part of your character. We all make mistakes occasionally. Each person can think of things they are not proud of. In my opinion, you deserve a second chance. And this is what I argued to the ethics committee."

"You did? Thank you so much, John," Anna said with tears in her eyes. At least he tried to defend her. He was always such a good guy. Even though they still decided to dismiss her, she would forever remember John as somebody who stood by her till the end.

"You're welcome. And I was not the only one who argued for you. Teresa Jameson and Bernard Kaye are your other big supporters. I had no idea, but Teresa is a big fan of your work and you as a person. Apparently, she had even known you in your 'prior' life as a tennis player. She explained to everyone what you had to go through—the terrible injury which cut your brilliant tennis career short. You are such a fighter! I admire you. I couldn't do what you had done."

"Thank you, John," Anna whispered.

"Teresa is a chief economist, so her vote had a lot of weight," John continued. "I suspect it might have been the deciding one... You were lucky to have her on your side, arguing so strongly for you. She put forward so many arguments in your favor that the ethics committee finally concluded that, you can return to your job next week."

"I can what?" Anna jumped up in astonishment. "But how is this possible? I just passed by my office, all the things in it were packed up! I was sure I was being dismissed."

"Oh, that's nothing. Our whole department is moving to another floor. If you work here long enough, you will move offices many times. We were not sure how soon you would be able to return, since this process has been dragging on forever, so Teri packed up your things just in case. The movers are coming in a couple of days."

"Thank you, thank you, John!" Anna exclaimed in delight. "I will be your most honest and devoted employee, forever and ever."

John nodded in agreement.

"I believe you. That's why we are giving you a second chance. I also think that your position in the Energy Institute was quite solid. It's exactly the type of job I would want a Global Associate to hold prior to joining Polaris. Our HR sets too high of a bar for the applicants, and people like you think they need to pretend to be somebody else in order to get in. The HR targets Ivy League schools and expects applicants with flawless credentials. It always makes me wonder, is that even the right approach? Lying on the application is not the way to go under any circumstances. But I believe that we need to re-consider our screening process, so that more folks like you have a chance to get an interview."

"I hope this will happen one day," Anna said.

"So, are you going to sign the full-time employment contract?" John asked with a smile as he held out a pen.

"I totally will," Anna replied proudly, as she signed her name with a flourish.

****

Anna was slowly walking around the Polaris cafeteria, peaking at the food they were offering at all the different stations, in search of something good to eat for lunch. She was in a dire need of a nice meal to cheer herself up.

That morning, she finally saw Olena leave at the Dulles Airport. After everything seemed to have resolved itself with Anna's job, it was time for Olena to head home and check on the rest of the family.

In the last weeks, Western news channels were talking more and more about the imminent full-scale Russian invasion, and Olena wanted to make sure she got to Kyiv as soon as possible. Both Olena and Anna were hoping nothing major would happen—Ukraine had been living under the threat of a full-blown Russian invasion since 2014—but just in case, they decided to speed up Olena's departure. They needed to make sure Grandma Maria was in good hands in the remote case that their fears did materialize. The plan was for Anna to visit Kyiv in the next months, once she got her Zanzibar project approved. Definitely in time for Grandma's birthday.

Anna finally stopped by the Asian station and zeroed in on the Cambodian noodle bowl. This was the best dish she had seen in the whole cafeteria, so she put it on the tray and started walking towards the cashier. Hopefully, someday, the Polaris cafeteria would also serve Ukrainian food.

"*Bonjour,* Anna," she suddenly heard a familiar voice from behind her.

Anna turned around and saw Jean walking up to her, a kind smile on his face. She had a feeling of déjà vu.

Just a year ago, they were having their first lunch in this very cafeteria and she had been looking forward to their first date. But everything had fallen off the rails. Anna rushed to rescue Katie's frog, then Emily stole

Jean, then David came into her life, and finally she was almost fired. Now they were back in the same cafeteria. But could they start all over again? Was Jean still interested in her?

"What a surprise," Anna said, unable to hide her astonishment.

"I hope a pleasant one?" Jean asked carefully.

"Very."

"It's been quite a while since our trip to Zanzibar," Jean observed. "I was hoping to hear from you after a week or two. But I figured you were not ready yet."

"A lot of things happened—I have so much to tell you. Most importantly, I broke up with David. I am free to see who I want now."

"Glad to hear that. How about we start afresh today?" Jean asked simply. "I'm searching for a companion to travel to the magnificent Africa with. To watch the serene sunrises and golden sunsets, hang out on the glorious beaches, stroll along the bustling streets, admire the might of the spectacular waterfalls, sail on the enchanted dhow boats in the clear emerald waters, with an occasional safari thrown in, that kind of thing… Just in case you might be interested."

"Anytime," Anna said. "I'd love to explore Africa with you."

Glossary

Bandura—the national musical instrument of Ukraine. It's a stringed instrument with an oval wooden body. Bandura dates back hundreds of centuries and used to be played by blind musicians who travelled from one village to another and performed various folk songs for their audience.

Bud'mo—"cheers" in Ukrainian. One can expect to hear this toast many times during Ukrainian parties.

Chervona Ruta—a mythological flower. A ruta flower normally has yellow blossoms. But according to a Ukrainian legend, on the summer solstice, it turns red ("chervona") for a brief period of time. If a person finds this red flower, he or she might receive tremendous luck, wealth, and ability to understand the animal speech. However, the flower is guarded by evil spirits.

Chudo—the Ukrainian word for miracle.

Cossacks—military men who initially protected steppe settlers against Tatar raids in the sixteenth century, but later also played a critical role in building an autonomous Ukrainian state. Ukrainian Cossacks are famous for their patriotism, courage, strength, and love of freedom. Many Ukrainian writers and poets have praised Cossacks in their works.

Dacha—a country house, usually surrounded by a nice garden with flowers, fruit trees, and bushes. Many Ukrainians own a country house, in addition to their regular apartment in the city. Ukrainian families spend their weekends and sometimes even vacations at their dachas.

Hata—the Ukrainian word for house or hut.

Hopak—a Ukrainian folk dance. The choreography

includes astonishing jumps, spins, kicks, and turns.

Horilka—a popular Ukrainian alcoholic beverage. If you attend a Ukrainian party, most likely there will be a bottle of horilka on the table. This drink, which can be both commercial and home-made, is often distilled from grain (wheat or rye) and also can have fruit infusion.

Kopijka—currency unit (1/100 of hryvnia, the Ukrainian currency).

Lapa—the Ukrainian word for paw.

Panove—the Ukrainian word for ladies and gentlemen.

Pushcha Vodytsia—an area in the outskirts of Kyiv. With its lovely forests and lakes, this neighborhood has always been known for a number of sanatoriums, hotels, and state cottages for government officials and the like. In July and August, large crowds gather at the sandy beach as the water warms up sufficiently for a comfortable swim. For those who cannot afford a vacation outside of Kyiv, Pushcha Vodytsia is an excellent vacation option.

Vyshyvanka—a beautifully embroidered Ukrainian shirt. The pattern of vyshyvanka differs depending on the region where the shirt was made. Each element bears a lot of symbolism. Vyshyvankas are a source of national pride. These shirts are also world famous. For example, Queen Maxima of the Netherlands wore a Ukrainian vyshyvanka shirt designed by Vita Kin to the Rio Olympic Games.

Zdoroven'ki buly! Zdrastujte! Dobrogo vechora!—common Ukrainian greetings.

Zirka—the Ukrainian word for star.

A word about the author…

Valeriya Goffe was born and raised in Kyiv, Ukraine and spent most of her adult life in the United States. She currently resides in Washington DC together with her husband and young daughter. Valeriya works for a large international development organization, leading financial sector development projects in various countries. She holds a PhD degree from the Kyiv National University of Economics in Ukraine and an MBA degree from the Kogod School of Business, American University in Washington DC. She is also a Chartered Financial Analyst (CFA) Charterholder. Valeriya is trilingual in English, Russian, Ukrainian and also speaks French and Spanish.

www.valeriyagoffe.com

Or follow her at:

Twitter: @GoffeValeria
Instagram: valgoffe_author

www.ingramcontent.com/pod-product-compliance
Lightning Source LLC
Chambersburg PA
CBHW051137030726
47504CB00004B/912